D A

HUNT

SHADOW AND LIGHT
BOOK ONE

KIM RICHARDSON

FABLEPRINT

This book is a work of fiction. Any references to historical events, real people, or real locales are used fictitiously. Other names, characters, places, and incidents are the product of the author's imagination, and any resemblance to actual events or locales or persons, living or dead, is entirely coincidental.

FablePrint

Dark Hunt, Shadow and Light, Book One

Summary: Rowyn is a Hunter and angel-born—a mortal with angelic essence flowing in her veins, and she's going after demons with a vengeance.

ISBN-13: 9781096659044
[1. Supernatural—Fiction. 2. Demonology—Fiction. 3. Magic—Fiction].

ALSO BY KIM RICHARDSON

SHADOW AND LIGHT
Dark Hunt
Dark Bound
Dark Rise
Dark Gift
Dark Curse
Dark Angel

SOUL GUARDIANS SERIES
Marked
Elemental
Horizon
Netherworld
Seirs
Mortal
Reapers
Seals

THE HORIZON CHRONICLES
The Soul Thief
The Helm of Darkness
The City of Flame and Shadow
The Lord of Darkness

DIVIDED REALMS
Steel Maiden
Witch Queen
Blood Magic

MYSTICS SERIES
The Seventh Sense
The Alpha Nation
The Nexus

DARK HUNT

SHADOW AND LIGHT
BOOK ONE

KIM RICHARDSON

CHAPTER

1

The demon smiled at me seductively. It wore the guise of a man, a very handsome one, with a chiseled jaw, straight nose and perfect hair. His lips curled toward his eyes, making his whole face shine—the face of an Armani model. It was no surprise with a face like that, and wearing a suit that promised tight, rippling muscles, women were following it like a blowout sale at BCBG.

But I was no ordinary woman.

Its black eyes were like bottomless pits, promising eternal agony, and it sent anger shooting through me. God, I hated demons. Especially the ones that preyed and fed on human souls. I'd been tracking it for two days now, following the death trail of single women in its wake. All the victims were found naked in hotel beds without any signs of struggle or indication of how they'd died. They all shared the same strange smile on their faces, a smile of pure bliss. But with one look at the bodies, their emaciated skin and lacking any echoes of their life-force, I knew what had killed them and what it had taken—their souls.

We were dealing with an incubus. The sex demon possessed the power to lure women to bed with it, promising endless pleasure, only to end up dead and their souls taken.

The New York City Police Department was looking for a serial killer—a *human* killer—and that had been their first mistake. But most humans didn't know what dangers lurked in the night, the demons and monsters that crawled through the Veil into our world from the Netherworld to feed.

The hairs on the back of my neck rose. It was trying to pull a charm on me. I felt its demon magic lace up my spine, warm and inviting, caressing me like the touch of a man's hands over my skin. My face was impassive, but anger burned within me, like the summoning of fire.

As a Hunter, tracking down and killing demons, along with all the other creatures that went bump in the night, was my usual line of work. It took a creature to catch a creature.

I'd been hired by Father Thomas, one of Thornville's local priests, for this job. Father Thomas was a modern-day Templar Knight, waging a secret war against the church's enemies—demons and half-breeds—which the church hid from the public.

Killing the incubus while inside the bar wasn't the best idea. I needed somewhere dark, somewhere quiet.

I smiled at the creature. The demon winked at me as it pushed itself from the bar and moved to the door, its every motion emanating a confident seductive grace. Then it slipped out of the Black Pony Irish Pub.

It was cocky, and it wanted me to follow. Whether I'd been made or not didn't matter. I gulped the last of my gin and tonic and followed it out.

The streets were quieter than usual for a Friday night, and my boots clicked against the sidewalk as I followed the demon. It looked over its shoulder, eyebrow raised, and smiled confidently as it saw me. I clenched my jaw and kept going.

The demon was leading me straight to a small, decrepit building with its exterior walls painted in graffiti and conveniently placed only a block away from the pub. My gaze lingered on the red flashing sign that read Charms Motel. Damn. It was taking me to the motel. The priest wasn't paying me enough for this crap.

This is pathetic, I thought, eyeing the dingy motel. I was way too good for this, but I needed the money.

The number seven was stenciled in black above the door. The demon pulled out a key, unlocked the door, and walked in.

It left the door open for me, a silent invitation. I hesitated as I watched it stride across the room to stand next to the bed. It removed its jacket and stood facing me, its human muscles peeking through the low-cut shirt. Oh, it was cocky.

Smiling, I walked in and closed the door behind me. No need to alert the neighbors. As I stood in the narrow room, I ran my gaze over the typical motel room—one double bed, striped beige and gray duvet with matching pillows and drapes, and tucked away towards the back was a single door, which I guessed was the bathroom.

It smelled of old cigarettes and musk. My predatory instincts stirred as I felt another prickling of demonic magic tugging against my skin.

It removed its white shirt effortlessly and tossed it in the nearby chair. "Come to bed, darling. Let me show you the pleasures you've never dreamed of. I know what you want. What all women want. I can give it to you." The demon's voice was low and seductive, like a lover's purr. I wanted to vomit.

"I doubt it." I knew I was supposed to play along, but I couldn't help it. I'd always hated handsome, overly confident men, who thought they could get women into bed with just a smile, a cheap meal, and lots of wine.

The demon's smile faltered just a little, its black eyes pinning me. "You're afraid? Don't be. There's nothing to be frightened of. I promise. Just relax." It crossed the room and closed the distance between us.

Close now, I could smell the mixture of sulfur and male musk. It was tall, taller than I'd expected, but nothing I couldn't handle.

It licked its lips as it lowered its head. I felt the same pulse of demonic magic coming from it, sending tendrils of pleasure over me. I smiled as its magic pulsed one last throb and then melted away, just like all demonic magic and hexes do whenever cast on me.

It pulled its head back. I saw the flicker of annoyance and then recognition as it realized its demonic magic had no effect.

"You," it said, its black eyes widened. "I've heard of you. The rogue Hunter… the angel-born…"

I flashed it my best smile. "That's me."

I pulled my soul blade from my waist. The angelic blades were given to us from the angels, forged from celestial metal and light, and as hard as diamonds. I whipped my blade at the demon, but it jumped back, slipping past me like a shadow, the tip just missing its chest.

I hissed as I missed and stumbled forward. It was faster than I'd anticipated. It moved like a cloak in the wind, dark as death and just as quick.

I could see its true shape. Now that it had to concentrate all its magic on surviving, a human guise required too much energy. With its glamour gone, it was naked with the shape of a man, but bent forward with long arms that grazed the floor ending in claws and hooves for feet. Its skin was marred with sores and open wounds filled with yellow pus. Hatred and bloodlust burned in its black gaze. Its leathery face had inhuman curves that most closely resembled that of a large lizard as they were illuminated in the soft light of the motel room. It reeked of death, and the smell of carrion filled the air.

"Damn," I said as I shook my head. "If only the women could smell you and see what you truly look like, there's no way in hell they'd sleep with you. You are one ugly mother—"

It shot at me. I felt its cold and powerful demonic magic rise against me, but I never let it finish.

In one fluid movement, I ducked, and then I was up and spinning, the tip of my blade whistling through the air. The demon pitched back, crashing into the wall. It howled and lunged again when my blade was past. It hit me in the back, and I went sprawling onto the bed, the brute force knocking the frame apart and sending the mattress to the floor with us on it. I twisted around, just as the demon loomed over me.

It howled as it shot at me again, yellow spit dripping from its mouth. My eyes burned at the stench of rot and sulfur.

"You dare disturb my feasting!" roared a voice that was many voices, mixed with the wails of demons and the cries of dying men. "I will feast on your soul, angel bitch!"

Its jaws met my jacket sleeve and tore into my flesh with its needle-like teeth. I swore as white-hot pain ripped through my arm. Hot ice ran through my veins—the demon's poison. I felt the muscles of my arm tighten and then go numb.

"Damn." Incubus demons were notorious for using their venom to paralyze their victims into a complete trance when their glamour didn't work. *Not going to happen.*

I kicked out with my leg and my boot vibrated as I made contact with its knee. The demon staggered back, but in a flash it went for me again.

I struck at it with my blade, black blood spilling everywhere, but it was too quick. The blow glanced off, and it snapped at my arm again. Tears filled my eyes. The bastard was going to chow my arm off if I didn't stop it.

I felt a rush of panicked anger as I yanked my blade into its side with a twisting cut to the sound of a wail. The demon let go and stumbled back, hissing and spitting. Black blood oozed from the cut on its side as the demon thrashed and spoke in the ancient demon language.

"I'm a little rusty on my demon dialect," I said as I spat some demon blood from my mouth. "But I think you just called me a *very* bad word. Am I right?" I frowned at the tear on my jacket sleeve. "Crap. Look what you did. This was my one good jacket. I can't afford a new one, not even with this lousy job's pay."

The incubus turned its head very slowly in my direction. Shit. It was really mad.

It sprang at me again, running like a streak, just a blur of black and shadow. Before I could stop it, we hit the wall together with a frightening force. The impact of pain took the breath from my lungs, and I felt my soul blade slip from my hand. A shower of wood fragments and plaster exploded into the air, falling over my hair, and dust blew into my eyes, blinding me momentarily. I was pinned to the wall and couldn't move.

The demon shrieked in laughter and its warm breath assaulted my face as it spoke. "I will rip the skin off your bones slowly, until you beg for mercy, until you cry out for your mommy... and then I will suck out your soul like water through a straw."

It pressed its body against me. I screamed as I kicked and struggled to get away. Hell, I was not going to end up soul-sucked by this incubus in desperate need of a shower.

It grabbed a fistful of my hair, pinning my head to the wall as it licked my face.

I gagged, my eyes watering at the reek of rotten meat. "Screw you."

It punched my side, knocking the wind from my lungs. "With pleasure."

I felt the demon going for my neck before it even moved. I cried out, panicking as a guttural laugh tore my ears. Its hand clasped around my neck and began to squeeze.

Blood rushed to my face. I couldn't breathe. Where was my soul blade?

There was only one thing to do when about to be soul-sucked by an incubus without a soul blade, and that was to hit it where it counts.

I raised my knee with as much force as I could muster and hit it right in its groin—well, what I expected was its groin. It worked. The incubus howled in pain and fell back onto the ground, hunched over.

It was male, after all. Even male demons had their weaknesses.

I snatched my soul blade from the orange-stained carpet, and a thrill rolled up my spine. The fight wouldn't be ending so soon. I would dance with the demon a little while longer and let my rage free.

"You'll never hurt another woman ever again, demon."

The demon laughed, a seductive kind of laugh. "Who said you're capable of killing me?" It raised itself to its full height.

"I just did."

With a flick of my wrist, I let my soul blade fly. It flew true and straight and hit the demon straight in its right eye socket.

The incubus burst into flames. It made a horrible scream as it thrashed around the room, its mouth opened wide and teeth snapping as flames burned all over it. Its howl made my skin crawl. Hunched over, it staggered toward me, still on fire, and I backed up.

"I know what you are," screeched the demon, pointing at me with a flaming hand. "I know! *They* know it too. They all know it! And they'll find you! Death is nearer than you think! I'll be back—"

The demon burst into a cloud of gray ash. I didn't even wait for the demon ash to settle as I stepped through the falling dust, crossed the room and picked up my blade. I wiped it clean with one of the drapes. It's not like anyone would even notice, not with the hole in the wall, the broken bed, and the pile of ash that would soon settle all over the room.

My soul blade gleamed. I could see the reflection of my thin face staring back at me, framed by a tangle of long brown hair. God, I was a mess. I needed a shower. Groaning, I sheathed my blade back to my waist.

"Nice work," said a voice behind me.

I flinched and whirled around.

A man stood in the doorway, and I never heard his approach.

CHAPTER
2

I kept my hand on the hilt of my blade as I gazed at the stranger. Demon? He didn't smell like a demon, and he was pretty, *very* pretty. How much had he seen? How was it that I never heard the door open?

But it was nothing compared to the shock I felt at his easy demeanor as he strolled into the room uninvited like he owned the motel. He moved with fluid grace, the way all predators moved. He was handsome with tousled hair and tanned skin, which meant he spent a great deal of time outside. His carefully tailored clothes, all black, finished the look with a black leather jacket. An enchanting smile curved over his clean-shaven features, giving him the look of someone my age—in the twenty-four-year-old range.

Warning bells were going off in my head at his casual entrance, making my stomach clench. I was certain he had just witnessed me murder a human— and he was smiling. It was a compelling smile, mixed with confidence and secrecy. Two blades hung from his weapons belt. Curious.

My eyes moved to the low V of his shirt, to the P-shaped birthmark on his neck—the archangel Michael's sigil. *Ah-ha.* The stranger was a Sensitive, an angel-born like me. Well… almost like me.

Sensitives, or angel-born, have been around as long as man has been walking the Earth. We're primarily human but have angel essence flowing in our veins—a secret race of humans created by the archangels, bred with supernatural abilities to be the eyes and ears of the Legion of Angels on Earth. Just like guardian angels, angel-born monitor mortals and protect them from demons. Unlike regular humans, we can see through the Veil—the supernatural layer that acts as a glamour or an illusion and changes the way things look to mortal eyes. It prevents mortals from seeing the true self of angels and demons.

I hadn't seen another angel-born in five years. I didn't recognize him as a member of Hallow Hall, the Sensitive safe house and workplace in Westchester County, about thirty miles north of New York City. But then again, I had left that life a long time ago. The Sensitives had safe houses in nearly every big city in the mortal world—from New York to England to Sydney, Australia. He could be from anywhere.

My stomach tightened, and I wondered if I'd have to fight my way out. How had the council found me? I had walked away from that life and never looked back. That was a big no-no in the demon-fighting world. It was against the council law. Being an angel-born meant a life contract. Leaving put a price on your head. As an angel-born in exile, I was an enemy of the council. I had known all this. Still, I had left.

The stranger looked around the room. "This place is trashed. You going to pay for the damages?" He smiled cheekily at me, like he knew I was broke.

My face burned with indignation. He was starting to tick me off. "What do you want?" I'd never taken my hand off the hilt of my blade, and I wanted him to know it.

The stranger pursed his lips. "Straight to the point. I like that." His eyes moved to where my hand still rested on my blade. "You're a Hunter for hire, right? Rowyn Sinclair?"

I shifted my weight and arched my brows. "Who wants to know?"

"We heard you were back in town," said the stranger, his voice rising and falling pleasantly as his eyes met mine. "I have a job for you."

"You mean the council has a job for me." I wasn't sure I liked where this conversation was going. My heart pounded, and I hated how just thinking of the council made my blood boil. I moved my gaze to my waist and to the dirt under my nails. "I don't care what the council wants or has to offer. I left that life a long time ago," I said, curling my fingertips over my blade to hide them. "I'm not going back. You might as well turn around and leave."

The stranger still wore that brazen smile. "I have something that might change your mind. Here." He reached inside his jacket and tossed me an envelope.

I caught it easily and looked inside at the thick stash of twenty-dollar bills. My heart raced. I'd never seen so much cash before. There must have been at least four thousand dollars in there.

"Five thousand dollars," said the stranger, reading my thoughts. "And there's five more *after* you finish the job. That's ten thousand big ones, darling."

"Call me *darling* one more time… and I'll cut off your manhood and feed it to a hell hound. Got it?"

"Yes, ma'am."

I didn't have to look at him to know that he was smiling. He was an ass. Pretty, but still an ass.

Damn. I needed that money. I was broke. Dirt poor. My last meal had been a bowl of Lucky Charms, and there was nothing *magically delicious* about them apart from the sugar rush. I was losing too much weight, too quickly.

I had sworn I'd never return. Not after how they had treated me. Because I was different…

But as I stood there, with the weight of the envelope in my hand, emotions were an expense I couldn't afford. I could pay my rent and get some new clothes. Damn it. My underwire was poking my ribcage again. I needed a new bra!

I looked up. The stranger was eyeing my ripped jacket sleeve. "It broke your skin," he said, slightly impressed. "But you don't seem affected by the demon's poison." When I didn't answer, he continued. "You move fast... for a woman." I knew he added the last part just to irritate me further. "I heard you were good, but I didn't know you were *that* good. I felt like I was looking at a younger version of Wonder Woman without the sexy outfit."

I glared at him. "Don't patronize me, pal—"

"Jax."

"—I don't know who you think you are—

"I'm Jax. I'm a Scorpio. I enjoy long walks on beaches, beer, women, and killing demons."

"—but after what the council did to me... after what happened to my parents..." I said.

He looked at me, seemingly sympathetic. It made him look appealing and attractive, and I forced the thought from my head. "If I wanted someone pulling on my leash, I would have stayed. As I remember, the council wasn't too keen on me in the first place, and I believe they were very happy to see me go. I don't remember anyone trying to stop an eighteen-year-old from leaving."

Jax's smile faltered. "I'm sorry about what happened to your parents. It was a terrible accident."

"It was *no* accident," I hissed. My face went cold and then hot. "Two highly trained angel-born just don't die from a fire in their own home. I don't care what the council says. It was murder."

My parents had died under suspicious circumstances. At least they were suspicious to me. And that was the reason I distrusted the council.

And one day I'll get to the bottom of this.

Ire flashed in Jax's eyes, and I could see that they were green. Whatever was going on in his head had nothing to do with me.

My temper burned. "It makes me sick that the council thinks they can buy me off." But it made me sicker that I was tempted by the amount of money in my hand.

"It's not a payout," said Jax persuasively as he tucked his hands in his pockets in a causal gesture. "They're not asking you to come back. It's a job. You don't have to deal with the council if you don't want to. You can deal with me. And after the job is done, you can go back to whatever it was you were doing." A wry smile wafted over him. "But I can see you're hanging on pretty tightly to that envelope."

I glowered at him. "Oh, shut up." Damn. Damn. Damn. "What's the mark?"

Jax smiled, raked a hand over his hair, and sighed. "A Greater demon maybe? We're not sure. But it's something clever and strong enough to kill highly trained Sensitives."

I started. "A demon's killing angel-born?"

"Murdered. A body was discovered in New York City three weeks ago, and then another one two days ago in Westchester County. We found the body in the woods just outside her home in Thornville."

My pulse quickened. Thornville was my hometown.

"All angel-born," said Jax. "Something's targeting us. And nobody knows why."

Fear gripped me. I'd never heard of a Greater demon targeting angel-born. It was so much easier just to kill regular humans to get at their souls, their life-forces. Why would a demon go through the trouble of tracking and killing a handful of angel-born, who could easily fight back and possibly kill it, when it had an unlimited supply of easy human kills? It didn't make sense.

"How are they killed?" I questioned, trying to keep my voice from showing too much emotion.

"Throats ripped out, skin left in ribbons, hearts gone, souls gone," said Jax. "All evidence points to a demon attack. It's the same MO for all of them. A demon mess. I can't wait to get my hands on the SOB."

"What does the Legion say?" I had to ask. The Legion of Angels was the council's boss, so to speak, or at least that's what it was supposed to be. The archangels had given the Deus Septem to the council. It consisted of a series of seven books with rules to help guide them in their roles as appointed warriors on Earth, to watch over humans from whatever evil slipped from the Netherworld. But angels rarely came to visit us mere mortals, so the council was pretty much left to its own devices and set of rules.

Jax's face flushed, and tension rippled over his shoulders. "What they always say. They have no idea, and it's better we figure it out on our own."

He was even handsome when he was mad. *God help me*. I glanced over his shoulder through the open door to the gleaming black Audi A5 parked in front of the motel that hadn't been there when I'd followed the incubus.

"How did you find me?" I asked, a little annoyed. I always thought I was pretty good at covering my tracks. But this guy had found me three days after I'd arrived back in New York. I was either losing my touch, or he was really good at tracking people.

Jax's sly smile had retuned. "I'm a friend of Father Thomas. The man's got a mean *Star Trek* collection. He's got this action figure of Khan that can—right, anyway," he added quickly as he saw my frown. "He told me he'd hired you to kill the incubus and that I'd find you here."

I raised a brow. "Really? In this motel? I think I'll have a chat with the priest."

"No, not *here*, here," Jax shook his head, his face flushed. It was a very nice face. "At the Black Pony Irish Pub. I followed you."

"So, you're a stalker. How nice."

Jax laughed. "Don't you first need to be a stalker to become a good Hunter?" He looked at the broken bed. "I have *other* skills too."

Heat rushed to my face and I put my hand on my hip in my attempt to crush it. But I also wanted to punch that pretty smile off his face.

"Why did they send you?" I eyed the stranger called Jax. He was very cute, no, not cute, but strikingly handsome. I knew then they'd sent a pretty face to tempt me. I doubt I would have stayed to listen to more than five seconds if they'd sent an average-looking man. I was a sucker for the pretty boys. "Did they think I'd go weak in the knees because of a pretty face?"

Jax beamed. "You think I'm pretty?"

Good lord. I rolled my eyes. "Shut up."

"You do. It's written all over your face. You think I'm hot. Don't you? You think I'm sexy."

What had I done? "Can you shut up a minute? Can you do that? I can't hear myself think. I need to think." *Please go away so I can think.*

Jax moved from the door and came towards me. "What do you say—" he extended his hand, "—partners?"

I looked at his extended hand but didn't take it. "I work alone."

"Not this time you don't," said Jax, lowering his hand, seemingly prepared for me to say that. "Listen, the job comes with a partner—me—and it's not negotiable. It's a take it or leave it kind of thing. You decide. But I come with a pretty price tag of ten thousand dollars."

"If I catch and kill the demon responsible."

"If you catch and kill the demon responsible," repeated Jax.

I swallowed wondering what the hell I was going to do. I've never had a partner before. I'd always worked alone, and that's how I liked it. My own choices. My own decisions. Never had to wait or compromise for the likes of anyone. That was what a Hunter was, a loner. It was the perfect job for me. I was born to be a Hunter.

But I was broke. Worse than broke, and I was nearly starving—not on purpose—I *liked* to eat—a lot. Hell, I needed the money, and if some Greater demon was out there killing us, I would gladly send it back to the Netherworld for a hefty paycheck.

And just maybe… this was my chance at sneaking back into Hallow Hall to search the records pertaining to my parents' deaths…

"You can start with buying a new wardrobe with that money." Jax's eyes rolled over the tears in my jeans, my leather jacket, and gray t-shirt that had once been black.

There he went pissing me off again. But he had a point. I looked like I lived on the streets.

My eyebrows rose. Jax blinked, seeing the inkling crossing me and not knowing what it was.

"You want this job or not?" he asked, seeming nervous for the first time.

"Fine," I said. "I'm in."

CHAPTER
3

The sound of purring slipped into my awareness, jarring me awake. I opened my eyes in a moment of panic, not remembering where I was and still unaccustomed to the white walls and L-shape of my new apartment. I blinked into two large blue eyes staring at me—

I screamed like a banshee and fell out of bed with a heavy plop.

"Ouch," I said to the floor. "Damn it, Tyrius! Why do you always have to do that? One day you're going to give me a heart attack. Is that want you want? Eaten away by maggots by the time Father Thomas smells my rotten corpse?"

"Always so dramatic." The cat leapt off the bed and landed expertly on the wooden floor next to my face. "I like watching you sleep. Something about the way your eyelids twitch."

"That is so creepy on so many levels." I rolled to a sitting position. "I think I cracked a rib."

"Nonsense," said Tyrius. "Maybe just bruised. You heal fast, anyway. Before you know it—you'll be right as rain."

I sighed and stared at the cat. "Why can't you just pretend to be a real cat? Cleaning yourself nonstop, chasing birds, throwing up hairballs? You know… the usual cat stuff?"

"Because I'm not a real cat, dearest," said Tyrius as he stretched to his full length. "I'm a baal demon. Hairballs are for amateurs. If you get your human to brush you regularly—no hairballs."

I shook my head, feeling a smile creeping up to my mouth. I could never stay mad at the demon. He was just too damn cute. The sophisticated Siamese looked dressed for an elegant masquerade ball in pale evening wear with chic black accessories around his face and paws. His deep blue eyes could hypnotize any mouse or bird. I'd always suspected cats were just way too clever to be just regular animals. I knew there had to be a demon in there somewhere. Well, some of them.

I rubbed the crust from my eyes. "Wait a minute—where's your collar?"

"Collar!" said Tyrius, and he shivered. "I'm not a pet. I *choose* human companionship. I'm not a slave.

I get free food, lodging, massages, and all I have to do is purr and blink and humans practically fall all over me."

I met the cat's blue eyes. "I'm not human."

"You are *part* human," said the cat. "And I'm one hundred percent demon extraordinaire."

A wave of irritation swept through me. "Grandma got you one, only to ward off the potential animal lovers, thinking that you were a stray. It's for your own protection, Tyrius."

"Me, a stray? Please, woman. Look at me. I'm fabulous. A Seal Point Siamese—it doesn't get better than that. In the cat breed world... I'm royalty."

I rolled my eyes. "Fine, Your Highness. But don't blame me if you get snatched up by some crazy cat lady. I heard they only feed their cats *canned* food."

Tyrius made a disappointed sound in his throat. "Speaking of your grandmother... why didn't you come home sooner?"

I kept my face blank, but my shoulders tensed. "I was busy."

"Four phone calls a month isn't enough, Rowyn. Your grandma deserves better. And she's not getting any younger either. She's the only family you've got left."

Ouch. That hurt. He was right. I was a complete ass, too proud to come back home with nothing to show for my five-year absence. There was no way I'd mooch off my grandmother. And that kind of thinking had kept me away.

The tiny cat shook his head. "You don't write. You don't call—"

"You don't have a phone."

"Right. The point is… your grandmother misses you."

My chest tightened. "I know. I've been a complete ass." I got to me feet, only slightly embarrassed that I was in my undies and t-shirt. It's not like I had anything worth hiding.

"Rowyn."

I turned and looked down at the worried tone in Tyrius's voice. "What?"

"When's the last time you had a real meal? You look positively famished."

A sigh shifted my shoulders. "Thanks."

"You're welcome." Tyrius sat back on his haunches, his tail curled around his paws. "I'm serious. You look like you've lost about ten pounds since I saw you two months ago. What's going on?"

"Try being broke." I moved over to the small night table and picked up my phone. No new messages. Being a Hunter wasn't glamorous. It was hard work and the pay sucked. I didn't have a steady income. Hunting was more like freelance work, and the pay—when I got paid—was barely enough to get by. With my Facebook page, app, and website DarkHunterforhire.com, I'd get a few hunting jobs— once I'd figured out how to skim through the fake messages—but it wasn't enough. Not nearly enough.

Times were tough, and it was one of the reasons why I came back. Father Thomas was a paying customer. The bonus was he offered me this loft-like apartment, the converted attic in his Victorian-style home, at a very reasonable price.

I knew by coming back to my home town I'd risk seeing familiar faces. But I didn't feel ready to deal with it. The pain was still fresh, even after five years.

I put my phone back down. "Things are looking up for me, though. I got a new mark."

"Another incubus gift from Father Thomas?"

"No." I moved my gaze over to the cat. "The council."

Tyrius wheezed like he had a hairball stuck in his throat. "The council Council? The one you hate? The one you blame for your parents' deaths? The one you ran away from and swore you'd never join again?"

"That's the one." I swallowed, feeling cold. "And I'm not joining them. I'm doing freelance work for them. It's different."

"If you say so." Tyrius watched me. Blue eyes wide, he bobbed his head, not dropping his gaze for an instant. "What was it that convinced you? It must have been something significant—no—don't tell me—they offered you *a lot* of money. Didn't they? Yes, that's it. Isn't it? How much?"

Damn that cat was too perceptive. "Ten grand. Five now and another five when I finish the job."

Tyrius swore. "Think of all the filet mignon you can eat with that kind of cash!"

I made a face. "I don't eat flesh."

The cat shook his head. "Maybe you should start." Tyrius changed the subject at the frown on my

25

face. "What's the mark? Must be a considerably large demon for that amount of money."

I quickly told Tyrius about my meeting with Jax and the Greater demon killings.

Tyrius was silent for a moment. "Why you?"

I blinked taken aback. "What?"

The cat's small features twisted in worry. "Why did they offer *you* this job? Why not just put more angel-born on the case? Why did the council single you out for this mark? Something smells fishy, and it's not the scallops I had this morning."

A frown pinched my forehead as I looked at the baal demon. Tyrius had a point. I sourly wondered if the council had an ulterior motive for getting me involved. Too late. I'd already accepted the money and planned on spending it.

I gave the cat a wary look. "I don't know. Maybe because I'm a damn good Hunter? What does it matter anyway? The demon needs to be stopped before it kills again, and I want to help any way I can."

"And what about this Jax character?" inquired Tyrius, his eyes narrowed. "You trust him?"

"Of course not. I don't know him." *I don't care how good-looking he is*, I thought. He was still a stranger. I smiled at the overprotective cat, my only true friend. "Don't worry. It's fine. I'm supposed to meet him this afternoon at some healer's clinic. I need to see the body before they cremate it, in case they missed something." I looked down at myself, suddenly wary. "But I need to go buy some clothes first. I can't keep going around town looking like a hobo. It's not good for business."

A hesitant look pinched Tyrius's eyes. "Are you ready to work with another angel-born?" His faint tone of worry tightened my shoulders another notch.

"I am," I lied. I wasn't ready. The butterflies in my belly wanted out. After Jax had driven off in his shiny car, I'd gone home to take a shower to wash the demon ash from my hair and skin and to catch some much-needed sleep. I was still uncomfortable with the idea of having a partner, but each time I stared at that wad of cash, I had to keep telling myself it was just temporary.

What would happen if he found out my secret?

CHAPTER

4

The fifteen-minute bus ride to Parks Hollow felt like seconds. I had left my apartment calm and collected, but every block deeper into town wound me tighter. I was so wrapped up in my own mind, going over what Jax had told me, that I almost missed my stop. Agitated, I pulled the request cord and got off at the next stop.

The clinic was a dark brown brick building with rows of neatly trimmed boxwood hedges. A large sign on the front lawn read, ALL SOULS REPAIR. With a name like that, you didn't have to worry about the occasional wandering human thinking it was an ordinary healthcare establishment.

Next to it was a Sensitive private cemetery and funeral home, and I guessed the clinic doubled as a morgue. All angel-born were cremated. Bones left in a grave were an invitation to demons and other supernatural creatures to possess and use. Gray headstones lined the small graveyard with fruit trees in full blossom, creating a colorful carpet of white and red petals on the ground. With my mind going to my parents' headstone, I felt the whispers of tears at the backs of my eyes, but I quickly shook them off. I couldn't afford a meltdown.

Instead, I inhaled the sweet smell of apple and peach trees—a far cry from the demon sulfur that I was accustom to—and calmed my breathing.

A black Audi A5 was parked in the lot adjacent to the clinic. Jax leaned against his car, arms crossed, with the same familiar cocky smile on his face. Today he had on jeans that showed off muscled thighs and a loose t-shirt. His weapons belt peered from under his leather racer jacket.

"Why are you smiling at me like that?" My stomach tensed as I walked past him, heading for the clinic's front door. I winced as I felt a blister forming on my right heel from my new boots.

"Nothing," said Jax as he appeared next to me, smelling faintly of aftershave and soap. "I just didn't know there was a pretty woman under all that demon ash and blood."

"God, you're so aggravating." My face burned. It felt damn good to be told I was pretty, even if I didn't feel it. "Are you going to be like this while we work together?"

"Like what? Charming?"

"An ass."

Jax laughed as he opened the door for me. "Après vous," he said in very good French, way too good to have been learned in school. Clearly he spoke it fluently. If I had to guess, I'd say one of his parents was French. This Jax was full of surprises.

I stepped into a cozy foyer with a small sitting area. A single wood desk, nuzzled between upright file cabinets, served as the front desk. Behind the desk was a dimly lit hallway with sterile walls and doors leading to a shadowed spot at the end of the hall. It was clearly a waiting room.

Jax moved past me and hit a small brass call bell. He turned around with his back on the counter and crossed his legs looking smug.

I looked everywhere but at his face. "How did you get this assignment, anyway? You must have seriously ticked off someone on the council to be stuck babysitting me."

"I asked for it."

I met his steady gaze. "You asked for it? Why? You don't look like you need the money?" He didn't come across as someone who needed any extra cash, not with his expensive car and clothes, and his pretty, well-fed body.

Jax looked at his boots and for a second his expression went distant before looking back at me, his smile returning. After a moment of silence, it was clear he wasn't going to answer. And it clearly made me want to know more. I would figure it out.

I stared at the vertical blinds, but my eyes moved to the collection of tiny troll figurines with wisps of purple, green, orange, and blue hair behind Jax. "What can you tell me about the deaths that you couldn't or wouldn't tell me before I took the job—?"

"Jaxson!"

A door in the hallway burst open. A plump, twenty-something woman came rushing down the corridor, her face flushed and beaming. The buttons of her white lab coat were stretched to their limits around her large bosom. Her bejeweled glasses slipped on her greasy face as she hurried towards us.

Jax pushed off the counter. "Hi, Pam. How are you? You look great."

Pam looked positively in heaven. I could see some drool forming on the corners of her mouth. She didn't even notice I was there as she careened straight toward Jax. She lifted her arms as though she was about to hug him but pulled them back at the very last minute, looking half crazed.

"Jax, they told me you were coming by today," she panted, pushing up her glasses. Her eyes widened. "You want to see the body?" she said excitedly. "It's still fresh."

I frowned, not liking the way she'd said that, like it was ripe enough to sink her teeth in. This one had spent way too much time manipulating formaldehyde.

Jax gave an uncomfortable laugh and turned towards me. "Pam, this is Rowyn Sinclair. She's a

Hunter hired by the council. She's working the case with me."

The woman turned around faster than I thought possible. "Oh. Hi! Didn't see you there." She giggled like a schoolgirl. "A Hunter. Wow. That sounds *exciting*," she shivered in delight. "You're here to see the body too?"

"Yes." I nodded my head slowly, not sure what else I was supposed to do or say. When Pam adjusted her glasses again, I saw a small r-shaped birthmark on her forearm—the archangel Raphael's sigil. Pam was from House Raphael. The angel-born from that house were always the healers and doctors, all jobs pertaining a medical-type field.

Pam looked up at Jax, beaming. "I've kept her nice and cool, just for you. Come on." Pam moved fast for a person with such tiny legs. Jax gave me a sideways grin before sauntering after Pam.

What had I gotten myself into? I wondered how many other Pams, Jax had doing him favors.

I followed Jax's tight behind down the hallway and then through one of the doors from the hallway. The cool air hit me as I walked inside a large lab-like room, like I had stepped into a freezer. It stunk of bleach and dead tissue. Yuck. It had the typical morgue layout with stainless counters topped with medical tools and devices, wall-to-wall cabinets with books and bottles and jars of fluids. A sheet-draped gurney holding a body waited for our attention—the angel-born's body.

Pam waddled over and pulled off the drape like a magician performing the tablecloth trick. She rolled up the cloth, pressed it against her chest, and stood still, looking at Jax for approval. But Jax wasn't looking at Pam. For the first time since we'd arrived, he wasn't smiling. His sole focus was on the body. He walked over slowly, his body tense and wired as he examined it. He said nothing as he leaned over and inspected it like he was looking for something. A flicker of disappointment flashed over his face as he pulled away.

It was as though he'd been looking for something specific, some mark on the body.

I looked over to Pam and was shocked to see she had tears in her eyes as she stared at Jax. What the hell was going on?

I stood in an uncomfortable silence. I wasn't paid to pry into other people's affairs. Making up my mind, I crossed the room and stood next to the body. It was female. Her throat had been slashed, and her skin had been so severely cut and torn, I couldn't tell where her clothes ended and her skin began. I swallowed, forcing the bile down. I'd never seen a body that torn up before. It was as though she'd fallen into a meat grinder.

"You know for a fact the victim was a Sensitive?" I asked as I made my way towards the head.

"Yes," said Pam. "Her name's Samantha Fairfax. Twenty-four-year-old female Sensitive from Thornville. Her face was the only thing that wasn't so badly damaged. Her boyfriend found her, poor soul. Must have been devastating."

My insides twisted. Why did that name sound familiar? When my eyes found her face, my blood ran cold.

I knew that face.

A tendril of panic unfurled like a leaf inside my chest. My breath caught, and I blinked a few times to keep the room from spinning. I pulled what was left of her hair out of the way and looked for a sigil on her neck, where the skin wasn't damaged. Nothing. Heart pumping, I rushed over and grabbed her right arm.

"What are you doing?" came Pam's voice, and I heard the sound of feet coming closer. "Jax? What is she doing?" she said, her voice lower.

I turned the victim's hand around, trying to keep the panic from showing on my face. "Defensive wounds," I said, my voice cracking. "She put up a fight. She wanted to live. But whatever did this to her—she was no match for it." I yanked the sleeve up and examined her arm. I swallowed, my throat tight. Again, there was no archangel marking, no sigil.

Shit. I ran over to the other side, ignoring Pam's voice. I could barely hear her anyway. A cold sweat trickled down my back as I flung a long brown strand out of my eyes. With my pulse hammering, I grabbed her other arm, careful not to press into the shredded skin. But there was no sigil either.

"Rowyn, what is it?" said Jax, his voice tight. "Do you know what demon did this?"

Panic pulled my skin tight. "What house does Samantha belong to?"

Pam grabbed a note pad from a nearby table. "Ah… just a second… oh, that's weird."

"What's weird," said Jax, real concern in his voice as he made his way next to her.

Pam frowned and then looked up at Jax. "It doesn't say. Now why would they miss something like that?"

I looked at both of them, my stomach knotting. "They didn't."

Jax frowned at me and then grabbed the note pad from Pam and began slipping through it, as though she had missed something. But Pam didn't look offended. She looked confused.

"The other victim," I said, as tension sang through me. I leaned against the bed, my vision darkening. "You said she was female, right? Do you remember her house?" I asked, a little too loudly. "Which house was she from? Jax?" I was practically yelling. Pam stared at me with wide eyes, her expression turned affront as she took a step back, like I was about to strike. But I didn't care.

Jax's expression was hard as he looked up from the pad. He shook his head. "They never said anything about which houses. They just said the victims were definitely Sensitives and not regular humans. Rowyn," said Jax, his expression went worried, "you know who she is. Don't you?"

I shifted my gaze to Samantha's face, to her blank expression. "I know who she is," I said, my voice faltering as it felt far away from me. "I know because she's from my home town. We grew up together."

I heard the scrapping of boots and then Jax was standing next to me. "Then you know what house she belongs to. Which is it?"

I released a breath that I didn't realize I'd been holding. "You don't understand."

"Then explain it to me."

"The other female victim," I said, my pulse racing. "Was her name Karen Finley?"

Jax flipped through the papers on the pad. "How did you know that," he said, frowning as he looked at me. "What's going on, Rowyn?"

"Samantha didn't belong to any of the seven archangel houses," I said sullenly.

Pam snorted. "Of course she did, silly," she said laughing. She brushed a red curl from her face. "An angel-born not having a house? Did you hear that, Jax? That's like a bird without wings, a horse without legs. It just doesn't exist. There's no such thing. We are all born with the mark of an archangel. It's what makes us what we are. I think you've had enough excitement for one day, Rowyn."

My breath came faster, and I shifted my weight. "They do exist. Just… a handful."

"Jax," said Pam, her voice a little high. "What's she blabbing about? Angel-born without the mark of an archangel? That's ridiculous. Isn't it? Jax? Tell her she's being ridiculous."

"How would you know this, Rowyn?" Jax looked at me. His face held shadows of interest and something else I couldn't make out.

Tension pulled my stomach tight. "I know because, just like Samantha and Karen, I was born without a sigil. I'm Unmarked."

Pam let out a squeal and took another step back, like being too close to me would make her sick. "Jax! Tell her to stop lying. Tell her!"

Pam was looking at me with the familiar mix of fear and disgust I'd gotten most of my life. I'd hoped to get away from all of that, but it seemed I could never truly run away from who or what I was.

I was an outsider as soon as I was born. I might as well have been branded by the devil himself the way I'd been treated.

Jax's mouth was slightly open as he traced his eyes over my neck and collarbone and then my wrists. I knew he was looking for proof, a birthmark, a sigil as evidence I was what I claimed to be—an Unmarked archangel descendant. A freak.

"You won't find anything," I said. Jax's face flushed a little. "Trust me, the Elder Guild have already poked and prodded me since I was born. There's nothing there."

I looked at Jax, his expression wary. I took his silence as an invitation to continue. "We were never born with an archangel sigil like you. We were never marked or branded. We were born without a house."

"Why wasn't I ever told about you?" inquired Jax. "About others like you, if you say there are others?"

"Fear maybe? Mostly because of shame. We're a defect, abnormal in the eyes of the council. They wanted to pretend we didn't exist. The council didn't want to bring any attention to us. How can we be part of the Legion of Angels if we don't have their sacred birthmark, without their blessing? Without an archangel sigil, what does that make us?"

"Practically human," Pam said flatly.

I glared at her and immediately regretted it, as I saw the shock and then the fear cascading on her face at the sight of my teeth. *Crap. I had started to like her.*

There was a short silence. "She's not human," said Jax as he tossed the note pad on the table next to him. The sound of the metal hitting the table seemed loud in the tight space. "I've seen what she can do, how she can fight. Humans can't see or kick the asses of demons and monsters like she does. Besides, both her parents were angel-born from House Gabriel."

I raised my brows at him. Had he been checking up on me?

Jax watched me with an empty look on his face. "She's not human... she's..." his expression tightened. "Something else."

My stomach clenched at his words. I didn't know why. It wasn't like I hadn't heard it all before. Rowyn the Freak was my nickname as a teen. I was bullied and beaten up every day until that one day, the year I turned fourteen, when I became stronger, faster, and cleverer than those my age and older, when Colin Donaldson came at me with a soul blade, flanked by his cronies Ben and Najib.

"Hold her still. I'm gonna carve a sigil on the bitch," he'd said, as his friends had laughed, holding my arms.

Something had awakened in me. Darkness. Light. A little bit of both. I don't know what it was. When it was over, the three boys lay on the ground, spitting out blood as they cried for their mommies.

My parents had scolded me. No one cared that the dumbass Colin had taken a blade to me. All they cared about was what an Unmarked girl had done to their precious boys.

That's when the fear had started. Angel-born began to fear me, mostly because they didn't understand where my strength and skill came from since I wasn't blessed by the archangels.

I didn't want to get into my life's story right now. Mostly because I didn't like the way Pam was staring at me, like something interesting to dissect.

"There's a Greater demon hunting angel-born all right," I said, my throat tight as I pulled my eyes from Pam to look at Jax. "If I'm right, it's not just targeting angel-born. It's targeting those like me. The Unmarked."

CHAPTER

5

The ride in Jax's car to Thornville was as uncomfortable as a crowded elevator ride, like strangers pressing in from all sides and I couldn't wait to jump out.

Although he was hot in all the right places, his physique wasn't what had me wired like a top about to spin out of control. It was the situation we found ourselves in. Me a Hunter, loner, introvert and poorer than your local street rat, and he some wealthy angelborn with a secret agenda. Yes, I could practically smell the money rolling off of him like he'd bathed in gold every morning and snacked on caviar lollipops. I'd pegged him as being from one of the first founding Sensitive families, probably from Europe somewhere, as soon as his perfect French rolled off his pretty tongue.

You couldn't find two more different people on the planet. And yet, here we were, paired together on the hunt to find a killer.

I'd walked out of ALL SOULS REPAIR without a backward glance at Pam and had waited outside for Jax. I was wired. Way too wired to have Pam goggling over me the way she did. I was afraid I was about to do something stupid that I'd regret later.

I'd waited beside Jax's car, not knowing what else to do. "We need your car." Was all I had said as he came out. "We need to go to Thornville."

He hadn't said a word as he unlocked the doors and got in. I didn't know him well enough to read his blank expression or silence. I'd slipped in the passenger seat, sliding on the smooth black leather. I didn't want to wait for a bus or waste my new cash on a cab to drive me around town. Jax had a car. I was going to use it.

Besides, I had the horrible feeling we were already running out of time.

With Samantha dead, I needed to find the only other Unmarked I knew existed, and I needed to get to her before the demon did. Trouble was, I didn't know where she was. Five years was a long time. Who knew if she was even still in the same state or country?

I sank into the seat, relishing the deep rumble of the engine as I stared at the familiar landscape of rolling hills, ponds, and farmhouse that lined Upper Brook Road.

I shifted nervously in my seat. Jax's cologne was a pleasant mix of spices and fruit that probably cost more than my month's rent. I hadn't been this close to a man since I'd elbowed a male witch in the gut after he'd attempted to spell my drink six months ago at a pub in Chicago.

Hunters were loners, and loners didn't get to go on many dates. Sure, I'd dated humans, but it always ended badly—usually with me running away in the middle of the night. How could I ever explain what they couldn't see or understand? That didn't leave a lot of males to choose from. I'd given up on the whole dating thing. I kept myself busy, so I didn't get lonely.

It didn't work.

"So, there were three more like you," said Jax as he slowed to go over a railway track.

"Yes." I sighed, and then added, "but only one now." *Here come the never-ending questions.* "And that I know of. We were all born without a sigil birthmark."

"Same age?"

"Close enough," I answered, rummaging through my brain for my memories. "A few months in between, give or take. But we were all roughly the same age."

"That's weird," said Jax, lines appearing on his brows.

"Why's that?"

"Think about it. All born within that same year… all without a sigil and all in the same town. Doesn't that strike you as a little bit weird? What are the odds of that happening when you guys are supposed to be rare?"

I opened my mouth to protest but closed it. He had a point. A very good point. I'd never really considered it before. But what did that mean? Why were our birthdates so close together? And why all in the same town?

Jax flicked his attention from the road to me and back to the road. His eyes held a mix of concern and disbelief. "What's the council's explanation for being born the way you were. You said they did tests. They must have come up with a theory?"

"Yeah, that I was dangerous," I said bitterly. "If they knew something, they never shared it. At least, not with me." My stomach twisted. I'd always felt as though my parents had known more about why I'd been born differently than they'd let on. But whatever they knew, they never shared it, and I never got the chance to ask them.

"The others," inquired Jax, his eyes curious. "Did you guys hang around with each other? Were you friends?"

I looked out the front windshield. "Not really. Cindy's parents never let her out of their sight, and Samantha and Karen were practically sewed at the hip. I knew them a little, but I wouldn't call us friends."

43

"Why do you feel what happened to your parents wasn't an accident?" he asked.

A flash of anger warmed me. "Why were you looking at that body like you were expecting to see something else?" I prompted.

I turned to see a muscle tighten along his jaw as he watched the road in front of him. But he never answered.

The car phone rang, loud in the overwhelming silence, making me jump.

Jax looked at me and pressed a button on his steering wheel. "Yeah?"

"Jax? It's Daniel," said a loud voice on the speaker phone. "I searched our records for the name you gave me... Cindy Wentworth... there's nothing man. No records of that name. You sure you have it right?"

I looked at Jax. Tension slammed back into me and I felt myself stiffen.

"Yes," answered Jax. "That's the right name."

"Sorry, man," came Daniel's voice. "I don't know what to tell you. Does this have something to do with the recent murders of those two angel-born?"

"Yeah, it does."

"Shit. I'll keep looking. I'll give you a call if I find anything."

"Okay," said Jax. "Thanks, man." He pressed a button on his steering wheel and turned towards me. "I guess you were right. Looks like the council doesn't want to admit that you ever existed."

I looked out the window. "Yeah, well, welcome to my world." I doubted that the council didn't keep records of those like me. I was sure they did. I guess this Daniel didn't know where to look or didn't have the proper clearance.

"Do you remember where she lived?" asked Jax. "Maybe we could ask her parents? If they still live there, I'm sure they'll tell us where she is now."

"Sure," I answered. "Yeah. Cindy's parents' house was only five houses down from my parents." My heart pounded as I recognized the old maple tree on Bellwood Avenue. "Turn left at the next intersection."

Jax did as I instructed. We drove along Riverside Drive, the long stretch of road that bordered the Hudson River. The blue waters sparkled in the sun, and white-topped waves hit the shores in a soothing rhythm.

"Do you know why a demon is after you?" asked Jax after a long moment of silence.

I shook my head. "No idea. I might be wrong. I hope I'm wrong. The idea of a Greater demon hunting us—the Unmarked—opens an entirely new can of worms…" My words trailed off, and this time the silence was welcomed.

"Turn right here," I said, after a two-minute drive along the water's edge.

We pulled onto a short country road with tall golden grasses swaying in the breeze along white fences. Majestic pine trees lined the street, and hidden behind them was the small neighborhood I grew up in. Twenty craftsman-style homes were evenly spaced along a ring road, with Highland Park nestled in the middle. Multicolored roofs, siding and pitched gables gleamed in the sun like a fairytale village.

My heart thumped painfully as we approached where my parents' house used to be. Jax felt my tension as he slowed down next to a square patch of land with tall grass. I could see the foundation through the weeds. It was all that had been left after the fire.

"This is an angel-born neighborhood, right?" Jax's voice was low and gentle. It surprised me. But I was grateful he didn't ask about the fire. I wasn't sure I could answer.

"Yes," I said as I cleared my voice and blinked my burning eyes. "When I lived here, most of these families worked in Hallow Hall. A secluded little getaway, nestled back in the trees and safe from spying eyes. A regular love nest."

Jax laughed and I turned around. His eyes met mine and he smiled. Not the cocky smile he'd given me or Pam, but a real, genuine smile. It transformed his face, making it spectacular.

Warmth shot up from my neck to my face and I quickly turned around. "Here," I pointed to a house. "The white house with the red door. That's Cindy's parents' house."

Jax pulled his car to a stop in front of the house and killed the engine. I popped the door open and was already up on the front porch by the time I heard Jax's car door close.

An uneasy feeling ran over me, prickles of sensation along the nape of my neck as I stood on the front porch.

"Something's wrong." I felt Jax behind me before I saw him.

He looked at the door. "The door's closed and there's no sign of a forced entry. You think someone broke in—"

"No." I felt the coldness in me, the tug of supernatural that I'd always felt whenever a demon was near. The pull of darkness was strong. My ears pulsed with it.

"Something's definitely not right."

Jax turned to look at me, brows furrowed. "How do you know?"

"I can feel it."

"You can *feel* it?"

I knew it was the wrong thing to say by the alarm that flashed across his face. Damn. Too late. He was bound to find out sooner or later since we were working together. Sure, angel-born could see the supernatural, but only angels could *feel* the tug of demon energies. Feel it in the angel senses, in their bones and core, like I did.

But I was no angel.

Jax was still staring at me as I pulled out my soul blade and pushed the door open with my other hand. With the feeling of panic increasing, I stepped through the small foyer. Inside the curtains were all drawn, giving the impression of nighttime in the house. The lights were off.

"Mr. and Mrs. Wentworth?" I called out into the semi-darkness. "Hello? Is anyone here?"

I moved past the wooden staircase and went into the living room. Cushions had been ripped from the sofa and scattered around the room. Some were torn lengthwise, feather and cotton innards spilling onto the floor. The flat screen TV was lying on the ground, smashed open like a wound. The bookshelves had been tipped over, their contents scattered. And blood. Blood splashes spotted the couch and pillows, and I could see bloody handprints smeared on the walls, as though someone had tried to pull themselves up.

To the human eyes, this would seem like a robbery gone wrong, but I wasn't human. And the obvious pulse of darkness dissolved the possibility that anything other than the supernatural was here—and had done this.

Jax and I shared a look and I noticed a long dagger in his hand. I followed the blood trail that led towards the kitchen at the back end of the house. The hair on the back of my neck pricked at the sudden rise of darkness. My skin tingled at the smell of blood. I listened for any floor board squeaks or sudden movement, but I only heard the soft pad of our boots.

As I crept towards the kitchen, the blood spatter on the floor became puddles. I felt Jax tense beside me as we obviously both came to the same conclusion that there was way too much blood for anyone to have survived whatever this attack was.

My breath caught when I saw them. Lying on the kitchen floor in puddles of their own blood, their faces were nearly unrecognizable, shredded into thin ribbons. Their chests lay open, their innards spilling onto the checkered linoleum floor. Their hands and feet were bound. Mr. and Mrs. Wentworth.

Horror spread through me at the sight, but also because now I knew I was right. Something definitely after us. My stomach contracted in terror as I took in the scene, the broken chairs and table, where they'd probably been tortured for the whereabouts of their daughter Cindy.

My eyes burned as I thought of my parents, burning alive, screaming for help that never came...

"Is that them?" asked Jax as he inspected the bodies, his voice hard.

"Yes, it's Mr. and Mrs. Wentworth. They were tortured by the looks of it," I said as I inspected the ropes around their wrists. "The demon was looking for their daughter."

"The way their skin is ripped, with the long, deep gashes, is the same as the other two victims." Jax moved to the side, careful not to step in the blood. "Do you think they told it where she was?"

"No," I answered. "The way they were always so protective of her, there's no way in hell they would have given up their only daughter. Maybe—"

The pull of darkness hit me, but it was already too late.

CHAPTER

6

I spun to a defensive crouch, my soul blade at the ready. Three figures stepped from the shadows in the hallway, just outside the kitchen. Igura demons. Yup, not one, but three.

Impossible creatures of nightmares with scales, claws and fangs, the cluster of black eyes was set dead center in the front of their flat skulls. They looked like a cross between a lizard and a rat. Their tails ended in a thick talon that whipped menacingly from side to side. Gleaming daggers with black blades hung in their grip—death blades, the demon daggers containing a demonic power that was poison to angels and angel-born. Just a small cut or even just touching the blade with a hand was enough to kill an angel. Fresh blood dripped from their blades as they lowered themselves, readying their bodies to spring.

"Move! The back door!" I yelled as I turned and pulled Jax towards the breakfast nook and the kitchen's back door. I knew these things' weakness was light. I hoped the demons wouldn't follow us in broad daylight. Still, if they did, we'd have better odds fighting them outside. Demons hated the light, as darkness fed them. Without the protection of a human body or a constant fill of human souls, the light would kill them unless they slipped back to the Netherworld. We needed to get outside.

Jax reached the handle and I saw him pull the door open, just as I slipped on the blood and went down. Damn. Of all the times I could have been a klutz, now wasn't the time.

Remembering my training, I rolled over, raising my knees to protect my stomach.

An igura demon crashed into me, the creature snarling and snapping. I gasped as its weight crushed my lungs, my breath escaping me. I kicked out with my legs, my boots connecting with its jaw, and the igura went sprawling backwards. I jumped to my feet just as another came barreling at me in a flash of claws and teeth.

I swung my soul blade, slicing into the demon's neck. Its warm blood splattered my face as it stepped back. I heard an angry, clicking growl. I took that half-second to search for Jax. The back door was open, letting in rays of light, but there was no sign of Jax.

The bastard had left me.

I let my anger spill inside as the same igura roared and then shot forward. From the corner of my eye, another demon leaped at me, and then came the other. Three against one. Great.

I steadied myself. "Come on, mouth-breathers!"

The kitchen echoed with the earsplitting cries of the demons, deep, savage, and vicious. I gripped my blade so hard it hurt, and then I let my instincts drive me.

I spun, hacked and sliced. Gasping, I hit the ground and rolled to the left, slicing as I came back up. I danced with death. I was death. I felt the warmth of their blood hitting my face, but I never stopped. If I stopped, I was dead.

My blade was an extension of my arm as I tried to cut my way through three demons. The smell of rot and sulfur filled my lungs, and I coughed. I could barely breathe.

Heart pounding, I knew I had to get out of the house. But my head spun, and I couldn't see past the scaled limbs and teeth and claws. The demons pulled back, as though something had startled them.

"Who sent you? Who is your master?" I shouted. I had no idea if iguras understood English. Iguras were stupid. These lesser demons weren't smart enough to tie up and interrogate a few mortals nor had they the patience to do it. These creatures were only out for blood. They wanted to feed on mortal souls.

"Who do you serve? Who is your master?" I asked. "Quis vos servies?" I figured they might understand Latin better than English.

The demons stilled. Their heads cocked to the side, as though they we trying to understand.

My heart throbbed. "Quis vos servies?" I asked again. I knew I was getting somewhere, their pause all but telling me exactly what I thought. They were sent by a Greater demon. But which one? And why?

All at once, they came for me again. I barely had time to swing my blade. I backed up and sliced through a set of claws. Something caught my foot, and I fell backwards, sprawling into something soft— Mr. Wentworth.

"Oh, hell no." I did my best to ignore the wetness and mush I felt. It was like falling into a giant raspberry pie that was still warm, but I was dead if I stopped to whine about the grossness of slipping into the innards of two dead people. My new clothes were ruined.

"Jax! You coward!" I yelled.

Growls reached me, and I instinctively brought my blade up. It sliced right through the demon's throat. I pulled back as it fell next to me. There was sickening pop as the demon burst into ash, sending dust right into my face. I heard the soft clang of metal as its death blade hit the floor. The blade would remain solid for an hour or so, until its essence returned to the Netherworld, just like the essence of demons.

Blinded, I twisted around, trying to get a solid grip and push myself up, but I couldn't. I fell back onto the bodies, and nausea twisted my stomach.

Sharp, wet teeth reached over me, snapping viciously at my face. I kicked and made contact with one of the demons as it stumbled back. I drove my blade up, but not fast enough.

Teeth sank into the flesh of my extended arm. I cried out as fire burned my skin where the demon's fangs had punctured it. I made a fist with my other hand and punched it in the head, but it didn't let go. I punched it again, and again, and again, and still the beast didn't turn loose.

Pain exploded through my side as I felt tiny knives rake my flesh. I smelled the rot of the other demon before I saw it clawing at my side.

A darting shape drew my eye. Jax.

He leaped forward and stabbed the demon with my arm pinned in its mouth. The demon let go and drew back with a howl of pain, Jax's blade still protruding from its back.

Jax pulled another blade from his waist. It was longer and thicker than a soul blade—more like a short sword—and swung it at the attacking demon.

With my blade arm free, I reached out and stabbed the other demon in the chest in quick successions. It hissed at me and stumbled back. I rolled to the right and felt the hard floor under me as I jumped up.

"Where the hell were you?" I yelled and braced myself for the demon to pounce again.

Jax ducked and spun around the other demon. "I thought you were behind me," he panted.

"I wasn't." I kicked the demon's gut, imagining it was Jax's face.

"I know that now."

Hot anger welled over my skin. The igura demons were starting to piss me off. One demon's mouth stretched widely with each roar. It leaned over me, black eyes glowing while snapping its huge teeth. I faked to the left, came up behind it, and slammed my blade through its skull. I felt it fall to the ground, and my attention whipped to Jax.

He moved fluidly and with the skilled grace of a killer. One moment he was next to me, and the next he was facing the last demon. There was a thud of metal hitting bone, and I saw Jax's sword running through the demon's neck. He yanked it back, and the demon fell to the ground, exploding into ash.

I raised my brows. Impressive. He fought extremely well, but I wasn't about to tell him. I reached down, picked up my soul blade, and bounded down the hallway.

"Where're you going?" Jax called from behind me.

I didn't turn around. "To see if I can find anything that'll tell me where Cindy is."

Because if I didn't find her quickly, she'd end up shredded to pieces like her parents.

CHAPTER

7

I sat on the wooden back porch, my hand resting on Cindy's parents' laptop next to me. It was the only thing I could find that hadn't been smashed by the igura demons. The Wentworths' house was strangely empty of anything that would suggest they had a daughter. There were no framed pictures and no photo albums. Even the rooms were creepy stale with ordinary and unremarkable furnishings that looked like guest bedrooms.

The sounds of voices over the loud humming of several vacuum cleaners drifted over to me from the open back door. The Sensitives' Cleanup Crew. Jax had called once we'd determined the threat of demons was gone. The bodies of Mr. and Mrs.

Wentworth had already been bagged and shipped. Now the blood and demon evidence was being cleaned away.

My legs dangled over the porch between rose bushes and hydrangeas, though their sweet aroma was completely lost in the stench of sulfur and demon blood.

A shape loomed above me, and I recognized his cologne. "You left me," I said angrily.

Jax lowered himself next to me, the deck boards squeaking under his weight as he sat. He looked at me, surprised. "I didn't leave you. I thought you were right behind me."

"I wasn't." I looked away from his mesmerizing green eyes before they could spell me.

"I came back as soon as I realized you weren't," said Jax, his long fingers folding in his lap. "Besides, it's not like you really needed my help. You were doing just fine without me."

I stared at him, incredulous. "I was getting my ass kicked by igura demons in there! Partners are supposed to watch each other's backs."

Jax eyed me from under his brows. "And I thought you didn't *want* a partner."

My face flamed and I looked away.

"You think you'll find something on that?" said Jax. I could hear the smile in the question, which only made me angrier. But right now my pride wasn't important. Finding the Greater demon was.

"I do." I tapped the laptop with my fingers. "If there's anything about Cindy's whereabouts, it'll be in here. I'm sure of it."

Jax leaned forward. "Then let's open it and find out."

"Can't," I shrugged. "It's password protected. I know my way around computers, but I'm not a hacker. But I know someone who is."

"Who?" asked Jax, but the answer to his question was interrupted by the appearance of a small woman with short white hair marching across the yard towards us like she meant business. Her tailored suit wrinkled at the speed of her short legs. Valerie, Head of House Uriel at Hallow Hall. She looked exactly the same, stern and always pissed off.

Next to her was another familiar face. Tall, athletic and voluptuous with the long, gleaming red hair of a princess in fairytales. Her short skirt showed off her long, lean legs, and the tight blazer did nothing to hide the large breasts that were busting out. She had a body that put all the rest of the females to shame, every man's dream.

"Shit," I breathed. "And I thought this day couldn't get any worse." Jax followed my gaze. His face was blank, but then he got up.

I didn't.

"Well," said Valerie, a little out of breath as she reached us. "They told me you were back here." Her eyes fell on me and rested there for a moment. "It's nice to see you again, Rowyn."

I raised my brows. "Is it? I seriously doubt that."

58

The woman's face never moved, never showed any kind of emotion. She didn't even blink. "How long has it been?"

"Five years," said the tall redhead as she moved next to Valerie. Her blue eyes took in my hair, my clothes, and every inch of me. Her smile widened at the sight of blood. "Why is it that whenever we meet, you're always *dirty*."

I matched her smile. "Why is it that whenever we meet you always look like a skank?"

Jax choked on his own spit. Amber's face darkened and twisted into something that was nearly *not*-good-looking. She promptly stepped in front of me, somewhat obstructing my view. Her hips were at my eye level, and I counted four blades around her waist.

She stood in her familiar "modeling pose" as I'd always liked to call it when we were younger, with one leg forward, chest out, chin tucked it, and hands on her cocked hips. The woman was insufferable.

Amber leaned forward. "I'll get you back for this," she whispered.

"Is that a threat?" I asked dryly, glad to have ticked her off. "You do know this isn't a photoshoot for *Vogue*. It's not about how good you look in a mini skirt or how well you can contour your makeup. It's about finding and killing monsters."

"It's always about how good I look in a skirt." Amber batted her eyelashes and gave a passing Sensitive from the Cleanup Crew a seductive smile as he waddled away with a transparent bag stained in red. He was old enough to be her grandfather. I threw up a little in my mouth.

"Does your face hurt from always smiling so much?" I asked.

"You're just jealous because you have the looks of a baked potato," said Amber, all without losing her smile and barely moving her lips. She was a damn good ventriloquist. "You're barely a one," Amber snickered. "I'll always be a ten."

Jaw clenched, and ticked off, I turned to look at Valerie, only to find that she was having a conversation with Jax, their eyes trained on me.

Amber caught me staring. "I don't know how you ended up scoring a job with Jax, but don't get too comfortable. It won't last. Men like that never stay with a woman like you."

I was about to tell her off, that I had no intention of anything with him, but she'd turned and left me with my mouth hanging open.

Amber's scowl evaporated, replaced again by her perfect smile. "Hi, Jax," she said, her voice sultry, smooth, and intimate. She was practically undressing him with her eyes. She touched his arm. "How are your parents?"

I wanted to vomit.

Jax gave her a tight smile, his face a shade darker than before. "Hi, Amber. My parents are fine, thanks."

Amber squeezed his arm and gave me a sideways smile before letting him go. She stood next to him, her hands on her hips. "I hear you're a Hunter now,

Rowyn," said Amber, and her face twisted in mock admiration. "Oh, is that the only job you could find? Because no one would hire you? Poor little Rowyn, vagabonding around the country, scraping up mindless demons for a few bucks. You did go a little crazy after your mommy and daddy died. So pathetic, you tried to convince the council that they were *murdered*. Murdered by their own, too. Wasn't it what you claimed? That angel-born killed your parents? You've always been too pathetic to be one of us."

"Amber," warned Valerie.

"What?" Amber questioned. "I'm just voicing what everyone is thinking. Everyone who matters knows she's a freak. I'm surprised she had the guts to show up after that fiasco she pulled at the council meeting."

My face felt like it was on fire. "It was the truth." I smiled, though I wanted to kick her in the shins. I felt Jax's eyes on me, but I wouldn't look at him.

Amber snorted. "Your truth, but not *the* truth."

"That's enough, Amber." Valerie's tone was final. "I'm beginning to understand why you wanted to come along. One more word out of you, and you're waiting in the car."

Amber crossed her arms but was silent, for the time being.

"Rowyn," said Valerie, her voice filled with exasperation. "The council is in chaos. The Heads of Houses are threatening to take matters into their own hands to protect their families. I can't have angel-born vigilantes on a demon killing spree. Humans could get caught in the crossfire. It's happened before, and I'm not willing to risk losing more innocent lives. Jax says you don't think these are random angel-born killings?" She looked at me, her eyes intent. "What do *you* think this is?"

I steeled my face, concentrating on keeping my voice from shaking. She'd never cared what I thought before. "Something controlled those demons," I said, trying to gather up what was left of my dignity. "Igura are stupid, mindless eating machines. They just want to feed on flesh and souls. They didn't tie up the Wentworths and torture them. A Greater demon did. They died because of what their daughter is—an Unmarked."

"Like Samantha and Karen," said Valerie. Her eyes met mine and then moved towards the kitchen window.

I shifted my weight. "That's right."

Valerie shook her head. "Why? Why would a Greater demon target them and not the rest of us? It doesn't make sense."

"That's what we need to find out," said Jax. "There's a reason. We just haven't figured it out yet."

I looked from Jax to Valerie. "Cindy's in danger. And she deserves to know what happened to her parents. Where is she?" I didn't believe for one minute that the council didn't know where she was.

Valerie pressed her lips together, shaking her head. "We don't have any forwarding address for Cindy. We looked everywhere. I even contacted the council when I found Daniel snooping around confidential files." Her eyes briefly moved to Jax. "They only had this address for her. I think her parents wanted it that way. To protect her."

"Well, we have to find her before the iguras do." My stomach churned. I was still covered in her parents' blood. The smell of human blood mixed with demon blood was making me nauseated. "I'll advise the council as soon as I find her," I said, trying to hide my disquiet.

"What about you?" inquired Valerie. I looked up at her worried tone.

I cocked an eyebrow. "What about me?"

"If what you say is true," said the older woman. "Then whatever's hunting Cindy is going to come after you too."

"She's right," said Jax, his voice wary. He rubbed his head anxiously, like someone had just slapped him.

I don't know why he looked so worried. The guy didn't even know me. "I'm used to monsters hunting me. I think it has something to do with my sending them back to the Netherworld. I can handle myself."

I'd moved twenty times in the last five years. If the Greater demon had tried to track me before, I hadn't made it easy. With my parents gone, the only way it could find me was through my grandmother…

Shit. I needed to check up on her. I thought of Cindy's parents and of my parents. I was certain there was a connection somewhere.

I gripped her laptop. I *had* to find Cindy.

"Well," said Valerie as she straightened the front of her jacket. "The Cleanup Crew should be finished in a few hours. In the meantime, I'll gather a team to see if we can find neighbors who might know something. There's always a snooping neighbor who knows something." Her light eyes found mine. "I'll pray to the souls that you find this demon. Be safe, Rowyn. Jax." Valerie gave a slight nod of her head and then waved her hand at Amber. "Come along, Amber. The angel Vedriel has asked to be kept in the loop. I must speak with House Ramiel. They'll want to inform him."

Amber sneered at me as she pressed her hand on Jax's shoulder and then swept it all the way down to his left bicep. "I'm sorry you're stuck with stinky over there." She laughed, and I made a rude gesture with my finger. "But when you're up for the company of a real woman," she inched her hips forward, "you have my number."

A grimace tightened my face as I looked away before Jax started to drool. I don't know why, but I didn't want to see that.

Not to mention that he didn't even have a splatter of demon blood on him. It was like the very sight of his pretty clothes deterred blood and guts, as though they were spelled to always be clean. I glowered. Even his damn hair was still perfect while I looked like I'd wrestled some decomposing zombies in a fighting pit of blood and guts.

I waited until Amber and Valerie had disappeared behind the neighboring house and slipped off the porch. My jeans stuck to my thighs and something pink rolled off my shirt.

My eyes found Jax. "Can you drive me home? I need a shower."

"You're not getting in my car like *that*," said Jax, mortified. And then the smallest of smiles appeared on his face. "Not unless you can wrap yourself in plastic."

Rage, so ferocious I almost threw up, pounded in me. "Really?" I said, my voice coated in venom. "Because of some demon blood and human guts? I wouldn't look like this if you had stayed with me."

"I didn't leave you." Jax smiled at my fury. "I really thought you were behind me. I swear." He moved towards the foundation of the back of the house, peering through Annabelle hydrangea bushes. "Maybe there's a garden hose here somewhere that I can hose you down with."

"Excuse me?" For a moment I could only stare. "Grab that hose and I'll kill you."

Jax laughed and raised his hands in surrender as he moved away from the bushes. "Okay, okay, enough with the scary eyes. I won't touch a hose."

Scary eyes? I glared at the SOB. No bus or cab would let me in, dripping human and demon waste all over their interior. There was no way in hell I was going to ask Valerie or any of the other Sensitives for a ride.

If he thought he could intimidate me with his posh smile and clothes and fancy car, he was a fool. I didn't intimidate easily.

"Fine," I said, setting the laptop down. Feeling defiant, I pulled off my jacket and shirt before kicking off my boots. Then I shucked my jeans and stood in my bra and underwear. I felt eyes on me from the kitchen windows, and one of the Cleanup Crew men, who'd happened to step out when I'd kicked off my last boot, froze, eyeballs gawking at my near nakedness.

Okay, so that wasn't such a great idea, but I was out of great ideas.

They could look all they wanted. I didn't care. I was toned and strong, though perhaps a little too skinny. Thank god I was wearing a new matching black bra and bikini briefs instead of a skimpy red thong. *That* would have been embarrassing. Nobody wants to see that.

I grabbed the laptop and looked at Jax, giving him a confident smile. "Is this good enough for you, Jaxon?"

Not waiting to hear his reply, and because I wanted him and all the others to stop staring at my half-naked body, I waltzed up to his car, slipped in and shut the door.

CHAPTER
8

Thankfully, Jax had stayed downstairs with Father Thomas, who graciously hadn't said a word as I slipped through my private entrance barefoot and in my underwear. I showered and changed into more of my new clothes—jeans, black t-shirt, boots, and a new leather jacket that had cost more than a month's rent. Ouch. Hopefully I'd get to wear this one longer than a day.

I checked my phone for new messages, but there weren't any. I set the volume to vibrate and slipped it in my jacket.

Jax was waiting for me in his gleaming Audi when I slipped out the front door. I swore it looked like he'd just polished it again. Were cars supposed to be this shiny?

I yanked the door open and slipped into the passenger seat, the laptop on my lap. The leather seat whined as I turned around. "Thanks for waiting."

Jax's smile had never left his face since I'd stripped down to my underwear. "No problem." His eyes were alight with humor. "Does that happen a lot?"

"What? Showering?"

"No."

"Stripping down to near nakedness in the burbs?"

Jax shrugged, his face twisting sheepishly. "Well, if you really want to do that again, I have no objections—"

"What are you talking about?" I hated how handsome he was and how good he smelled. That blend of spices and musk was driving me insane, but then I remembered that he probably had Amber's number on speed dial.

"The grime you get covered in whenever you're fighting demons," answered Jax. "Twice I've seen you fight demons, and twice you've come up covered in ashes and blood."

I checked my fingernails. They were clean. "I don't care about a little dirt, as long as I get job done."

"I can see that."

Flustered, I turned and looked out the window. "The address is 7997 Maple Drive, Thornville. It's not far from here. Five minutes, tops." I waited for Jax to enter the new address into the car's GPS. "Thanks, by the way. Thanks for giving me rides. I wouldn't want to spend all my cash on cabs. I'll get my own car once I've saved up enough." I felt a little guilty about ordering him around with his car, but he didn't seem to mind.

"Not a problem." Jax pressed a button and the Audi roared to life.

Cars flowed past us as we drove south on Riverside Drive. The street was still busy, and people hurried to get their last-minute shopping done before the stores closed for the day.

I rolled down my window and inhaled the warm air. My hair slapped against my face as we rode through the town. The evening sun was warm on my face, and a part of me wondered what it was like to live a normal life, as a human maybe—blissfully ignorant of the dangers around me, just working to pay the mortgage, living the happy married life…

Who was I kidding? I wasn't bred for the normal life. Hell, I wasn't *born* into a normal life.

I pretended to fix my hair elastic around my high ponytail as I snuck a peek at Jax. He was all smiles and usually composed, but I had seen some real sadness in those beautiful green eyes. I was certain his grief wasn't for Samantha. He hadn't known her like I did. But Pam knew what it was. It had to be something personal. He'd taken the assignment to work with me. He'd *asked* for it. Who did that? Only someone as desperate as I was. Except I was desperate for cash… Jax was desperate for something else…

Anticipation pulled me tightly, and I gripped the laptop. There had to be answers in here.

The car ride was short, and after five minutes we pulled up into the driveway of 7997 Maple Drive. I got out and shut the door.

A tiny gray cottage with white trim sat at the end of the street. It had a brown craftsman front door and neatly trimmed boxwood hedges that lined the small stone walkway leading up to the front porch. A white rocking chair sat empty next to a flower box spilling over with purple and white pansies. I heard Jax shut his door as I made my way up the path and bounded up to the front porch. I smiled at the familiar doormat that read, WELCOME MORTALS.

Before I had time to knock, the front door swung open. An elderly woman, white hair fitted loosely in a bun and wearing a flowered house dress and pink slippers, stood on the threshold.

"Hi, Grandma," I said, and my chest squeezed. "Told you I was coming to see you."

"You look so much like your father," she said. My throat throbbed as her eyes watered. *Please don't make me cry in front of Jax.*

My grandmother reached out and pulled me into a tight hug. "I'm glad you came," she said, and I could smell the wine on her breath. I let myself fall into her hug, the laptop heavy in my right hand as I struggled not to drop it. I hadn't realized until that moment how much I'd missed her, and I hugged her back.

When she pulled away, her eyes were wet. For a moment I thought she was about to cry, but then her lined face rippled in delight as her eyes moved past my shoulder.

My grandmother clapped her hands. "You've brought a boy home! A *real* boy!"

I smacked my forehead as I heard Jax laugh. "He's not a boy, Grandma. He's my partner."

"Yes, I know. It's what you young people call it now." My grandmother beamed. "Dear me. He's as handsome as the archangel Michael."

"Oh. My. God. This isn't happening." I rolled my eyes at the knowing smirk on Jax's face. He was enjoying this way too much. "He's my *work* partner. We're not together, together. Oh, never mind." I sighed since my grandmother was goggling Jax. "Grandma, this is Jaxon…"

"Jaxon Spencer." Jax moved to shake my grandmother's hand. I realized that I had never even bothered to ask him his last name. "You can call me Jax."

"Are you a relation to Mark Spencer from House Michael? The old founding Sensitive family from France?" inquired my grandmother as she took her hand away, her face holding a trace of interest.

"Yes, that's right. I'm his son." Jax gave my grandmother one of his smug smiles, but there was a new glint to it. I thought it might actually have a tinge of real warmth.

I loved to be right. Jaxon Spencer was from an old and rich Sensitive family. Interesting.

"Please! Please, come in!" My grandmother ushered us through the doorway. "I'm making my famous chili," she kept talking as she moved towards the kitchen. "The secret's not *in* the sauce, it's in the meat! You're staying for supper," she ordered. "And I won't take no for an answer. Jaxon—there's red wine in the cellar. Grab a bottle of Novelty Hill Merlot and Apothic Red. It's Rowyn's favorite."

"You heard the woman," I said, smiling and kicking off my boots as I shut the front door, "the wine's that way—"

"Look who the cat dragged in," said a Siamese cat as it came strutting down the hallway from the kitchen. Its tail was straight up in the air, long legs moving with the confidence of a lion.

Jax tensed. "That's a baal demon," he said. The tension in his voice pulled me to a stop, and his hands moved to his weapons belt.

"Hey, look who actually paid attention in demons 101?" mocked Tyrius. "Maybe he's not just a pretty face. Maybe there's an actual brain underneath all that hair. Wait a minute—are those your *real* eyelashes?"

Jax's hand was still at his waist. "Are we going to have a problem?" I asked, moving away from the door and placing my body protectively in front of Tyrius. I was prepared to defend Tyrius if need be. I didn't care how pretty Jax was, Tyrius was my longtime friend and he came first. "If you have a problem with Tyrius… then you have a problem with me. A big one."

Jax looked at me confused. His lips parted in wonder.

"I think he's having a meltdown," whispered Tyrius. "Is he having a meltdown? What did you do to him, Rowyn?"

"Nothing."

Jax's features twisted in shock. There was nothing of his usual, cocky self-glimmering in his straight posture. "I don't understand? Why does your grandmother have a baal in her home?"

"Because I *live* here," mewed Tyrius. "I take it back. This guy's definitely a little slow."

Jax had gone pale and very still. "Does the council know you have a demon in your home?"

"Screw the council," I spat. "Why should I care about them? They've been nothing but hypocrites. The lot of them. I took their money for this job, but I don't follow their rules. It doesn't mean they own me. They don't control me."

"But—there are laws about aiding a demon," said Jax. His eyes jerked to mine and a shocked look of revulsion crossed over him. "He might look like a pet, but he's no ordinary cat."

Tyrius lifted his chin. "Damn straight. I'm spectacularly magnificent."

"What is the matter with you?" Jax hissed. "Demons are born from the depths of the Netherworld. They are evil incarnate. There's nothing more foul and evil than a demon. Having one as a pet is ridiculous. It'll kill you in your sleep!"

Tyrius sat, his tail swishing behind him. "Wait a minute? What is he saying?"

I gave Jax a false smile and rested the laptop on my hip. "So, you're the type to believe what is light is good and what is dark must be evil, yes? Like crows are the Netherworld spies because their feathers are black, and doves with their white feathers are angelic birds that spread the word of God? Am I right? You think all angels are good just because they *are* angels? Well, let me inform you, Jax, that not all angels are good. I've met some. Trust me. And let me tell you something else... where you think there's evil... there is also good. Some demons are not the monsters you think they are."

"Are you mad? He's a demon. A trickster." Jax's tone was hard, and I didn't like the tension rolling off his shoulders. His fingers still twitched too close to his weapons.

A tiny growl escaped from Tyrius's throat. "Rule of the house—guests shut their pie holes."

Jax shook his head. "You can't trust them. I'm not sure what spell he has you all under, but it's clear to me he's been fooling you."

"Hey, just a minute there, Clark Kent," said Tyrius. "I haven't spelled anyone! Tell him, Rowyn."

Part of me wanted to kick Jax's stupid ass out of my grandma's house. But his face stopped me. There was something in his eyes, something that looked like a mix of desperation and terror that broke my heart. Something had happened to him, and my instincts said he was just trying to protect us. No matter how stupid he was being.

I took a breath and calmed myself. "Tyrius is my friend and has been part of my family since I was twelve years old. He's been there for me when no one else was. When my parents died in that fire, the council didn't come to see me, to console me or ask if they could do anything to help. No one did. But Tyrius was there. He was there next to my pillow when I cried myself to sleep for an entire year after the fire. Tyrius's soothing words helped me fall asleep. His encouraging words helped me get out of bed when all I wanted to do was curl up and die." I took a step forward and stared Jax down. "So, you see, Jax or Jaxon, or whomever you are, you are a stranger to me. Tyrius is my family. And families stick together."

"Here, here!" said Tyrius.

"No matter how strange it might seem to you, it's normal to us. If you can't accept that. If you can't deal with my family… then I suggest you turn around now and go home. We can work separately on this case."

I pushed the laptop higher on my hip. My eyes went to Jax, the width of the entryway between us.

"What's it going to be?" I inquired flatly.

Jax said nothing, jaw clenched. I told myself he could think what he wanted. I didn't care. I didn't have to live up to his standards or the council's. Who my family members were should have nothing to do with our professional relationship.

His head didn't move, though his eyes tightened in the corners. "We need to work together on this case. You obviously have connections and insights that I don't, that I never thought possible. It's going to help us. I want to find this demon as much as you do. I don't want Cindy to end up like her parents." He looked at me, and I could tell this wasn't easy for him. "It won't be a problem." He wouldn't look at Tyrius.

I glanced at him, my mood softening. "You sure about that?"

"I am." Jax's voice was tight, but I could tell he was being truthful.

"Okay then. Tyrius," I said as I showed the Siamese cat the laptop. "I need you to do your magic and crack the password on this laptop." I heard Jax's sharp intake of breath behind me.

Tyrius jerked upright, tail in the air. "Did you steal that from the council? Oh... please tell me I can finally get my hands on their dirty little secrets. There's also a file on me I'd like to erase—you know what I'm saying?"

"No, sorry, Tyrius. I wasn't that lucky," I said as I tried hard not to smile. "It belongs to a Sensitive family that was killed today. Long story. Their daughter's still alive somewhere, and this laptop is the only chance we have at finding her before the demon that killed her parents does."

"Say no more," said Tyrius as he bounded back towards the kitchen. The scent of chili peppers rose around us and my stomach growled. "Bring the laptop to the kitchen, if you please. I'll crack this baby like an egg."

I turned around. Jax watching me carefully, and I nodded to tell him to follow. His solemn green eyes went to Tyrius as the baal trotted happily down the hallway looking every bit like a real cat.

Jax gave me a tight-lipped smile, took off his shoes, and then made his way towards the back of the house. He looked tall in the tight space, the soft thumps of his socks resonating on the wood floor. Somehow even in his socks, Jax managed to move with a confident, seductive grace.

I turned to follow him, my steps slow and calculating, with my hand on my weapons belt, just in case.

CHAPTER
9

After we finished our meal of chili con carne—my grandmother had insisted we eat before letting Tyrius get his paws on the laptop, and I'd washed down every bite with a nice gulp of Apothic Red because I hadn't the heart to tell her I didn't eat meat—I set Tyrius up on the table next to me with the laptop. I was surprised when Jax pulled up a chair next to me. His shoulder grazed mine as he pulled himself forward, our chairs knocking together.

"Anyone want some coffee?" my grandmother's voice came from the kitchen just beyond the French doors. I could barely hear her over the loud Big Band music playing. She'd insisted on doing the dishes alone. Her face was flushed, and I didn't want to argue with her when she'd had way too many glasses of wine.

I looked at Jax and he nodded. "Two coffees please," I yelled back. When I was sure she'd heard me, I leaned forward in my seat and flipped open the laptop to press the power button.

Tyrius pressed a paw on the keyboard next to touchpad, and his eyes darkened to a deeper blue before closing. My skin prickled at the pull of demon magic, and I smelled the faint scent of sulfur as Tyrius sent his magic through the computer's hard drive. The dining room's chandelier lights flickered, and I felt Jax tense next to me.

"How long will it take?" Jax leaned close to me, his warm breath tickling my neck, and I felt a rush of blood heat my face.

Flustered, I reached out to grab my nearly finished wine glass and sipped the last of it, very aware of our knees touching. He didn't pull away, so neither did I.

"Patience, pretty boy," said Tyrius, his eyes still closed. "You can't rush perfection."

I burst out laughing and immediately regretted it. Where was that coffee? The lights flickered again and then went off.

"Tyrius! Lights on!" commanded my grandmother. "I can't see a darn thing in here!" I couldn't make out the rest of her words over the crash of dishes.

"Sorry," shouted Tyrius, and then the lights in the kitchen flared to life. His tail whipped from side to side as it always did when he summoned his magic.

An awkward silence followed as we all waited for Tyrius to crack the password. I felt the warmth of Jax's thigh press into mine through my jeans. He was really close to me. Too close. I stifled a shiver. Trying not to fidget, I sent my attention to the laptop as faint tendrils of demon magic rippled over the screen like black vapors.

"How did you two meet?" said Jax so suddenly I twitched.

I turned around in my seat, careful to keep my shoulders from brushing against his. "When I was twelve," I said and saw Tyrius cock his head towards us, eyes open.

"Yes, you said that… but how? Baals are usually kept as a witch's familiar, to assist them with their magic. And you're not a witch. Why did you keep it?"

I smiled at the shift in Tyrius. "You don't keep a baal demon. It's more like the other way around. Just like real cats, they *think* they own you and you're there to serve them."

"Nothing wrong with that," said Tyrius.

I laughed. "Tyrius and many other baals have been witches' familiars for thousands of years. Through their sharing of energy, of life energy—both mortal and demon—most baals can stay in the mortal world indefinitely. Well, until their energy runs out."

Jax's features creased in thought as he addressed Tyrius. "So why an angel-born and not a witch? You have magic. Why not be with a witch?"

Tyrius huffed. "I got bored of all their hocus-pocus."

Jax leaned back and looked at me. "I'm curious. How did you find the baal demon?"

"I didn't find him," I said. "He found me." Confusion cascaded over Jax's face and I felt my chest tighten.

Tyrius looked at me for approval, and I gave him a small nod. "Tell him." I knew someday Jax would find out since we were working so closely together. Better it come from Tyrius than someone else.

"I sensed her," said Tyrius, his blue eyes alight with demon magic. "It was like nothing I've ever sensed before, like two separate energies, like shadow and light all bundled together in this tiny girl package. I was curious, so I followed her home. Her parents fell in love with me—can you blame them?—and the rest is history. We've been besties ever since."

Jax had a frown on his face, and his eyes met mine. "Just like you can feel a demon's presence?" His eyes ran over my face. "Like the way angels do?" His voice sounded wary.

My heart pounded. I'd never told anyone about this. Only my parents, my grandmother and Tyrius knew about my abilities. No ordinary angel-born could sense the presence of a demon. It was why I was such a damn good Hunter. I could track *any* demon.

I watched Jax's curious expression, praying that I hadn't made a mistake in confiding my secret to him. I needed that mark. I needed that money. If he told the council of my gift, they might cancel the deal. Or worse, they might consider me enough of a threat to hunt me down and kill me.

Jax leaned back in his chair and crossed his arms over his chest. "Can Cindy sense demons too?"

"I can't be sure," I said as Tyrius lowered his head in concentration, his attention back at the laptop. "But if she's like me, if the others were all like me, then yes." Movement caught my attention and I saw my grandmother shuffling about the kitchen. The roast of coffee filled my nostrils.

"If the Greater demon knows this," said Jax, "it's motive enough for it to track you down and want to kill you. These black-eyed bastards will want to kill anything that stands between them and free human meals. And that means Cindy… and you."

What Jax said made perfect sense. Still, I didn't want to believe that a Greater just found out about us when we were pretty rare. I couldn't suppress the feeling that someone or something had told it about us.

"Bingo!" said Tyrius, making me flinch. "We're in."

I leaned forward. My chin brushed over Tyrius's head, and I rested my elbows on the table. Using my right index finger and thumb, I moved the curser over the folders on the desktop screen. I double clicked on the email icon, and a window popped open. Tyrius leaned into my shoulder and I welcomed the heat from his body and soft fur.

Scrolling down, I scanned through the inbox and frowned. "There's only one email." I double clicked on it. "It's from Walmart," I said. "Asking to leave a review for their recent purchase. They deleted their emails, covering their tracks."

A chair screeched against the wood floors. Jax was next to me, his body doing more than the wine did to warm me. "Check the deleted folder."

"Yeah," said Tyrius. "And if there's nothing there, check the 'sent' folder. People always forget to empty their sent email folders."

I doubled clicked on the deleted folder, only to find it empty as well. My pulse hammered. I knew if we didn't find anything here, it would take weeks or months to find Cindy.

I moved the curser to the sent folder and doubled clicked. "Jackpot," I said as I began to scroll through the hundreds of forgotten emails. One with the subject line "Miss You" caught my attention. "This one's dated three days ago," I said as I clicked on it.

"*Hi mom and dad,*" I read, my pulse a shade faster. "*Sorry I haven't written in a while. Things have been pretty hectic on my end. But I'm safe now. Remember my friend Danto I told you about? I'm staying with him at his club V-Lounge. Don't worry. He's keeping me safe. Love you. Cindy.*"

"Holy shit," I breathed.

"If this Danto is the same Danto who owns the V-Lounge club," expressed Tyrius, "that does pose a problem."

I leaned back feeling numb. As if sensing my quickened pulse, Jax turned to me. "What?" he asked. "Who's this Danto?"

I shook my head. "That can't be right. She can't be that stupid. Can she?"

"Looks like it," mewed Tyrius. "Very stupid."

"Guys?" demanded Jax, practically shouting. "Who is he?"

I looked at Jax, a knot forming in my gut. "He's the head of the Vampire Court here in New York City. And Cindy's with him."

CHAPTER
10

Going to a vampire nightclub in the middle of the night was not one of my best ideas, but with time being of the essence, we needed to find Cindy as soon as possible. And if that meant we needed to face a gang of hungry vampires in the middle of the night at their own club—then so be it.

After saying our goodbyes and thanks, we'd left Tyrius with my grandmother, safe in her cottage, while Jax and I drove downtown, high on fear and excitement. I'd left the laptop with Tyrius and asked him to keep looking for clues on it, hoping that we'd been wrong and this was just a mix-up.

Vampires were half-breed demons, part human and part demon with the thirst for blood—the hunger. It was easy for them to slip past angel-born since they looked human. That was until their eyes went black and out came the fangs. Vamps didn't mix with other creatures, even other demons, and especially not humans. Warm-bloods were food.

Jax's knuckles went white as they gripped the steering wheel. He looked wired. He hadn't said a word when he punched in the address I gave him as we pulled out of my grandma's driveway, and I didn't like the silence. I especially disliked the deep scowl on Jax's face and the way his shoulders tensed, his aggression emanating from him. I could see it in his eyes. I recognized that look. Hell, I wore it often. He wanted to kill something.

"Are you okay?" I asked, twisting in my seat. "You look tense."

"I'm fine." His voice was cold.

My brow rose at his tone. "You don't *look* fine. You look pissed." I watched as he clenched his jaw. "How about you share a little information? I shared some with you… it's only fair that you share some of whatever's happening in that head of yours with me."

Jax's face slacked as he looked at me. "I'm just anxious to find Cindy and send that SOB Greater demon back to his hell." His eyes became distant in thought before he turned around and looked at to the road in front of him.

"You're a terrible liar," I said. The flinch in his brow told me everything I needed to know. "The first rule of a good lie is *not* to break eye contact. I'll teach you sometime." I almost smiled at his refusal to look at me again.

"It's something else," I said, watching his face for more clues as to whatever was bothering him. "I can tell just by looking at you. I can help you if you tell me what it is. We're going to be partners for a while... at least until we find the Greater demon." I wasn't sure if this was just my obsession to know everything, or if I was genuinely concerned since I'd witnessed that moment of true sadness in his eyes.

"Fine. Keep your secrets. But they better not interfere with this case." Frustrated, I turned back and stared out the window. I was pissed. I'd shared something with this man, something that I'd kept from everyone, even the council, and yet he wouldn't share any of his secrets.

The sun was long down and traffic had thickened. The city lights illuminated the sky in blues and silver, making it appear to be on fire.

"I don't understand Cindy's actions," I said, wanting to change the subject before I lost my temper. "Her reasoning. No mortal, sane person would ally themselves with vampires. It makes no sense. She had called him *friend*. The only friends vampires have are other vampires."

"They tricked her," said Jax, and the faint worry lines around his eyes deepened. "Making her think they're keeping her safe until they rip out her throat and have a feast of her blood."

I grimaced at the intensity in his voice. "Then we better get there before they start to get hungry."

I kept to my cold silence as Jax drove us out of Thornville and headed south towards Manhattan.

We made it to Greenwich Village in about an hour. I gripped the door handle as Jax made a sharp right turn, pulling up on West Houston Street right before the club and parking at the curb. I opened the door and got out.

The street was unnaturally dark, and I looked up to find the street lamps all out. Traffic hummed two streets away, but here it was quiet. Too quiet. Along the street was a row of several cramped buildings, all but one an unremarkable mix of gray stone, metal, and iron. One had a red door. The name V-Lounge was illuminated in red lights above it.

The only indication that it was a club was the mummer of music and the rhythmic pulsing that came from inside.

"How did you even know about this place?" Jax stared up and down the quiet street. "Does the council know?"

"About the club? I doubt it," I answered and hitched up my jeans to where they were supposed to be. "The council doesn't bother with the few vamp clubs. As long as the vamps play by the rules, the council leaves them alone."

"If they don't kill any humans."

"They don't have to," I said as I made my way towards the red door, Jax following me closely. "Trust me. They have more than enough human donors, humans that beg to have their blood sucked out of them. I think it's sad, but that's not against the law."

I pulled open the door and walked in. The club was hot, like tropical weather hot, full of cigarette smoke and the familiar smell of booze. And yet, I could still smell the familiar stench of sour milk mixed with old blood that all vamps gave off. The pull of darkness was strong, and I knew even before I turned the corner that there had to be at least a hundred vamps in the club.

The hallway opened up to a larger room. Red lights played over a small dance floor, turning it into a hellish, blood fest of reds. The music was the loud echoing of drums, like the sound of beating hearts. We passed a bar to our left as we sauntered through, bottles of red wine littering the black granite bar top. Men and women were sprawled on red couches, some in conversation, some entangled in passionate kissing and touching. Their flawless faces were painted in pure bliss, and their black eyes were the only indication they were vampires. My skin tightened at the way they were looking at Jax like he was sex on two legs.

I saw a door behind the DJ booth towards the back of the club and made for it. A human man in his thirties with face piercings and tribal tattoos eyed us suspiciously as we made our way across the dance floor.

My skin pricked in warning as a vamp stepped from a recessed nook. I jerked to a halt, startled. He was tall and as thick as two grown men with ebony skin and a shaved head, and he was standing in our way. He looked more like a werewolf than a vamp.

"This is a private club," he said, his voice deep and raw like he didn't use it often. "No angel-spawn allowed," he added, looking at Jax, and I wondered why he wasn't looking at me. "You need to leave." He crossed his arms over his powerful chest in a show of strength.

I smiled, moving my hip so he had a clear view of my blades. "We're not here to join, if that's what you think, big boy. We have business with Danto. Tell him it's council business."

The vamp's black eyes rolled over us, his face frowning as he took in Jax's hands on the hilt of his weapon before he turned around and disappeared behind that door.

I turned and looked at Jax. "You need to relax," I said, seeing his grip tightening as he scowled at any vamp that looked his way.

"I'm fine. Never been better," he said, giving a gorgeous female vamp in a short black dress who'd started to walk his way a murderous look. She looked put off as though she'd just missed out on a night of passion as she returned to her couch. She crossed her legs very slowly, her eyes still on Jax.

Jax's earlier easygoing and sultry demeanor had evaporated into an angry, soldier-like expression of strength, dignity and menace. It gave me the creeps.

"What do you know of vampires?" I said, feeling a cold sweat drip down between my breasts. I wondered if Jax had crossed paths with vamps before. It would explain his uptight behavior.

"Most vampire lore is crap," said Jax, eyeing a male vamp with a black, racoon-like tattoo across his eyes, who was rolling his tongue in a sexual gesture at him. "Crosses don't work. They don't like sunlight, but it won't kill them. But the Hunger, the bloodlust—that part's true. They can feed on animal blood, but their preferred meal is fresh human blood."

I watched Jax's face, his features alternating in the shadow and red light. He looked red-faced and even angrier than before.

"Just remember," I said loudly, over the beating drums. "We're here for Cindy. Nothing else. There are a lot more vamps here than the two of us. Keep your cool. All right?"

The big black vamp came back moments later and motioned for us to follow him. We entered a lounge-like room with red carpets, red sofas with plush black pillows and long, black velvet drapes. A large flat TV was mounted over a roaring fireplace. The black vamp closed the door behind him and stood guarding it like a bouncer.

My heart hammered, and I looked around the room. About twenty vamps sat or lounged comfortably on sofas and chairs. There was no human girl here, no sign of Cindy.

I calmed my breathing. Vampires had an acute sense of smell. If they smelled fear, we were done for. There were laws, but if no bodies were left or witnesses…

Their black eyes were narrowed and full of hatred and anger. A male vamp stood up as we entered. He was barefoot, dressed only in black slacks. The red light illuminated his muscular bare chest and porcelain-like skin.

Everything about the vampire radiated sensual grace. My breath caught. He was mesmerizing—lethal, beautiful, and merciless. But he also had traces of a gentle elegance, like the pale beauty of the snow. He looked to be in his twenties, but I knew vampires had the gift of longevity. While not immortal, I'd heard of a few over eight hundred years old. He could be any age, with his strong jaw and full, very sensuous mouth. His long black hair gleamed like a raven's feathers, offsetting his pale skin. And unlike the other vampires, his eyes were gray.

The vampire brushed his long black hair out of his eyes, and the smile he gave me made my pulse quicken.

"Rowyn, baby, it's been a while," said the vampire, his eyes twinkling with amusement as he beheld me. His sultry voice sent my skin riddling in goose bumps.

Jax cut me a look. "You know him?" I didn't like the implication in his tone. Besides, my past life had nothing to do with this job.

I gave the vampire leader a bob of my head in way of greeting. "Danto."

Danto prowled closer, a half smile playing on his lips. "You've lost weight. It doesn't suit you."

"Tell me about it," I said as I shifted on my feet.

"Who's this? A gift?" Danto said, his attention on Jax, still smiling a predator's smile.

A muscle feathered along Jax's jaw as I said, "This is Jax. He's helping me on a case."

"Really? I never thought you the type to have a partner," he mused and began circling us. "Well, at least the years I've known you. Hunters are always alone. You're loners." I looked up to find all the other vamps as still as statues, waiting for one of us to slip up so they could feast on us. I was good. Hell, I was damn good, but there was nothing I could do against twenty vamps.

Danto pulled his gaze away from Jax and homed in on me. "And this case, you say… brought you here? I thought you came back because you missed me."

I bristled at his arrogance, but I never moved. "Don't flatter yourself." I took a breath, and when I flicked my gaze over to Jax, my bowels went watery. His face was strained with emotion, and he looked like he was about to spring into attack mode.

Shit. We needed to get out of here before the fool did something stupid.

"Where's Cindy?" I asked, very aware of Jax's increasing anger.

"Cindy?" asked Danto, his smile widening. "Cindy who?"

"Cut the bull, Danto." I wiped the sweat from my brow. *God. Why is it so hot in here?* "I know she's here. She needs to hear what I have to say. It's important."

Danto paused his circling. He now stood between me and the twenty other vampires.

"Something happened," I said quickly, knowing that I had caught his attention now. "Something happened to her parents. She needs to know—"

The black drapes behind one of the couches across from us flew apart, and a woman stepped through. Her eyes were wide as she looked at me and Jax. I recognized her large, pretty brown eyes and dark, luscious hair.

"What's happened! What happened to my parents?" Cindy's face was flushed and as she closed the distance between us.

Danto was next to her in a flash, and his hand clasped her wrist. For a moment I thought he was going to pull her away, but he stood shielding her from us with his half-naked body.

"It's Rowyn, right?" Cindy's eyes were glimmering. "I recognize you." Her bottom lip quivered, making me feel worse for what I was about to say.

I looked away from her big eyes. "I'm so sorry, Cindy. They've been killed—"

"No, no, no, no!" Cindy shook her head, her long brown hair cascading in waves. She fell into Danto's arms, and I was surprised at the tenderness on his face. Did this vamp love her? Couldn't be.

"I should have stayed with them," she sobbed. "It's my fault they're dead. All my fault."

Danto wrapped his arms around her and whispered something in her ear. The sight of his genuine affection was making me uncomfortable.

I shook the thoughts from my head. "Listen, Cindy." I waited until she turned her head so I could see she was looking at me, though still cradled in the vampire's chest. "I'm sorry about your parents. Truly, I am. I know how it feels to lose them both… so suddenly." I swallowed, my mouth dry. "But you have to listen to me. Whatever killed them, is *still* looking for you. To kill you. It's not safe for you here anymore."

"You need to come with us." Jax moved forward, surprising me, his voice cold and commanding. "We can protect you. Let's go, Cindy."

"Are you kidding me?" laughed Cindy as she wiped her eyes with her hand. She moved from Danto's embrace. With her face flushed and her eyes alight with fire, she was truly beautiful, a mix of *Gone-With-the-Wind* type old Hollywood beauty. "I've been protecting myself just fine without you around. Forget it."

Jax opened his mouth but shut it as Danto pulled Cindy behind him. "Cindy is staying right here with me." He blinked, and the gray of his eyes disappeared to be replaced by black.

Jax tightened his grip on his weapon. "She's coming with us."

Crap. This was not going well. "Cindy," I said, "I don't know how many are after us. Maybe it's only one, maybe it's more, but I do know they want to kill us. And I don't know why. They're clever and strong. They'll come for you, and they'll kill you. These vampires won't stand a chance. Not after what I've seen. Don't you think you'll be safer at Hallow Hall?"

Cindy gave tiny smile. "You of all people should know that the council doesn't give a rat's ass about us."

My chest tightened.

"What are you even doing here? You left, like five years ago."

"The council hired me to hunt the demon that's doing this."

"Really?" Cindy's voice had a touch of belligerence. "My parents are dead. Guess you're not cut out to be a Hunter either."

My anger resurfaced. "I didn't have to come here and try to rescue your sorry ass, but I'm here. Now, are you going to stay here and wait for your death sentence, or are you coming with us."

"She is not." Danto stood like a lethal predator. "She's staying with me. She's my mate."

I choked on my own spit. "She's your what?"

Cindy stood tall, defiance written all over her face. Her large eyes were clear. She wasn't spelled or glamoured. She loved him. And Danto loved her too.

I knew vamps mated for life, so this was serious. He would defend her if we tried to take her by force.

Jax looked at me. "Is that even allowed? I mean… can they… you know?"

"Yes." I glanced at Cindy, knowing all too well what would come of this if we didn't leave now. This was bad, really bad.

"As my mate," said Danto, his voice dripping with venom. "She will never leave my side. Besides, she's safer here with me than she'll ever be with you. Let me give you fair warning. If you try to take her, I *will* kill you. And I'll be well within my rights."

I felt the air shift behind me as the vamp bouncer move closer to us from behind.

"Fine," I said looking at Cindy. I didn't want to leave her with a bunch of vamps, but we were seriously outnumbered. "It's your funeral. Come on, Jax. She made her choice. Let's get out of here."

I watched in disbelief as Jax pulled out his blade.

"No," he said. "We're not leaving her here. She's coming with us."

My heart was hammering so hard I felt like I was about to have a heart attack. "Are you mad?" I whispered. "What the hell are you doing? Don't be an idiot!"

Glancing over the room quickly, I could see the long, gleaming black claws that had sprouted from what had once been manicured human fingernails on each vampire's hands. They had turned. They weren't hiding behind their human shells anymore. They were full on vamps.

Shit. Shit. Shit.

My breath came rapidly. The bouncer vampire was so close I could smell the blood he had for dinner on his breath. "Danto," I said as I met his black eyes and expression of ire while blinking the sweat from my eyes, "call off your dog. We're leaving—"

The air shifted behind me again as I felt a hand reach out and grab my arm.

Ah, crap.

I went to yank it away, but Jax was already there. I caught a glimpsed of his face, a mixture of fury and madness, and then he stabbed the big black vampire through the heart with his short sword.

Jax pulled out his sword as the vampire stumbled back. The large vamp looked more shocked than hurt. His black eyes moved past me over to Danto.

My pulse pounded. I knew what was coming. I took a breath. The adrenaline hurt.

Danto's expression was livid as he raised his arms—and snapped his fingers.

And then a horde of twenty-plus vamps barreled towards us.

CHAPTER
11

"**Y**ou idiot!" I yelled at Jax. "Why the hell did you *do* that?"

"I thought he was going to bite you. I was wrong."

"No shit, Sherlock." But it didn't make any difference. Jax had spilled first blood, which meant we were now fair game.

We were already at the bottom of the pool of deep doo-doo. We were surrounded by hisses and teeth and death.

I drew my blade in a rush as a huge, dark shape lunged from behind a chair. The ringing sound of steel was drowned out by horrible screeches and roars. Mouth spread wide, a female vamp dove for

99

me. For an instant, I saw Jax with his sword in his hands, slicing and dicing until he disappeared under a mass of fangs and bodies.

Why hadn't he listened to me?

My thoughts evaporated as I went into self-preservation, self-defense, hell, *survival* mode. The female vamp's jaw seemed abnormally large, like she'd dislocated it to better swallow me whole. Yikes. I ducked and spun, cutting her in the abdomen, and she fell off to the side just as another vamp took her place.

A male vamp, with Asian features and claws that would make Freddy Krueger proud, came at me in a flash of claws and fangs.

I knew I had to get Jax and escape through the door we came in before we ended up as an all-you-can-eat vampire buffet.

I gripped my blade, the one my father gave me, and took courage from that. "By the way, the remake *sucked.*"

Vamp-Freddy snarled and lunged, but I was ready for him.

I went down into a crouch. Claws gleamed in the red light, and I came up, whirling my blade, and swung. The blade flashed in the light, taking off a few claws in a spray of blood.

That only enraged Vamp-Freddy into lunging toward me.

"Don't worry," I grinned. "It'll grow back."

Vamp-Freddy hissed. Long, wet fangs ripped at the night air. Its eyes were ablaze with a furious black glow. Damn vamps were ugly when they turned.

In a shift of demon energy, another female vamp came at me from behind. Claws swept on either side of me as she grabbed my shoulders, and I gave her a head-butt to make her see stars. She stumbled back.

Vamp-Freddy wasn't done. He lunged, spraying the air with his bloodied stumps for claws. Heedless of the other vamps, his demon energy pulsed through me, demanding blood. Instead of dodging the advance, I ducked. Heart pounding, I sprang up, driving the tip of my blade through Vamp-Freddy's chest. I yanked the blade back with a twisting cut to the sound of a scream of mortal pain.

Vamp-Freddy thrashed on the ground, but it wasn't over.

"Jax!" I screamed as I saw a flash of silver sword and a matt of brown hair. For a moment I forgot the dangers that surrounded us as I watched him move in an elegant dance of death.

My breath caught when Jax stumbled and tripped over a fallen vamp at his feet just as he lurched back to escape the swipe of a massive claw. He came up swinging his sword in fury. The tip of the sword sliced a vamp across the smooth, taut, stomach. The vamp howled in rage as he rushed him again and again. Red-faced and sweat pouring, I knew it was only a matter of time before they'd drag Jax down and kill him—or worse—bite him. You were either born a vampire or you were created through the demonic virus. Once the vampire virus was in your system, there was no coming back from it.

Fear twisted my gut. I didn't want that for him. "Jax!" I cried as I dodged another vamp coming for me and ran towards him. I was going to drag him out with me if I had to. "We need to get out—"

Pain exploded from my side and left arm as vamps tackled me. I slashed my blade out with a powerful stroke as I went down. My arm jerked, and I knew I'd hit something. I looked up to find a male vamp with a toad-like face, claws clutched to the gushing wound at his chest. It teetered a moment and then toppled heavily onto its back.

"Jax! You fool! If we get out of this alive, I'm going to kill you!"

As I pushed myself up, a weight crushed into to me, causing me to hit the ground hard. Rolling, teeth and claws thrashed at me, shredding and tearing through my clothes and skin. It burned like a hundred white-hot knives slicing into my flesh. Boots slammed into my stomach, and the air shot out of me. I rolled on the ground and spat out a mouthful of blood, but I was up in a heartbeat.

The female vamp that looked like Elvira on steroids gave me a shocked expression.

"What?" I shrugged at the vamp. "I heal fast."

"We'll see about that," she said, stretching her mouth widely and showing off her pointy pearly whites.

I gave her a smile. "Bring it on, Twilight."

The vamp hissed and spat, springing back with a startling quickness, her eyes black eyes flashing. She leaped at me like a feral cat, slashing with her claws in a blow that could have severed through bone and flesh. I ducked past her guard and onto the unforgiving stone. I heard a groan over the shouts of the swarming vamps. Jax. My heart stopped.

Vamp-Elvira brought her fist down onto my face. Stars plagued my vision as I stumbled. My cheekbone howled in pain, but all I could hear was that sharp pain in Jax's voice, the fear. I reeled back and kicked with all my strength, hitting her in the knee. There was a crack and she went down.

I felt the warm trickle of blood from my nose, and I blinked the wetness from my eyes as the shadow of more vamps loomed over me.

Even with the angel essence that flowed in me, I was no match for a vampire's supernatural speed. They were still way faster than me, stronger, and dodged my attacks with fluid ease.

My head throbbed, and I felt it swelling up like a balloon. A male vamp lunged at me, now standing so close with his teeth bared. I spun around, but not fast enough. He grabbed me by the front of my jacket and his fist connected with my head.

I stumbled, barely aware of my legs that were miraculously still supporting me. Blood pounded in my head as the same vamp snarled, grabbed me, and threw me to the ground.

I was *so* going to kill Jax.

The air whooshed out of my chest, blood trickling out of my nose as I tasted it in the back of my throat.

"I'm going to rip out that pretty little throat," snarled the vamp male, looming over me. He bared his fangs. "You understand? Angel bitch?" He started to sit on me, but I got my legs around him and shoved with every ounce of strength left in me. I pinned him to the ground, his eyes wide with what could only be fury and surprise.

I raised my blade to his face. "Looks like I'll be doing the cutting."

I sliced with my blade in my right hand, just as I hit with my left fist. Again. And again, I hit him. I lifted my aching fist once more, but there were hands at my wrist and under my arms, hauling me off. I thrashed against them, still screaming, the sound wordless and endless.

A keening wail came from the shadows. Jax. And I felt my heart stop. For a second, I thought I saw, hunched on the ground, what looked like Jax. But my attention was immediately seized by the immense vamp descending on me as he pinned me to the ground.

I tried to move, but it was pointless. There were other vamps' hands pinning my arms and legs. Anger welled inside my core. There was no way in hell I was going to die like this, sprawled spread-eagle on the floor of some dingy vampire club.

Sour, hot breath tickled my face, his glowing, black eyes locked on me.

And then he sank his teeth into my neck.

I don't know what the fuss is all about, being bitten by a vampire. I didn't feel any warmth down in my groin. I didn't get the feels or the shakes, and I didn't explode into a lust-frenzied female.

It just hurt like bloody hell!

I felt the immediate release of my arms and legs as the others pulled away. His hair brushed my face and I got a whiff of Head & Shoulders, which left me wondering if vamps could actually get dandruff.

Pissed, I raised my left hand and jammed my fingers into his eyes sockets. He yelled and let go. That trick always worked.

I rolled to the ground and came up with my blade in tow. I could feel something wet trickling down my neck. I pressed my hand to my neck and when I pulled back, it was covered in my own blood. My knees went weak, but I pushed my fears away. This wasn't the time to freak out. And as soon as I saw the blood, the rest of the vamps did too.

They all turned my way, their noses in the air with nostrils flaring, like dogs on a scent. My freaking scent. They crouched low, ready to pounce.

But the frown on the vamp that bit me had real fear racing up my spine. He licked his lips, tasting my blood, and his eyes narrowed in confusion, almost like he wasn't sure *what* he was tasting...

"Enough!"

As one the vamps pulled away.

I looked up to find Danto still standing at the exact spot I'd last seen him. Cindy was nowhere to be found.

And then I saw Jax. He was splayed on the ground with his limbs strewn awkwardly. His face was red and swollen, his eyes closed. Blood trickled from the corners of his mouth and seeped through the tears from his jacket and shirt. His chest rose and fell, so I knew he was still alive, but a shiver spiked through me, pulling my insides tight.

"Take him," said Danto as he jerked his chin towards Jax, "and get out. If you ever come back here looking for Cindy, I'll kill you myself. And I'm going to take my time." The muscles of his chest shifted as he stepped forward. I noticed that his eyes had returned to their previous gray. "I won't say it again."

"You don't have to," I said, my throat raw. I sheathed my blade to my waist and rushed over to Jax. Damn. He looked worse up close. I dropped to my knees. "Jax?" I gently rubbed his arm. "Jax?" I said more urgently. "You need to get up? Can you get up?" Jax was well over six feet and nicely muscled. There was no way I could carry him. If I couldn't get Jax up and out, he was dead.

His eyes fluttered open and strained to focus on me. "Rowyn?"

"Yes." Panic filled me at the tension in his voice and the confusion that crossed his features. "We need to leave. Can you get up? I don't think I can lift you." I took Jax's hand, and his rough fingers squeezed mine. His skin was as cold as stone.

Jax nodded as I reached behind him and gripped him under the arms to lift him. God help me, he was heavy. But he was also wet. He smelled of male perspiration and blood. I tried not to think about the possibilities of where he might have been bitten. I needed to get him out.

Together, we managed to get him on his feet, and he groaned as I wrapped his arm around my shoulders. "Holy crap. How much do you weigh?"

"Do think twice before barging in on me again, sweet Rowyn," came Danto's voice. "And next time, do me a favor and leave your boytoy home."

"Screw you," I said as I heaved Jax towards the door. I heard Danto's laughter as I reached out and yanked open the door. I kicked out my leg sideways to give me enough room to pass.

"Come on, Jax." Bearing most of his weight, I managed to heave his stupid ass across the dancefloor, past the sneering vamps that still lounged on the sofas, all the way to the front of the club and out the door.

When I saw his car, my knees wiggled in relief. The adrenaline rush was feeding me with super powers as I managed to drag him to his car.

I shoved my hands in his front pockets, wincing at the wetness, and pulled out his keys. I unlocked the doors and shoved Jax into the back seat. I heard a thump as his head hit the side of the door.

I shut the door and slipped into the driver's seat. Fear cascaded down me in waves, ice cold and chronic. I tried hard not to think about the bite that throbbed and seared on my neck.

The Audi roared to life as I pressed the push-button start. I slammed my foot on the gas and floored it.

CHAPTER

12

Thankfully, I didn't get stopped by the NYPD for going fifty over the speed limit. There was also no one on the road, so my crazy ass driving went unnoticed. It's not like I'd had lots of practice. I barely glanced at the cars that passed me on my way out of the city. The sun wouldn't come up for another three hours, and I was glad for the cover of darkness.

I was panicked, afraid, and clueless when it came to caring for other people. I had always been alone, so I only worried about saving my own ass. I never had to worry about anyone else's.

I glanced in the rearview mirror. Jax was out cold. He didn't even let out a groan when I took a sharp right and his head smacked the side of the door.

If he died it would be my fault. I'm the one who dragged him out to the vampire club. I should have told him to wait for me in the car. I should have realized that he was no good with demons when he freaked at the sight of Tyrius.

I let out a strained breath when I eased into the lot and killed the engine. I yanked open the door and ran out.

I jogged up the stone path and practically threw myself on the door. I rang the doorbell, shifting my weight from foot to foot like I needed to pee, which come to think of it—I probably did. I rang it again. And again. And then I made a fist and started to pound on it, over and over—

The front door swung open.

Pam stood in the threshold, sleepy-eyed and wearing polka dotted pajamas. "Rowyn?" She slipped her fingers under her glasses to rub her eyes. "What are you doing here? It's like two in the morning. Are you crazy?"

"It's Jax," I said, and then added in a blabbering rush, "he's hurt. We were attacked by vampires. I—I didn't know where else to take him. I couldn't take him to a human hospital. You know what they would do. This was the only place I could think of." Unless I wanted the human police asking questions.

Pam's eyes widened like saucers and moved past me to Jax's car. Her mouth dropped open, and then she was running. She had pulled open the back passenger door even before I had made it next to her. For a larger woman, she was light on her feet.

"Jax? Jax, it's Pam. Can you hear me?" Pam reached in and felt his forehead before grabbing his wrist. "His pulse is really weak. Help me get him inside."

Together, we hauled Jax out of the car and through the front door. We put him in one of the rooms across from where I'd inspected Samantha. I didn't want to think about whether she was still there.

We heaved Jax as carefully as we could, Pam swearing profusely as we pulled him up and then dragged him over to a bed with white linen sheets. The room was small with a single window and built-in cabinet and drawers. An old TV set hung from the ceiling and two chairs, frayed with wear and tear, sat in the corners. It was a typical hospital room, sparse but functional.

Jax let out a small moan and I let go, staring at him. "His skin's turning gray. That can't be good, right?"

Pam pushed me out of the way as she cut through his shirt with a pair of scissors that had magically appeared in her hand. She pulled the shirt pieces apart and moved her fingers over his skin and the lesions. I watched her work in silence, fear flashing through me hard.

Please don't be a vamp. Please don't be a vamp. Please don't be a vamp.

My stomach was in knots. "I couldn't tell if he was bitten." My eyes rolled over Jax. "If he is…" I didn't want to think about what would happen to Jax if he was infected with the vamp virus. "Do you have anything that could counter the virus? Maybe a vaccine?" I knew it was a longshot, but I had the feeling Pam dabbled in things other than Sensitive medicine.

Pam moved to the head of the bed and inspected his neck and clavicle area. She dabbed a white cloth around his neck and then moved to his arms and wrists and finally inspected his thighs and lower legs.

Pam pressed her arms on the edge of the bed and let out a long sigh. "He hasn't been bitten."

"Oh, thank God," I said smiling and then regretted my smile at the shock and anger on her face. "He's going to be okay, right? You can heal him?"

Pam gave me a look that said if she could burn me alive with just her eyes, she would. "There aren't any bite marks, but he's been cut up pretty badly. By the looks of it, their claws did this. He won't turn into a vampire, but he's been infected with something. Maybe their claws were venomous. I don't know. But whatever it is… it's killing him." She whirled on me, furious. "What the hell did you do?" Spit flew out of her mouth. "Why was he attacked by vampires?"

"He went a little crazy. Okay?" I yelled, not appreciating her tone. I *did* try to save his life. "I don't really know why he did it. He just went a little crazy-ass on me. And then all hell broke loose. Literally." I looked at Jax's face, remembering the fury in his eyes at the sight of the vampires. It was like he'd been at war in his own head. My eyes reached his face. Even with gray corpse-like skin, he was still beautiful. I felt my knees go weak again. "Can you help him?" I said, my voice low.

"I don't know," said Pam rubbing her eyes again. "He's in pretty bad shape." She glanced over her shoulder. "Give me a hand with this IV" She rolled an IV stand to me as she went to a drawer, pulled out a transparent bag with blue fluid and hung it over the stand. "Hold his arm," she ordered, as she came forward with a catheter.

I did what she instructed and held down his arm. My thumb rubbing against his skin gave me the chills. "What is that?" I asked as I jerked my chin towards the blue substance.

"It's a demonic counter virus serum." Pam poked the needle into Jax's arm and then proceeded to check that the substance was feeding into the tube from the bag to his arm. "It's like an antibiotic for us Sensitives. It wouldn't work on a human. They don't have the correct DNA for it." At the confusion she saw on my face she added, "We use them all the time. Most of the time it's to fend off minor demon poison or from bites that have been exposed for too long without proper medication. It can reverse the effects of a demon's death blade poison if caught in time."

My mouth was dry. I let go of Jax's arm and leaned over the bed, careful not to accidentally bump into it with my hip. "How long will it take? How long until we know it's working?"

Pam moved her eyes to Jax's face. "If he's still alive in half an hour, we know it's working."

I clamped my mouth shut. I didn't know what to say to that. My heart seemed to catch at what she said. I didn't want to be responsible for the death of another Sensitive. It was another reason why I preferred to work alone. I didn't handle the loss of anyone very well. It brought up the feelings I had about my parents' deaths, and the rest all went to hell. I'd be a mess for months.

I shouldn't have accepted that damn job. I should have refused the money and gone after the demon myself.

Damn. The council should have sent the ugly one.

Pam shifted next to me, and together we watched Jax. "Tell me exactly what happened," commanded Pam, a tremor of anger reflected in her voice.

I let out a long sigh through my nose and recounted the events that led us to the vampire club. "We were only there to collect Cindy, but then things went really bad, really fast." I swallowed. "Cindy refused to come with us. Apparently, she's Danto's mate. Don't ask. And when it was time to leave, Jax went crazy. He couldn't accept that Cindy didn't want to come with us. And then he went ahead and did something really stupid." I sighed again. "He stabbed one of the vampires."

Pam hung her head. "Oh, Jax," she sighed.

"All hell broke loose after that," I said, remembering the onslaught of vamps. "It was a vampire feast fest. We almost didn't make it. If it hadn't been for Danto holding off his vamps, we'd both be dead." I searched Jax's face. "I don't get it. It was like a switch went off in his head. He went into kill-all-vamps mode. All he wanted to do was slaughter the vampires. He drew first blood, Pam, and there was no reason for it. The vamps had every right to kill us."

"Thank the souls they didn't," said Pam, her voice muffled. "He wasn't always like that, you know. He changed after his sister was killed." She hesitated, taking a ragged breath. "His twin sister."

My lips parted in surprise. *A twin sister.*

Sorrow flashed before settling into a churning burn in the pit of my stomach. I didn't have siblings of my own, but I had heard stories and seen with my own eyes how close twins were. They were two of the same. They practically shared the same soul. Remove one and you were left with half of yourself.

"Jax and I grew up together," said Pam, "until his parents moved away after the incident. Jax and Gillian were inseparable. Always together. Always laughing at some secret joke that only they knew. Both Jax and Gillian had always been nice to me when the others teased me because of my weight. Gillian was the one who untied me when Stuart and Tim had tied me to a tree for two hours." Pam's face shifted in a mask of pain. "She didn't deserve to die like that."

My insides twisted, and I saw fresh tears spill down her face. "What happened to her?" I clutched my arms around myself.

She inhaled quickly and held it for a moment. "She was killed by a demon when she was thirteen."

More tears fell freely. "There wasn't much left of her. After the demon had taken her soul, it had ripped her apart and taken her heart. They found her remains two days after she went missing. They never found the demon that did it."

"A rakshasa demon," I blurted. Seeing her questioning brow, I added, "They're a class of shape changing demons whose specialty is feeding on the souls of the young and then offering their victims' hearts as a sacrifice to their master. It's one of the only demons I know that takes the heart of its victims."

Pam pressed her lips together. A shadow crossed her features as she looked over to Jax, who was still unconscious. "Well, whatever it was, it practically killed Jax. He didn't say a word for a year after they'd found his sister. His parents took him to Europe for a while to stay with his grandparents, hoping to get him to talk. When he came back he was... different. Not with me," she added quickly, and the smallest of smiles pulled on her lips. "He's always been good to me. But different in the sense that there was a darkness in him that hadn't been there before. All he wanted to do was destroy any demon he could find. He became obsessed with finding his sister's killer and has been ever since."

My eyes burned as I looked at Jax's face, only now understanding his mistrust and hatred for demons. It all made sense—his apprehension when he first met Tyrius, which was still an ongoing issue, and his violent outbreak with the vampires. He was more screwed up than I was.

"Is that why he asked for this job?" I asked, as the pieces all started to fall into place. "Does he think there's a connection with his sister's killer?"

Pam nodded, looking solemn. "Knowing Jax, I'm sure he does," she said with a sigh. "One of these days, this crusade he's on is going to get him killed… if it hasn't already."

"Don't say that," I said, my throat tight. "He's going to pull through because he deserves some serious ass whooping from me when he does."

Pam made a choking sound that was a laugh. "Well, at least now he has someone looking after him. That makes me feel a little better knowing you're with him." She looked at me and gave me a half smile. But then her smile disappeared into a frown, and her brows fell to the top of her nose.

"You're hurt." Her fingers brushed my neck as she pulled down my t-shirt's collar. "You're bleeding—"

She let out a screech and fell back, eyes wide and finger pointing. "You've been bitten! You're a vampire!"

My hand whipped to my neck. I could feel the tiny bite marks, two tiny holes each about the size of a small pea. The flesh was sore and tender where the dumbass had bitten me. Crap. I'd forgotten. How the hell does one forget they were bitten by a vampire?

I stood in silent shock. I was still me. I was sure of it. I'd seen a human bitten by a vamp once, and it took a matter of minutes before he had turned. Kind of like with zombies, as soon as you were bitten and the virus was in your blood stream, aided by the pumping of your heart, you turned in a matter of minutes.

Vampires that fed on humans were destroyed, and that's when the Vampire Courts were formed. They protected the half-breeds but also protected humans from bite-happy vamps. Vampires had their own set of rules to follow.

Newborn vampires had to be supervised until they had the Hunger under control. Otherwise you'd have newborn vampires on a killing spree in New York. Not pretty. Humans turned vampire by bite were rare because once a vampire got the taste of human blood, they usually didn't let go until their prey was completely drained of blood. The victim almost always died.

But I hadn't turned.

Pam grabbed a surgical knife and waved it at me. "Don't come any closer! I know how to use this thing! Don't underestimate my skills with a blade! I was trained to cut things up!"

"I'm not a vampire," I said, mostly to myself. "I haven't turned. See?" I opened my mouth and showed her my teeth. "No fangs. Just regular human teeth."

"But you've been bitten!" she screeched. "Those are bite marks! And don't you try to convince me that's a hickey because I know it's not!"

"It's not a hickey." I shook my head. "Do people still do those? I thought only kids did that," I said, hearing the thread of fear in my own voice. "Pam, listen to me. I'm not a vamp. I'm the exact same person you met yesterday. Nothing's changed."

Pam's face was flushed. Her hand trembled and I could see that her mind was working a million miles a minute. "You were bitten a least an hour ago. I know the vampire virus works fast. You should have been turned by now." She seemed to relax a little as she lowered the knife. "How—how is it that you're *not* a vampire?"

The fact that I *hadn't* turned was more disturbing to me than if I *had* turned. Something was definitely not right with me.

I dropped my hand. "Honestly? I don't know."

"Is it because you're… you're… you know…" Pam waved the knife in my direction and made an outline of my body in the air.

"Unmarked?" I answered for her. "Probably."

"What *are* you?"

"Hell if I know." I pressed my lips together to keep them from trembling. I felt cold and hot all at once and that had nothing to do with the vampire bite. I wish I knew what I was. I knew I could heal faster than the average Sensitive, and that I could sense demon energies like an angel. So what was I?

I could feel my angry tears burning at the backs of my eyes. *I will not cry in front of this woman.*

I was a Hunter. Hunters didn't cry. They killed things.

I took a slow breath, watching her pretend not to notice my disquiet. It was more than not wanting to lose the only partner I'd had in the past five years or the possibility of a real friend. It was the fear of not knowing who or what I was.

How was I supposed to keep on going when I didn't know what I was capable of?

If Cindy didn't want our help, that was her problem. But I was going to find out why we were being hunted.

And I knew just where to start.

I don't know how long we stood there watching Jax breathe, his handsome face perfect even close to death, but the next thing I knew Pam reached out and touched Jax's forehead. "Oh, thank the souls," she breathed. Her eyes filled with tears as she looked at me. "His fever's broken. He's going to be okay."

I looked away so she wouldn't see the almost-tears that were threatening to leak out of my eyeballs. I mustered every bit of strength to keep them at bay, and it hurt. *Why am I even like this?*

"What are you going to do now?" asked Pam after she'd calmed herself and saw that I wasn't going to spontaneously transform into a vampire and rip out her throat.

I only turned once I had my almost-tears in check. "Now? Nothing. But I'll come back in a few hours to check on him," I said. And then added. "If that's okay with you?"

Pam smiled. "I think he'd really like that."

My face flushed. I wasn't sure I liked the way she said that. "Okay, then," I said as I moved away from Jax. "See you in a bit."

I spun around and left her staring at my back. The cool air hit me as I stepped outside, making me shiver, and I realized how tired I was. I hadn't slept. But sleep would have to wait.

There was something I needed to do first.

CHAPTER
13

"**Y**ou do realize this is the stupidest thing you've ever done," said Tyrius as he sat on the floor next to me. "And you've done your share of stupid."

"Thanks for the support," I grumbled and then took a healthy gulp of coffee and winced. It was cold. I set my mug on the floor. "What are you doing at my place anyway? I thought you were staying with grandma tonight."

"I wanted details about Cindy and to see if you'd gotten any closer to finding out what demon's after you." Tyrius's tail lashed anxiously behind him. "And by the looks of what you're about to do... you're no closer in your investigation."

I sat on my heels, knees pressed against my living room floor. I reached out and took a piece of chalk. "Don't start with me, Tyrius. It's been a rough night." I reached over and flipped the pages of an old book, using two hands to manage the unwieldy tome. The binding had been torn off the spine, and the smell of dust and leather rose to my nose as I searched the page for the next instructions.

Tyrius got up and padded over to the book. He took one sniff and jumped back. His hair stood on end like he'd been electrocuted.

"Rowyn!" Tyrius shrilled, tawny fur sifting from him. "Are you out of your angel-born mind! I recognize this book! It's a dark witch's grimoire. Are you crazy? This is really, *really* stupid, Rowyn. Do you know how dangerous they are? I should have stayed with Granny. You're going to get us killed!"

"You can't die. You're immortal."

"I can still feel pain." His blue eyes danced with fear. "How did you manage to get your hands on it?"

"I stole it from a dark witch."

Tyrius froze and then keeled over on the ground with a loud *thump*.

"Can you stop with your hysterics," I breathed. "It's perfectly safe."

"Says the girl with a dark magic book as old as dirt!" said Tyrius. He rolled over and sat. "Well, it was a pleasure knowing you."

"Leave or stop talking, Tyrius. I'm serious," I said, drawing my attention back to the book. "I need to concentrate." It was hard to read the Latin on the pages. Some of the words had worn off, and it was crucial that I read the spell right. Too many times I'd heard the stories of humans trying to summon demons and other creatures, and too many times the humans disappeared.

"Do you even know what you're doing?" quipped the cat. "Witches summon demons to draw powers from demonic forces, not angel-born. I know what I'm talking about. I'm a baal demon. Witches have used us for thousands of years as their familiars. You don't know the spells."

"If witches can do it, so can I."

"Newsflash," said Tyrius. "You're not a witch."

"No, I'm not." *I'm something else*, I wanted to say. With the chalk in my hand, I turned to him and said, "Okay. I'm going to draw a seven-point star. Inside each point, I'll draw one of the seven archangel sigils. Stay where you are. Don't walk over it, okay?" At the annoyance on Tyrius's face, I added, "I'm not sure what would happen if you did, but I'd rather not take that chance. Just stay put. Got it?"

Looking skeptical, he nodded. "Yes, master."

I made a face. I kind of liked seeing him so overprotective. It was nice to have someone other than my grandmother care about me. I drew the seven-point star, making it large enough to fit a person in the middle. And then I drew the archangel sigils inside each point.

I leaned back, admiring my handiwork. I also had to make sure there were no gaps. All the lines had to be connected. Otherwise it wouldn't work. I went over the star twice, no gaps. It was perfect.

"Is that it?" Tyrius's eyes were wide with curiosity.

"Not quite." I placed seven glasses filled with water—one above each of the sigils. Then, I got to my feet and went over to the kitchen. I grabbed the two large metal buckets I'd found in Father Thomas's shed and filled them with water. When they were both filled, I set the first one carefully inside the seven-point star, and the other one I placed about six feet from the star's outline.

Tyrius leaned back. "What are you doing with all that water? Please tell me you're not about to try and trick me into taking a bath again. I'll have you know that cats are meticulously clean. Why do you think we get hairballs all the time? We're obsessive compulsive about cleanliness."

"I thought you said you didn't get hairballs. The water's for the spell," I said as I stood up. "Water's important. It's the key element for the transition, to crossover into different realms and planes. It's the doorway to other dimensions."

Tyrius made a face. "I don't recall ever seeing any of my witches use water." He perked up. "I believe you have piqued my interest, you crazy mortal. What's next?"

"Blood." I reached my weapons belt and pulled out my soul blade. I hated that part, but without blood of the summoner, the spell wouldn't work. I took a deep breath and ran the blade along the inside of my left palm. Dark blood oozed out of a long cut. Quickly, before I spilled my blood all over the place, I held my left hand over the bucket of water inside the seven-point star and spilled seven equal drops of blood. Then I moved to the other bucket and did the same.

My heart pounded against my chest. "All right, then…" I murmured and pulled the dark witch's grimoire next to the bucket.

"Rowyn, are you sure about this?" said Tyrius, and I recognized the fear in his voice. It had the same intonation I'd had when I was leaving town. "Maybe summoning a demon's not the best solution. You know they won't give any free information. There's always a catch. They'll want something in return… like a part of your soul or something. Which demon are summoning?" His eyes widened. "Please tell me it's a lesser demon and you're not trying to summon a Greater demon? Rowyn?"

My face went cold. "I'm not summoning a demon," I said. My head throbbed as the adrenaline pulsed through me at what I was about to do. "I'm summoning an angel."

Tyrius hacked like he was about to cough up a lung. "You're going to do what? Have you lost your mind? Wait a minute—is that even possible? No—I don't even want to know… well, is it?"

I pulled off my socks, rolled my yoga pants to my knees and stepped into the bucket of water I had placed in front of me. "We're about to find out," I said as I wiggled my toes. The water was calming around my feet.

"I have a bad feeling about this," whined Tyrius. "Have you even done this before?"

"No," I answered, hoping he didn't hear the faint tremor in my voice.

"Who are you going to summon? Do you have a name? You need a name, that much I do know. Without a name it won't work."

"I have a name." I knew exactly who I wanted to summon, but I wouldn't chance uttering his name out loud until I was ready. I didn't know what would happen if I screwed this up.

I took a slow breath, willing my mind to focus while I said the incantation. I looked down at the text and began reading. "Angelus enim ego voco super Vedriel, ut esse subiectum ad voluntatem animae meae. Placant, spatium ad angelum Vedriel, in conspectu oculorum meorum."

I call upon the angel Vedriel, to be subject to the will of my soul. I invoke the angel Vedriel, in the space in front of me.

I felt a little foolish saying the incantation out loud in front of Tyrius. I'd never cast a spell before, and I'm sure he'd seen his share of witches casting spells.

I stood in the bucket of water, taut and wired, waiting for whatever was supposed to happen. My head throbbed with the pressure of my blood, making me dizzy.

KIM RICHARDSON

"Nothing's happening," whispered Tyrius. "Maybe you did something wrong?"

"Shhh," I snapped. But that was exactly what I was thinking. I was an amateur. Maybe I'd misread one of the Latin words. What if I didn't summon an angel... what if I'd summoned something else?

Just as I began to second guess my witch-casting abilities, a wind that came from inside my apartment, with all the windows closed, lifted strands of my hair. The light from the candles flickered, sending looming, twisted shadows to dance on the walls. My nose wrinkled at the smell of lemons and oranges—the scent of angels.

Immediately I felt a pull in my chest all the way down into my toes. Panicked, I looked down to see the water swirling into a whirlpool around my ankles. The pull crushed my lungs. I couldn't breathe.

Searing pain jutted through me, and for a moment I thought my insides were burning like hot wax as a force surged into me. I tried to get out, tried to lift one of my legs, but it was like trying to lift a giant concrete block. My body was cemented into place. I couldn't move.

What the hell have I done?

Over the pulsing power in my ears, I heard Tyrius calling out to me, but I couldn't even move my lips. My skin prickled from the wind blowing around me. The power of the spell ran through me like boiling water.

And then the pull subsided, and I felt the use of my body return to me, but the water at my ankles

128

kept a constant swirl. The heat rushed from me, leaving a sick, cold feeling in my stomach. I was dizzy and nauseated.

My throat was raw, my mouth dry and when I reached up to touch my face, it was soaked and sticky.

"Hold on to your butts—it worked!" cried Tyrius.

I blinked the black spots from my vision and my breath caught.

There in the middle of my chalk-drawn star was an angel.

CHAPTER
14

At first, I wasn't sure it was an angel, just a shifting blur of shadow, but then a figure solidified out of the darkness.

The angel was male, tall, his muscled body covered in dark leather that reminded me of the scales of a dragon. A long sword was strapped down the column of his spine. His face was human, blessed with unnatural good looks, his features sculpted to perfection. His face was too perfect, and it gave me the willies. Long white hair spilled down his back past his waist. His skin was fair, so much so that at first glance I thought he was an albino. But his eyes were the color of the morning sky. And like all angels, his skin gave off a brilliant glow, as though light illuminated him from inside. Strangely, he reminded me of Legolas from *The Lord of the Rings* movies.

Surprise sparked through me, driving my pulse faster. *It had worked.*

The angel's face frowned when he caught sight of me, standing in the bucket of water before him. His face was masked in shadow as he growled and said, "What is the meaning of this? Where am I?" His voice was cold and cut through the room like lightning on a stormy night. He tried to pull his legs from the bucket, and his face went a few degrees angrier when he realized he was trapped.

I knew he couldn't step out of the water, not until I said the words to release the spell, just like I wasn't able to step out either. The angel and I were connected, bound together through blood and water.

I watched as his blue eyes roamed down me to the floor, tracing the seven-point star and then to finally rest on the old book on the floor next to me. His eyes were fixed on me as I felt a spark of fear ignite inside my soul. I was sure he would have killed me right then and there if he wasn't restrained by the water.

His intelligence was obvious as he looked Tyrius and me over, fingers curling into fists at his side. "Who are you?" he said, his voice laced with quiet thunder. "You're not a witch. Your star is too sloppy to be made by one of the earth's children. A stupid human female perhaps?"

My fear evaporated, replaced by the increasing dislike of this Legolas the angel. "My name's not important. But yours is. You're the angel Vedriel. With a name like that, and with those clothes... I'm guessing you're one of the original angels. The Order of the First? Am I right? Sorry we had to meet under these circumstances, but I'm tired of waiting around for the council to give me answers. I want my own answers. And I want them now. That's why you're here."

Vedriel's stare was cold. "You're an insubordinate Sensitive child. You've broken one of the most sacred laws by trapping me to this star. Do you even know what you've done? The council will hear about this, and you will be severely punished. Say the counter spell, and I will be lenient. Release me."

"Maybe he's right," whispered Tyrius, making me flinch. How had he gotten so close to me without me even noticing? "Call it off, Rowyn. I don't like the way he's looking at me, like a baal-fillet."

As soon as Tyrius had said my name, I saw the angel's eyes narrow. I could have sworn I saw a flash of alarm in his eyes before it disappeared.

I straightened. This angel was really starting to piss me off. "Cut the scare tactics. It won't work on me. I know you can't harm me while your ass is in that water," I lied. Truth was, I had no idea. "You might be able to scare other Sensitives with your *Lord of the Rings* elf outfit—but it's not going to work on me. I don't give a rat's ass about the council, so cut the crap. I'm working freelance for them. That's it. Which is why you're here."

Vedriel eyed me suspiciously. "You're a rogue?"

"I prefer the term Hunter." I kept my voice even. I needed answers, and I knew if I pissed him off too much, he wouldn't answer my questions. "What Greater demon is killing the Unmarked?" I knew I'd hit a nerve by the shift of his face. It was subtle, but I saw it.

Even with his skin glowing, his face darkened. "Release me," he ordered, his voice rippling with darkness. The threat in his voice made my insides tighten. "Release me now or I will break free from this spell and I will rip the soul out of that soft body and end you."

Tyrius hissed and spat at the angel. His sharp white teeth glimmered with the light of the candles. I felt a warmth of gratitude. God, I loved that little demon.

"Release me now," threatened Vedriel as his eyes sparked with fury and his fists shook. "Release me!"

I placed my hands on my hips. "Not until you answer my questions," I said as he continued to seethe in anger. "You can't break free, so you can stop with your idle threats," I said, hoping I was right. I didn't remember reading anything about that in the grimoire. "You're bound to that star—to me. You're mine, angel. Just answer my questions and you'll be free to go."

"How do you know he won't kill you the minute he's free?" Tyrius's voice had a little tremor in it.

Vedriel sneered. "Your pet demon is right. I might not be able to kill you now… But once you release me. I shall return and snap your short life between my fingers. I'll leave your body to be eaten by maggots."

Swell. A heavy weight pressed into my chest and I swallowed. "You can't kill me," I said, thankful that my voice was steady. "I'm an innocent. A mortal. I'm protected under the Angel Code. If you harm me in any way, it's a ticket to Tartarus for you. I hear the angel prison is far worse than the Netherworld." I saw Tyrius tense beside me.

If things went sour, I hoped he was fast enough to run away and escape. This experiment was not going as I had planned.

"Rules are meant to be bent and broken," said the angel, a smile tugging on his lips. "I'll tell the Legion that you tried to kill me. All I have to do is show them this room. The energy from the summoning will still be here, proof that you'd trapped me against my will, for this is not the usual way angels and Sensitives communicate."

"You angels *barely* communicate." When I looked at him, his blue eyes were as ruthless as the churning of a winter storm.

"I killed you in self-defense," argued Vedriel, looking smug. "Even angels are allowed to kill mortals to save their own lives." He saw me look at Tyrius. "And then I'll kill your disgusting little pet. No witnesses. All very neat and tidy."

"Rowyn," moaned Tyrius. "I don't like this. His milky skin is giving me the creeps."

"Don't worry," I said, though my stomach gave a giant heave. "I've got this." I met Vedriel's glare with my own. I wouldn't show this angel fear. If I showed fear, my plan wouldn't work.

"I've sent a letter to the council in the event of my death," I said to the angel, hoping he would buy my bluff. "It's in the hands of a trusted friend. If you kill me, they'll know it's you. It's all written down. Every last detail."

Vedriel's jaw clenched, but he remained silent.

"I'll ask you again," I said, as I tried to calm my breathing. Tyrius was trembling next to me, and when I glanced at the continuous whirlpool at my feet, it was making me dizzy. "Give me the name of the Greater demon that's killing the Unmarked."

"What gives you the impression that *I* would know such a thing?" Vedriel crossed his arms over his powerful chest, sending his long hair in glorious waves cascading down his back. I knew a few women who'd kill for hair like that.

I raised my brows. "A gut feeling? I overheard someone from Hallow Hall say that the angel Vedriel—that's you—wanted to be kept in the loop with the killings, when you angels *never* get involved with our business. I knew something was up." I looked the angel square in the face. "Who's killing the Unmarked? I know the Legion knows more than they let on. Come on. You're angels. It's your business to know what's happening in the mortal world. And my gut feeling tells me you know something."

Vedriel's pale face was tight with repressed anger. "I have no idea what you're talking about, *human.*

Greater demons? Human killings?" he shrugged. "What's that got to do with me? With the Legion?"

A low growl escaped from Tyrius. "He's lying."

My heart leapt. Now we were getting somewhere.

"I'm not lying," Vedriel said tightly. "The Legion has more important things to do than worry about a handful of human deaths."

"Tyrius?" I questioned as I looked at the Siamese cat.

"Yup, the bastard's lying," said the cat. "Angels... they're not as holy as their human creations think."

Vedriel pulled out his sword and pointed it at Tyrius. "Your fur will make a nice hat, come this winter."

"Shut your pie hole, angel," said Tyrius. "You can't touch me while you're in your toe bath."

Vedriel's smile was crazed. "I will cut out that filthy tongue, puny demon," he snarled.

"Shut up, both of you!" I howled. I was so tired, and I was getting grumpy. I had had enough of this. I wanted my bed. My eyes closed as I gathered my strength.

"Cut the bull, Vedriel," I said as I opened my eyes and then gave him a thin-lipped smile. "There's one thing most people don't know about baals. They're truth detectors. They can sense when someone's lying. Tell me the truth."

The angel made an ugly noise deep in his throat. "And why, pray tell, would I do that?"

I stiffened at his anger. The sharp tang of citrus filled my nose, and I knew the angel was struggling with his angelic powers against the bond. He was trying to get loose.

"Well, for one thing," I said cocking my hip, as I tried to calm my rising panic. "I can keep you here all day and night if I have to. You see, the last part of the incantation binds the summoned for as long as I want," I lied. "Basically, I *own* you." I smiled at his visible hatred at those words. "It's up to you, Vedriel. You can give me what I want, and you can go home... or keep being a little bitch and you'll be stuck here with me for a very long time. I freelance. I don't have to go anywhere."

I waited as I kept my eyes on the angel, his white eyebrows going high. I could see his thoughts jumping and scrambling as he assessed the situation.

Finally, he sheathed his sword, looking murderous. "You're looking for the Greater demon Degamon."

"See, that wasn't so hard," expressed Tyrius, looking smug, and I knew the angel had spoken the truth.

"And where can I find this Degamon?" My heart thumped with excitement. Finally, I was getting real answers. I knew my demons, but I'd never heard of one called Degamon.

Vedriel's piercing blue eyes met mine. "I don't know."

I cut my gaze to Tyrius who nodded. "What can you tell me about it? Weaknesses? Strengths? How do I kill it?"

Vedriel gave me a chilling look. I could see his angelic power surging through him. If he wasn't bound, I knew he'd kill me the first chance he got.

I knew I was pushing my luck with the angel, but I saw the resolve in his eyes as he started talking.

"Just like all Greater demons," said the angel. "Degamon has significant power and intelligence compared to the lesser demons. He's clever, cunning, ruthless, and rules over an army of lesser demons."

"Like the igura?" I inquired, remembering my encounter with them. My insides clutched at the memory of what three had done to the Wentworths.

"Yes," said the angel. "Among others. Degamon cannot be killed, as you say, not by any means you possess." He eyed my soul blade against my hip. "But it can be defeated. Its body will return to the Netherworld. While it may take it centuries to reform and rebuild its physical form, it eventually will. But it will remain weak for decades."

I pursed my lips. "I'm okay with that if it means it'll stop killing us." I watched the pale angel, my unease growing because there was something I still needed to know. He was here now, and I knew I'd never get the chance ever again. As soon as he was released, he'd find some spell to keep himself from ever being summoned again.

"I've answered your questions," said the angel, recognizing something on my face. "Release me."

"No," I said, and I felt Tyrius jerk in surprise. "I have one last question," I said, my voice trembling. Then I asked the question I'd been wanting to know for the past five years.

I took a shallow breath. "What am I?"

I saw the tension flow through Vedriel, almost visible it was so strong. *He knew.* Anxiety slammed through me. Nausea gripped my stomach, and I could feel my pulse pushing against my skin.

The angel narrowed his eyes but said nothing.

I took an angry breath. "Why am I Unmarked?" I demanded, feeling myself warm. My voice rose with my sudden irritation, my hands curling into fists. "Why don't I have a sigil like the rest of the angel-born. Why am I different? *What* am I?" I repeated.

Tyrius stood up next to me and the tension rose. "He knows," breathed the tiny demon.

Exuding confidence and satisfaction, the angel stared at me without blinking. Clearly the angel wouldn't talk. I knew it was pointless. Somehow I knew he'd never answer that question.

"You bastard!" I yelled. "What am I? What's wrong with me?" I raised my fists, swinging them like an idiot, as though it would do any good. But when a smirk crossed the angel's face, I lost it.

"Tell me!" I screamed. I could feel the desperate, angry tears now. Too long I'd been going around the world feeling like I didn't belong anywhere—not with angel-born—not with humans. Too long had I felt ashamed of who and what I was. And this bastard knew, yet he wouldn't tell me.

"Tell me!" I swung my fists. I was out of control. I leaned forward—

"Rowyn!" screamed Tyrius, but it was too late.

The weight of my body pulled me down, and I crashed onto the floor. I used my hands to stop my fall, but I still hit the wood floor like a dead log. My breath escaped me. I heard the smash of the bucket and felt the water splash under my legs. I propped myself up on my elbows and I looked up to find a satisfied smile on Vedriel's face. I was so close to him I could reach out and touch him.

A wind rose, and my hair flapped in my face. Crap. Vedriel gave me a knowing smile. He knew the spell had been lifted. His pale skin flickered and then waved like water, and I could see right through him to the old cottage painting on the opposite wall.

As Vedriel stood in the bucket, tiny sparkles of light peppered over his skin, making him look like he'd doused himself in glitter.

The deep fury in his eyes scared the crap out of me. He raised his leg. Shit. He was going to kill me.

With my heart lodged in my throat, I pitched myself backwards, scrambling on the slippery wet floor, but he reached out and snatched my wrist.

I cried out as my wrist flamed. It hurt—as if the hounds of hell were chewing on it. I howled in pain, over and over again as his fingers burned into my flesh, and I gagged at the smell of burnt flesh. My flesh.

"I'll be seeing you again soon, Rowyn," said Vedriel, still holding my wrist.

Hot white light shone through the angel's body. And with a final flicker, his solid form burst into a million brilliant little particles. The angel Vedriel was gone.

"Well, that went better than expected," said Tyrius, and I felt his cold nose nudging my cheek. "Rowyn?"

My breath came in a ragged gasp. I opened my mouth to answer, but then my vision blurred, and the darkness took me.

CHAPTER

15

The bus ride south to ALL SOULS REPAIR came with the usual snide remarks I'd gotten before when riding with Tyrius around my shoulders, his legs draped around my neck like a living scarf. But when he jumped to my lap, he got the most attention.

Tyrius *loved* the attention, purring as loudly as he could whenever someone sat next to us and scratched his head or raked their fingers down his back. People were in awe of the beautiful cat, and I often wondered if he was using his demon magic to get more belly rubs. The little demon meowed loudly, demanding even more attention, true to the Siamese species. People laughed. Some even clapped and cheered, and I frowned, disgusted. Unlike my friend, I hated attention.

I'd always known Siamese were extremely vocal cats, but this was a performance by the Phantom of the Cat Opera. The more people oohed and aahed, the more colorful Tyrius's recital was. *Tyrius the celebrity*. To think that he wasn't even a real cat was an understatement.

I pulled Tyrius away from an elderly woman whose nervous fingers told me she was about to catnap him, and we jumped off at our stop.

"Did you enjoy yourself with that performance?" I asked as my boots hit the stone walkway that led to the front door. "We should have had a hat and asked for tips."

Tyrius jumped out of my hands and landed gracefully on the ground. "You're always grumpy when you don't get enough sleep. That or when you're hungry. Yeah, you're *exceptionally* grumpy when you're hungry. You're like a Rowyn-zilla."

"I have a fast metabolism," I said, smiling, because I knew it was true. I was a real monster if I didn't get my bagel with cream cheese in the morning.

"Or maybe you have a tapeworm," suggested the demon.

I made a face. "Now, why would you say that? You know I have a thing about bugs."

"Says the woman who fights monsters for a living."

"Bugs are not monsters," I said, grimacing at the idea of a tapeworm in me. "They're bugs. They're gross."

"Well, I've seen my share of bugs that look like monsters," argued the cat. "Big, nasty critters with too many eyes and too many legs." I shivered as Tyrius padded next to me, his tail high in the air. "Why couldn't you sleep? Thinking of Degamon?"

I had thought of the Greater demon Degamon and where to look next for it. But that wasn't why I couldn't sleep. I pulled the sleeve from my jacket. My right wrist had a nasty purplish-red bruise. I could make out four lines that wrapped around it, Vedriel's fingers. The pain had been excruciating when he'd grabbed me, and it still hurt like hell. The pain kept me awake most of the early morning. I'd applied ointment and bandaged it up before bed, mainly to keep Tyrius from staring at it like it was about to burst open. But when I took off the bandage this morning, it looked worse. It was as though the bruise was still bruising, like it hadn't finished spreading.

The abnormal bruising wasn't the only thing that kept me up all night. It was the deep rage in Vedriel's eyes and the promise I saw in them. One day soon he would avenge himself.

I suppressed a shiver as I felt eyes on me. I stopped and looked down to find Tyrius's blue eyes narrowed as he stared at my wrist.

"It's just a bruise."

"And I'm just a cat," said Tyrius, clearly not convinced. "Tell me, when was the last time you had a bruise that actually stayed? Eh? Try like *never*, that's when. The only time I can remember a bruise on you was when you fought with that big red werewolf in the underground fighting pits two years ago, and he'd given you a smack across the face. Your right cheek and eye got all big and swollen and red. You should have had a nasty bruise then, but after a half hour, your face was back to its normal pretty self. You don't bruise, Rowyn. You never have."

I clenched my jaw, an uneasiness settling in my stomach. "Just drop it, all right?"

Tyrius jerked his head at my wrist. "That is not a normal bruise. I might be wrong… but I think that's a mark."

I forced a pleasant expression. "I've always wanted an angel mark."

"Don't be a smartass," snapped Tyrius. "If that thing doesn't disappear in the next few days, I'm really going to start worrying."

"You're starting to sound like my grandmother," I said stiffly, knowing he had tagged along because he was worried for my safety. "I can take care of myself."

"I'm not leaving you alone," said Tyrius. The worry in his voice made my skin prick. "Not after what the angel did to you. He marked you, Rowyn. And I have no idea what that means. I thought only demons marked mortals and other demons. But that," he jerked his head up again towards my wrist, "is an angel's mark. What do you think it means?"

I pulled my sleeve over the nasty bruise. "I don't know. Nothing. He was just trying to scare me. Possibly kill me. Don't forget I did trap his sorry ass in that star. Given the chance, he would have killed me."

"Which is exactly what worries me bout that mark," said the tiny cat as he sniffed the side of the walkway. "A male German Shepard urinated here."

I shook my head, not sure how he could possibly know that. "Good to know." I glanced at the front door and I felt my pulse quicken. I didn't know why I was nervous. It's not like I hadn't been here before. Twice. When I'd left, Jax was still unconscious but alive. Pam had said the serum was working. Jax should be fine.

"Remember," I said, taking a breath, "Pam's a little…"

"Flaky?"

"No," I said. "Edgy? Overly sensitive? She really cares for Jax and I think I scare her a little. Just be on your best behavior and try not to freak her out. Okay?"

"Piece of cake," said Tyrius, the tip of his tail curling. "Women *love* me."

I pulled open the door and stepped into the small foyer. "Hello? Pam?" I ventured. There was a scuffled of feet on tile, and Pam appeared in the hallway.

"Rowyn!" she beamed, her large breasts bouncing as she rushed towards me.

"Hi, Pam—" the breath escaped me as the larger woman squeezed me into a bear hug. My arms were

146

pinned uselessly against my sides. I hated hugs. They were way too personal, and there was touching involved.

I wanted to pull away, but she kept on squeezing and squeezing. Her hair tickled my face, and she smelled of potpourri and coffee. Finally, she drew back, her oily face flushed. "Jax is going to be so happy to see you."

"So, he's conscious?" I asked, the relief evident in my voice.

"Yes, he is." Her eyes found Tyrius, who had been watching the exchange with a strange expression that I knew was amusement, but to everyone else would seem like a normal happy cat.

Pam's eyes widened in delight. "You brought a kitty for Jax? Oh, look at his eyes! A Siamese! He's glorious. They're a highly intelligent breed. I always wanted one growing up, but mom's allergic." Pam was down on her knees faster than I thought possible. "Hello, kitty, kitty."

Tyrius flicked his tail. "The name's Tyrius, lady. Hello Kitty is a fictional character with a red bow on its head. Do you see a bow on my head?"

Pam screeched and scuffled back on the floor, pointing with a trembling finger. "He's a… he's a…"

"Demon," I finished for her. "A baal. He's harmless. I promise. He happens to be one of my closest friends." Her eyes kept on getting larger and larger. "He's already met Jax. It's totally fine," I said as I saw her starting to panic.

Tyrius padded over to Pam and sniffed her. "I think she's about to seize," he said, turning to me.

"Give it a rest, Tyrius," I said moving over to Pam and helping her up. "He can be a complete ass sometimes, but he can also be useful. He's very good with computers."

"I've never seen one before," said Pam as she brushed the hair stuck on her forehead from her eyes. "Only images and what I've read about witches and their familiars. Is he a witch's familiar?"

"The correct term is baal," said Tyrius, as though he were talking to a child. "And there's an accent on the second a… ba-aaa-l."

Pam clasped her fingers. They were shaking, and so were her lips like she wanted to say something, but the words were stuck in her throat. Her face was flushed and getting redder. Guilt cascaded over me. I had put her through enough stress as it was. She didn't deserve Tyrius's pestering. The woman's eyes were red, and dark shadows marred the skin beneath. I figured she hadn't slept. She'd probably watched over Jax the rest of the night. I felt worse.

"Tyrius," I growled when Pam turned and headed down the hall. "If you don't behave yourself, I'm going to strap a collar on you… with *bells*."

Tyrius stiffened, his mouth open, clearly appalled. "You wouldn't."

"Watch me, Hello Kitty." I smiled at his horrified look and followed Pam.

CHAPTER
16

As soon as I entered the room, I felt my tension ease out of me. Jax was sitting up in the bed, his skin a beautiful golden color, not the sickly gray I'd last seen on him. He looked healthy. He met my eyes and flashed me a smile that made me catch my breath. My face flushed. Why did he have to be so damn pretty?

"Rowyn? You came?" His voice was a little bit rough, like he had a sore throat.

"Of course I came," I said as I crossed the room. "The last time I saw you, you looked like one of those extras for a zombie movie."

Pam said nothing, but she was smiling as she pulled away the TV that hung from the ceiling so I could stand next to the bed.

"That bad, huh?" Jax said. He tugged at something behind his right ear, which had turned a little pink.

"Yeah, that bad," I said, leaning against the bed. I took him all in—his large shoulders and thick arms. My mouth went dry, and I dragged my gaze down his muscled chest I spied through the low V of his t-shirt, which was probably from Pam, over the planes of his chest and to the thickness of his thighs. When I realized I had been staring for far beyond what would have been an acceptable amount of time to look at someone, I pulled my gaze back to his face to find his smiling eyes on me.

"See anything you like?" he teased as he studied me.

My face flamed, and I knew my skin had darkened two more shades of red. Tyrius jumped up on the bed, saving me from further humiliation.

"You look pretty good for a nearly dead guy," said Tyrius as he nudged up against Jax's knee and made himself comfortable on the bed. Cats.

"Hi, Tyrius." Jax smiled. Even though it was tight, with no teeth, I could see it was still an improvement over the first time they'd met. "I can see now why Pam came in here looking like she'd seen a demon. Because she did."

If it were humanly possible, Pam turned another shade of red. "He surprised me, that's all. I wasn't expecting him to speak." She glanced at Tyrius, her fingers twitching like she was dying to pet him but still couldn't.

"Yes, you do look good—" *Oh, my God. What am I saying?* "You look well," I added quickly, avoiding his eyes. *I'm such an idiot.* He was enjoying this.

Jax's eyes moved to my neck and I knew what he was looking for. "Pam told me that you were bitten," he said, his eyes gleaming with concern. "But you didn't change. You weren't infected with the vampire virus?" I could see his mind turning, trying to work out why I was so different from everyone else. "I didn't know anyone could be immune to the virus."

I gave a little shrug. "That makes two of us."

"Three," said Pam, holding her fingers in the air.

"Four." Tyrius sat up in the bed, his ears back. "You were bitten by a vamp and you didn't think to share that with me?" he said in a low voice that had more concern in it than anger.

"Nothing happened," I dismissed with another shrug. "I didn't vamp-out, so I didn't think it was worth mentioning."

"It *was* worth mentioning," said Tyrius. "All these things, Rowyn. What's happening to you... it's all connected. How could you be so selfish?"

"I was busy," I seethed, not wanting to get into what I had done last night. "It must have slipped my mind."

"Nothing slips your mind, Rowyn Sinclair. Ever."

I flinched at the way he said my name, like it was a curse in itself. "Leave it alone, Tyrius. I'm tired. Too tired to argue with you right now. Okay?"

Tyrius glared at me as he settled back against the comfort of Jax's knee. "Fine. But this conversation isn't over."

"Well, I'm glad you're here," said Jax, trying to cut the tension. "You saved me. I don't think Rowyn the vampire would have brought me here."

"No, I would have bled you to death and then eaten you." I smiled at him, broad and without restraint. His eyes fell on my mouth, and my pulse throbbed. "I'm just relieved you're okay and happy your crazy ass is here and resting, where Pam can watch over you," I said quickly. *Why is he still staring at my lips?* "I can't believe you stabbed that vamp. We're lucky to be alive." His eyes peeled away from my lips, and he silently stared at his sheets like they were going to give him answers.

My chest tightened at the pain I saw on his face. I knew he was thinking of his sister. It didn't excuse his actions, but I still felt sorry for him.

For a long moment, I just stared at the raw emotions on his face—maybe his true face, the one beneath all the masks he wore to keep his people safe and to find his sister's killer.

"I'm sorry about your sister," I rasped. I watched him as he shot an accusing glare at Pam, who didn't look at all taken aback by the subtle attack. She looked at him and shrugged as she leaned against the wall across from us.

"And I'm sorry I still haven't found the demon that killed her," Jax said with equal quiet.

"If you had been open with me, as I was with you," I said, leaning forward to get a good look at his face, "I would never have let you come with me to see the head vampire. I should have known demons were a sensitive issue when you flipped out at the sight of Tyrius at my grandma's."

"I don't bite, you know," said the cat as he yawned. "Well, only if aggravated."

Jax was silent for a moment. "Are you saying you don't want me as a partner anymore? I told you. I come with the job. You can't have it any other way."

I stiffened. "I have a troubled past, and so do you. But I don't let mine affect my job, my life, or the lives of others. When you let your emotions take over, mistakes happen. In my line of work, mistakes get you killed. And I intend to keep on living."

"I'm sorry." A tightness wound around Jax's shoulders, and tension coiled around him like a blanket. "I never meant for that to happen. I wasn't thinking."

"Clearly," mumbled Tyrius, and I shot him a glare.

I sighed through my nose. "Hell, I do need the money. But I value my life more than a few bucks. If you can't control yourself in front of demons— because there'll be more, a lot more—then I don't want you as a partner. I'll still look for Degamon on my own, though. So help me God, I'll find that SOB Greater demon and finish it."

"You got a name?" Jax sat up straighter, looking from me to Tyrius. "How did you find that out?"

"We got lucky," I lied. I wasn't about to get into the details of my stupid stunt of performing an illegal angel summoning and getting a nasty bruise in the process. "I've got connections."

"And you're sure it's this Degamon demon?" inquired Jax.

I nodded. "Yeah, I'm sure. Degamon rules over an army of igura. The Greater demon must have left the Wentworths just before we got there, probably leaving the three iguras in case Cindy came home."

"Do you know where to find this demon?" Jax's tone was all business, and I saw the anxiousness on his face, the mounting fury in his eyes.

"No." I frowned at the heavy sigh coming from him.

He peered at me with his brow furrowed and tightened his grip on the sheets. "You must have an idea of where to look, though, right? How else do you plan on finding it?"

I breathed through my nose. "I don't. I don't know where it is."

"Um, Rowyn?" Tyrius stretched, elongating his body and crossing his front paws. "Isn't it your job to *find* the demon? I mean, didn't the council pay you half up front to find it?"

"Yes." I shifted my weight and waited to get everyone's attention. "But I'm not going to go *looking* for it. I know it's hunting me... and now that I have its name..." I said, confidence pouring out of me as I ignored the sudden change in Tyrius. "I can *summon* it. I can trap it and kill it. I'm not waiting any longer. It's time. I'm doing this."

I looked at Jax and waited for his reaction. Apart from the slight frown on his brows, his face was blank.

"You crazy woman!" shrieked Tyrius. "Didn't you learn anything from what happened last night? Stupid. Stupid. Stupid. Tell her, Jax. Tell her how ridiculously stupid this plan of hers is. Jax? Are you with me?"

Jax was silent for long enough that I lifted my head to scan his face. But his eyes were bright, and I didn't understand what was there.

"I've done it before," I continued, and I saw Pam shifting nervously from the corner of my eye. "This isn't the first demon I've summoned. Demons can also be bound if properly summoned and trapped by the use of their true name. I have its true name." I could feel the strain rolling off of Tyrius. I hadn't told him, but I had already made up my mind about it.

I'd decided on that plan the moment I came to after Vedriel had left. I knew the only reason the angel had given me the demon's name was because he knew I would try and summon it, and he hoped I would die in the process. He didn't believe I would survive the encounter with a Greater demon. He was wrong.

Moreover, summoning a demon on my own terms made more sense to me than roaming the city in search of it. I knew soon it would come for me if I didn't kill it first.

"Have you ever summoned a *Greater* demon, oh wise one?" said Tyrius dryly, his whiskers flinching and his front teeth sharp as needles as he curled his upper lip in a snarl. "You've only just summoned lesser demons. This isn't the same, Rowyn. You're going to get yourself killed!"

"If I don't do something soon, it will kill me. I have to do this. I am doing this. There's nothing you can say that'll change my mind."

"You're going to summon the demon using its name and bind it," said Jax, in more of a statement than a question, shaking me out of my thoughts.

"Yes, that's exactly right," I said and felt a flutter in my stomach. "In order to cast the dark binding spell, I need to know its true name. We have it. I'm not waiting for Degamon to jump me when I'll least expect it. I'm going to summon this demon and then..." I added, smiling, "... I'm going to *kill* it."

CHAPTER
17

"Can someone please tell her this is crazy talk!" yelled Tyrius as he leaped up on his four legs, his body a crazed fluff of beige and black fur. "What's wrong with you mortals?" His blue eyes flashed with his demon magic, and my nose wrinkled at the smell of rotten eggs. "Can't you see how dangerous this is? No one in their right mind wants to summon a Greater demon! It's too dangerous. It's like putting a bunny inside the lion's cage and expecting it not to eat it. It's madness—"

"It's brilliant," said Jax, and Tyrius rolled his eyes back into his head and keeled over.

Pam, surprising me, was right next to him in a matter of two seconds, carefully stroking his fur and massaging his shoulders and back, which I suspected was why Tyrius stayed down longer than was necessary.

Shock shifted through me at Jax's reaction, and I didn't care that it showed all over my face. It was not what I'd expected, not even close. I looked at him and saw the silent understanding and eagerness to join in my mad plan.

Jax's smile was a promise of terrible things to come. "It's brilliant because the creature will never expect it. And when its lesser mind makes the connection, it'll be too late."

"Exactly," I answered, feeling a little smug at my own brilliance.

"And where do you plan on doing this crazy stunt?" expressed Tyrius, still lying on his side enjoying Pam's expert hands. He looked from me to Jax, his eyes bright and his face worried.

My self-satisfaction puffed out a little at the concern on his face. I bit my bottom lip. "My place—"

"The priest's attic?" laughed Tyrius, and he slowly came up and sat. Pam looked a little put off at not touching him anymore, and she began to fold the edge of the sheet. "Just because he's a priest," expressed Tyrius, "doesn't mean his building is sanctified and will protect you. Because let me tell you... it won't."

"I know that," I said, "and it's a risk I'm willing to take. I know what I'm doing." Adrenaline pumped through me. "I'm doing this tonight."

"Tonight?" inquired Tyrius, his eyes narrowed into slits.

"Yes. Tonight."

Tyrius shook his head, mumbling in some demonic language.

Jax clapped his hands together making me flinch. "Then we better start preparing."

"You?" I looked at Jax's face. He was still a little pale and his voice a little too hoarse for my liking. "You're not ready—"

"No, she's right." Pam's tone gave me a clear indication she didn't approve of Jax's decision. She hovered over the bed looking like a concerned parent. She reminded me of my grandmother. "You're not completely healed yet. You need to rest for another couple of days at least—"

"No way." Jax lifted the bed sheet off his legs, covering Tyrius with it, and swung his legs over the edge. He was wearing only a pair of black briefs, and my eyes traveled down muscled, golden legs that were practically hairless. Those were some damn fine-looking legs. I knew I should have looked away, but I didn't. So sue me.

My gaze pulled up to Jax's face, his smile confident at knowing I had liked what I'd seen. It sent flutters through my chest. My face warmed as Tyrius fought his way out of the sheets.

"Not cool, man," the cat said angrily as he jumped off the bed. "Not cool at all. No respect. None. You'd think I was a street mutt and not a pure-bred, treated in this fashion."

"I can't allow it, Jax," said Pam, her eyes filled with terror. The amount of concern for him touched me. "You were almost killed just last night. I know you... I know you're doing something gallant here. No one's disputing your bravery. But *use* your head. Please, just this once. Your body isn't ready. It's too soon. Why would you put yourself in danger again?"

"I'm fine, Pam. I swear," said Jax, looking between her and me. "I'm not passing up this chance to kill this demon before it kills again." He raised his hands in surrender at the sudden anger on Pam's face. "I promise if I didn't feel up to it, I'd tell you. You know me, Pam. I swear I'm fine."

I had a feeling he was lying, and Pam knew it too. He wouldn't give up the chance of finding his sister's killer, even if it wasn't the same demon. Jax was up for the opportunity of slaying any demon.

"Jax," I breathed, not wanting to be responsible for another mishap of his. He was unpredictable. "Maybe Pam's right. Maybe it's too soon for you." I shook my head as I took a step back.

"No, Rowyn, listen to me—" He reached to grab my hand, and his fingers curled around my right wrist before I realized what he had done.

My wrist flamed. I wrenched my hand away and flinched back, holding it against my chest.

"Rowyn?" Jax's stare dipped to my right hand as I clutched it, his brow furrowed in worry. "What's wrong with your wrist?"

"Hmmm?" I said, trying to rid my face of the pain. God, it still hurt like hell. Pam was right up next to me before I could blink.

"Is it a reaction from a vampire bite?" asked Pam, her face shifting abruptly to fear and worry. "I never checked your wrists. Were you bitten there?"

I dismissed her with a shift of my shoulder. "It's not from a vamp bite." Then I added, because I knew what she was about to say, "and this is not from a scratch of their claws either."

Pam reached out. "Let me see. Maybe I can help—"

"No!" I shrieked as I jumped back. Crap. Now I just made it worse by not letting her examine my wrist. All they'd be focused on now was what was wrong with it. I could see the same conclusion in Tyrius's knowing expression. He cocked his head and tapped his foot, yes, he could actually do that.

Flustered, Pam put her hands on her hips. "I'm a Healer. If you're hurt, I'm obligated to do everything in my power to help you heal and mend you." Her eyes moved to my hands. "What's wrong with your wrist?"

I pressed my lips together. I'd hoped to avoid this conversation and the embarrassment of what I'd done. At the time, I hadn't been *completely* sure it was forbidden to summon an angel, since I'd never even heard of it until I overheard an old dark witch bragging about it to another witch on one of my jobs down in a New Orleans pub. I'd followed her home and stolen her grimoire.

But it had been clear by Vedriel's face that I'd broken one of the most sacred rules. Crap.

"Are you going to tell them," asked Tyrius, "or do I have to tell them."

"Tell us what?" Jax hadn't moved from the side of the bed. His half-naked body was very distracting, but so was the worried expression that marred his face. Pam looked more exasperated than worried that I had refused her help, as though I was the very first person to do so.

"Rowyn?" pressed Tyrius, and anger flashed in me. I started to regret that I let him tag along with me.

"Fine." Seeing as I knew they wouldn't drop it, I pulled my sleeved up and showed them the ugly red and purple bruise that plagued my wrist. "This," I said, slightly irritated, "is what you get from summoning an angel." I pulled my sleeve back down. "I don't recommend it."

Silence. They were both looking at me like I was nuts. Okay, so maybe I was a little nuts. You had to be in my line of work. Nuts kept you thinking outside the realm of possibilities.

Shoulders slumping, I sighed heavily. "I know it was stupid, but it's too late for that. At least we got the name of the Greater demon out of it." My throat tightened, knowing all too well that my motivation had been more selfish. I looked at the worried faces of Pam and Jax. "It doesn't change anything. I'm still doing this tonight."

This time Pam moved towards me and raised her brows. "I want to see," she ordered, and I reluctantly obeyed. I eyed Jax, but he was thin lipped, staring at me as though he'd never seen me before. *Great.*

Pam carefully grabbed my elbow as to not touch my wrist and turned it, her brows low, close to the bridge of her nose. "I've never seen this before. But if it hurts, it can't be good. Especially from someone who's immune to vampire bites and I'm assuming other demonic viruses and curses." She eyed my wrist again, and Jax folded his arms over his chest. "I thought only demons could leave a mark like that on a mortal?"

"That's exactly what I thought," said Tyrius. "Apparently not."

Pam let go of my elbow, and I didn't like the nervous look that passed between her and Jax. "Which angel did you say did this?"

"Vedriel," I answered, suddenly feeling more stupid, if that was even possible. But when I saw the horror on Pam's face, I felt I deserved the stupidest-person-in-the-world award.

"What?" I said, looking from her to Jax. "What!" I said again, goosebumps rippling my skin.

Pam pushed up her glasses with her finger. "Rowyn, Vedriel isn't just an angel—"

"I know, I know," I cut her off. "He's probably one of the originals—" I stopped at the shake of her head.

Pam's expression was tight. "He's an archangel."

Ah, hell. I *did* deserve that award. How could I have been so stupid? His clothes and the way he looked should have tipped me off from the beginning. I was in deep shit.

This was what happened when you didn't complete all your schooling at the Sensitive academy.

My eyes met Tyrius's. "Don't look at me," he exclaimed. "I can't keep track of all the angels and archangels in Horizon. That's your job."

Pressure rose to my head, and blood pounded in my temples. I looked at Jax, his silence only making me feel worse. I could sense his tension, his wire-tight reactions balancing on the possibilities of what was going to happen to me.

"How you were even able to summon him is scary—but remarkable," expressed Pam, the skin around her eyes tightening. "Dark witches can channel that kind of energy… but you're not a witch… you shouldn't have been able to do it."

"I shouldn't be able to do a lot of things," I said, my eyes still on Jax. "But here you have it. It's done. I can't take it back."

"How did the archangel leave you that mark?" Jax asked finally, his jaw clenched with a mix of determination and unease.

My gaze shot to his, dread in my gut. There it was. The question he wanted answered, the one they all wanted to know.

Pam exhaled, her hands on her hips again. "With the basic summoning I know from reading, you should have been far enough apart during your encounter. He shouldn't have been able to touch you. It's why the summoning circles are drawn at least six feet away from the summoner."

Stomach roiling, I said, "I fell, all right? Yes, it was that stupid. I fell, and he grabbed my wrist and then he was gone."

"That's it?" Jax's tone told me he knew I was holding something back. "He didn't ask for anything? A piece of your soul?"

"You're confusing angels with demons," I answered. "Demons would have required payment. But this wasn't the case."

"No, it wasn't." Jax raised his brows. "And the archangel Vedriel answered all your questions without you giving him anything in return? He gave you this freely with no attachments? Nothing at all?"

I nodded, lips tight. "Yes." It wasn't a total lie. I let out a breath. I was getting annoyed that he wasn't letting it go. I looked at Tyrius. He was smiling as though he was enjoying this. I was going to give him a bath when we got home.

I put my hands on my hips, scowling. "Forget my wrist, all right? Because I have," I said, my voice harsher than I intended. "I'm doing this. Are you with me or not?"

Jax slipped off the edge of the bed, looking healthier and stronger by the minute. "We're doing this."

"Good." My eyes went everywhere but to Jax's very tiny, tiny briefs.

Pam's face was red, her lips in a tight line. "I'll get the bags of salt," she said. "You're going to need a lot of salt to trap a Greater demon. And I must have some silver pendants somewhere that you can use for protection... just in case..." She never finished her sentence, but I knew she meant if I screwed up again. Her gaze moved to Tyrius. "I'd offer you one, but I think you can't wear silver?"

"No, milady," said the cat, "but I'd kill for some milk, if you've got some."

Pam's shoulders relaxed a little, happy to be of service to the baal demon, and she headed out the door. Tyrius trotted happily behind her, his tail up in the air.

I would have smiled if I wasn't so tightly wired.

Soon this will all be over, I thought. I would kill the demon, and my life would be back to normal. The hair on the back of my neck pricked. My angel mark pulsed, as if to tell me this was only the beginning.

CHAPTER
18

Holding the twenty-pound bag, I poured salt over the pre-drawn circle I'd made with the chalk earlier. The amount of salt was excessive, but I wanted a solid circle, and some of the salt might get accidentally rubbed off. I couldn't take that chance.

The Seal of Solomon was a circle within a closed triangle, with three additional demonic symbols drawn inside each triangle corner. It was the usual sigil to summon all demons and I drew it from memory. That was the easy part. That I had used this sigil to summon demons before didn't fill me with any confidence.

"Most of these spells are illegal," said Jax, his eyes never leaving the large leather-bound book. Jax was sprawled on my couch, reading the dark witch's grimoire attentively. A strange smile appeared on his face. "Now this is interesting—there's a spell that can make your... you know..." his face reddened, "... *parts* a little larger."

He looked much better after tearing into two Big Macs and a helping of fries and washing them down with a large soda. I'd offered to drive, seeing as he was still on the mend, but Jax wouldn't hear of it. I had the feeling he felt like I was about to wreck his sparkling Audi or—God help us—scratch it. But it could be that he didn't want anyone to see him being driven around by a female.

It was hard to concentrate with him here, with him looking like that, like an edible piece of male perfection. From what I could tell, he was giving off the singles vibe, and not once did he mention that he had a girlfriend. Not that I was interested. Still, Pam would have said something, right? Or maybe not. Maybe Jax asked her to keep his personal life private after she dropped the dead sister bomb. Who knows? Maybe he had a secret fiancée in France somewhere, waiting for him, a gorgeous voluptuous one like Amber.

Jax had warmed up to Tyrius too, offering him some fries. Crap. If he was going to start being nice to the baal demon, I was going to be in trouble...

"You missed a spot," informed Tyrius as he pressed his paw next to a sharp point on the sigil. He shrugged. "Just saying."

My face burned as I realized that Tyrius saw me looking at Jax. *I've been single way too long.* I said nothing as I moved to the spot. I exhaled through my nose, keeping my arm steady, and dumped some salt over the stroke of chalk. I was glad to have another pair of eyes on my sigil drawing skills, but I wouldn't tell Tyrius that.

The spilled water from my botched summons ritual with the archangel Vedriel had wiped away any trace that I had ever drawn a seven-point star. The only proof that it ever happened was the fingerprints around my wrist.

I cursed myself for being so clumsy. What were the odds of that happening? I lit three candles and positioned them on top of the three demon symbols near the tip of the triangle corners.

Unfortunately, after going through the entire dark witch's grimoire three times, I didn't find any summoning spells for a Greater demon. There were only the usual incantations for the lesser ones—imps, shadow demons, morax demons, even hell hounds. I didn't have time to look for another dark magic spell book. I was doing this now. I had the demon's true name. The rest was just inconsequential.

Most witches used all sorts of trappings to summon and contain a demon, but seeing as I already had its true name, I could easily summon it by simply saying its name and willing its presence.

I wiped the sweat from my brow with my forearm before it dripped into my eyes, and I took a breath, my temples pounding.

"You look a little pale," stated Tyrius, and I flinched. Damn that cat was too observant. "And you're sweating. You never sweat."

"I'm fine," I lied, just as my vision blurred and I blinked until I could focus. "I'm nervous. It's normal to be nervous, for God's sake. I am about to summon a Greater demon, so sue me if I'm a little sweaty."

I wasn't sweating because I was nervous, though I *was* nervous... I was sweating because I felt ill. The truth was, I woke up with a light fever this morning, and as the day progressed, it was getting worse. Now my fever had married itself with a pounding headache. Great. My heart was pounding, and I hadn't even done anything yet. Super-duper.

"You forgot the mirror," muttered Tyrius. Then he made an annoying sound as though he was clearing his throat. "Mirrors are essential when it comes to summoning demons, ghouls and wraiths. Without the mirror, they can't cross over into our world. Mirrors are portals, like water is to angels—"

"I didn't *forget* the mirror," I snapped. "And I know what mirrors signify in the supernatural world. I've done this before, remember?"

"I don't actually," said the cat. "I wasn't there. Because if I was, I would have stopped you from doing something so utterly stupid... like what you're about to do now."

"By annoying the hell out of me?" Huffing loudly to show him how annoying I thought he was, I reached behind me and grabbed an oval-shaped mirror, which I had taken down from the bathroom. I placed it in the middle of the triangle, careful not to break it. Not that I was a superstitious person, and I didn't believe in the whole seven-years-of-bad-luck thing. I just didn't want to spend the money to buy a new one.

Scanning the Seal of Solomon with everything in place, I noticed only one thing left to do. My favorite part. Once again, I yanked out my soul blade and lifted my left palm. That got Jax's attention as he snapped the book shut, leaped to his feet, and came to stand next to me. My skin pricked at his nearness.

The pressure was on now with two extra people witnessing my talents in summoning. I would have preferred to be on my own in case it didn't work. But in case it *did* work, having Tyrius and Jax as backup was a better option.

My hand shook as I stared at the small white line across my left palm that had been open and spilling blood just yesterday. I took a breath and, using the line as a guide, slashed through the soft flesh. It stung, but I keep my face blank as I squeezed some blood into a small puddle on the floor.

Using my own blood like ink, I wrote the name Degamon on the mirror, careful to spell it out correctly. Writing the name incorrectly would have disastrous consequences—like not working at all or giving the summoned demon free reign over the summoner. Not good.

Wiping the blood from my hand with a cloth, I leaned back. "Water and blood for angels... mirrors and blood for demons."

Tyrius's ears swiveled above his head as he looked at me, his tail lashing behind him. "What about the incantation?"

"It's coming." I stood up and regretted it almost immediately. My head swam, and my hands started to sweat as an uncomfortable sensation of being both hot and cold overcame me. My pulse pounded behind my eyes. I took a moment to steady myself, and hopefully it looked like I was preparing myself mentally for the final spells. If Tyrius knew I felt like I had the flu, he wouldn't let me continue. A wash of angst took me, but there was no turning back. When the dizziness subsided, I took five steps back, my soul blade hanging in my hand.

Jax followed my exampled and moved back too. "When do we kill it?" He rested his hand on the hilt of his soul blade, a slight tremor in his fingers.

My pulse quickened as I stared at the flickering candles. "After it answers my questions. We need to know why it's killing. Why it's targeting us. Because even if we destroy it, who's to say that another one won't take its place? Cindy and I won't be safe until we know for sure." My gaze moved over his face. "You're going to be *okay* with this, right?" I said, not liking the tension I read over his face and body. "You're not going to lose control and do something stupid, right? Because this Greater demon is far more powerful and evil than a vampire. We can't screw this up. We might never get another chance."

"I won't." Jax's eyes grew intense. "I won't do anything until you tell me to. I promise."

I frowned. "Why am I not convinced?"

Jax exhaled and turned his body to me. "I know what I did was stupid. I'm sorry."

"You almost died."

"I almost died," he agreed. Jax took a breath and then let it slowly out. The guilt in his eyes told me he'd regretted his recklessness. "I know I was an idiot. I won't let my emotions get it the way again. I promise you. I know how important this is, and I won't screw up again. I swear it." I could tell he was being truthful, or at least he believed he was.

His eyes caught and held mine. I felt a warmth that had nothing to do with my fever. His confident grin told me he knew something I didn't want to admit to myself.

I stilled my emotions as I stared at him, feeling my heart pound. "Good. Remember, the demon will be bound to me, bound to the circle, but it's still *very* dangerous. Don't get too close, and whatever you do… don't give it too much personal information about yourself. This is a Greater demon. It's got thousands of years of cleverness over us, and it's going to use it."

"Some demons are known to break free from the circle, Rowyn," said Tyrius, his eyes on the Seal of Solomon. "And drag the summoner with it back into the Netherworld."

"That's why we have our soul blades, in case something should go wrong. But it won't." I didn't like the fear in his tone, but I was more irritated that he didn't think I could do this. "I have the demon's true name, and that's power. Once I summon it, it can't hurt me."

"Maybe," said the little cat. "But I've seen my share of disastrous summoning with witches. I'd hate for you to spend eternity being tortured in the Netherworld as a demon's slave. The horrors they could do to your soul... to your body..."

"I'll kill it before it touches Rowyn," said Jax, and there was a dangerous note in his voice. I looked at him, surprised at the fierceness I saw in his eyes.

"I applaud your courage, young mortal," said Tyrius, his voice tight, "but if the demon latches on to Rowyn," his eyes flicked between me and Jax, "there's nothing we can do to stop it."

"I'm not dying today," I said, swallowing hard and doing my best to ignore the past few hours of uncertainty and fear as I had prepared the summoning ritual.

Tyrius lowered his eyes, his ears swiveling back. "There are worse things than death, dear Rowyn."

"Maybe you should let me be the judge of that." Fear licked down my spine making me shiver. "It's not going to happen," I said, my voice not sounding as convincing as it did in my head. The thought of me or my soul as some demon's sex slave made me want to vomit.

"Can't you just banish it with a spell and be done with it?" questioned Jax.

"No," I breathed. "It doesn't work that way. You need to summon it first and then banish it."

Jax scrubbed a trembling hand across his face and said, "Then, I want to know if it's the same demon that killed my sister."

His expression was unguarded, stripped of its usual distance, and he looked both very young and very old. He lowered his hand and curled his fingers around the hilt of his blade, his eyes moist.

Adrenaline shot through me, making me shake. I reached inside my pocket and pulled out the scrap of paper I'd written the two spells on, in case my nerves might make me forget.

"Ready?" I looked from Jax to Tyrius.

"For the record," said Tyrius, "let me say again how incredibly stupid this is."

"Noted." My chest clenched in guilt at the sight of real fear in the baal's eyes. Tyrius was acting like an overbearing parent because he was scared and because he loved me.

I took a slow breath, fighting off another spell of dizziness, and read the spell again in my head. Then I hid it in my pocket.

Maybe this was stupid, maybe I was stupid, but I'd rather meet the demon face to face than wait for it to jump me while I was sleeping.

I swallowed as I let the words flow through me. "Voco super daemonium Degamon ut esse subiectum ad voluntatem animae meae," I called, my heart pounding. "Degamon meum et vocavi te in spatio et in conspectu oculorum meorum." And then for good measure because I really didn't want to mess this up—and all without taking a breath—I repeated the spell in English. "I call upon the demon Degamon, to be subject to the will of my soul. Degamon, I summon you in the space in front of me."

My heart was beating fast, too fast. I felt like I was about to throw up. Swell. I wasn't sure why but I preferred to fight a demon than be sick in front of Jax.

I took a calming breath. My gut clenched when a small gust of wind broke through my apartment, just like when I'd summoned the archangel. With my gaze fixed to the name, I waited.

The breeze lifted my hair around my face and then died almost as soon as it had risen.

A frown creased my brow. "I think I did it wrong," I said, reaching inside my pocket for the written spells. "Just a sec—"

"Shit," Jax swore, and my hand froze. "Something's happening. Look!"

I looked up to find him staring at the floor. The hair on the back of my neck pricked. My bruise gave a pulse before my wrist flamed.

The blood with the name Degamon written in it bubbled and steamed above the mirror, the cloud of reddish vapor billowing up to follow the confines of a body not yet taken shape.

I waited, my tension growing. I had no idea what shape the demon would take. I'd never heard of it. The demon could look like a great big worm, a giant hairy spider, or a little old lady. I opted for the old lady.

The mist whirled, taking on what I could see was definitely a human shape. The red mist coiled and then coagulated to reveal the demon.

My breath hissed in through my teeth. But it wasn't a demon. It was my dad.

CHAPTER
19

"**W**hat the in the world?" Shocked, I stood goggling like an idiot at the creature that was my dad.

The demon straightened and said, in my father's voice, "My darling daughter, how nice to see you again," sending chills fluttering through me.

Standing on the mirror was my father's doppelganger. He looked *exactly* the same, had the same scar just above his eyebrow that he'd gotten when he'd fallen as a kid, the same thinning streaked gray hair and matching beard. He hadn't aged at all in the last five years, as though he'd been frozen in time. He wore the clothes I'd last seen him in, beige khakis and a polo shirt.

But his eyes... those weren't my father's hazel eyes staring back at me...

"You're not my father," I said hesitantly, my grip slipping on my soul blade as I tried to recover from the shock of seeing my father again. The familiar scent of rotten eggs and death rose thick and musty, overpowering the stale air from my apartment. "My father doesn't have black eyes, demon. Or should I call you by your true name... Degamon?"

My demon-father pressed his hands to his chest, and the familiar motion sent a spark of torment at my heart. "You wound me. How I've missed you. You're the splitting image of your mother when she was your age. Did you know that? Oh, she says hi, by the way... she's with me, you know, in the Netherworld... waiting for her only daughter. Your mother loves you very much. Don't you want to be reunited with her? Don't you want to join us?"

"Shut up! Just shut up!" Shit. Shit. Shit. This was not going like I had planned. Sweat poured down my temples and forehead, and I rubbed it with the back of my arm trying to remember what I was supposed to be doing. *What's wrong with me?*

"That is *not* your father," warned Tyrius, and then a deep growl formed in his throat as the demon grinned at him. "Don't listen to it. It's just trying to confuse you. Don't forget why we're doing this. Why we're here."

"This is so messed up," said Jax, and I recognized the fear on his face because it mirrored my own; he feared that if the demon decided to turn into his sister, he would lose it.

The adrenaline seemed to push my fever down for the moment as I gathered myself and straightened. The demon would not get the better of me, not while I still drew breath.

"Why did you take the shape of my father?" I asked, with a terrifying calm that surprised me. "What do you know of my parents?" I hissed, my pulse thumping against my forehead.

Degamon grinned to show startling white teeth, chilling me with its confidence. "I know they suffered an untimely death."

"How do you even know that?" Rage rose up in me in such a mighty wave that I had no thoughts in my head other than wrath.

"I share a direct link with my summoner," said the demon. "With your blood, I share your memories, your fears, your most *intimate* thoughts. Oh, my, my, my... how naughty." Its black eyes went to Jax and I felt my face burn. Hopefully, Jax and Tyrius hadn't noticed.

"How nice," I grumbled.

Degamon leaned close. "Humans who summon demons are bound to them, usually in exchange for eternal youth, eternal life, fame and fortune... but that's not why you summoned me, is it?"

"Enough with the chitchat," I commanded, afraid of what the demon might reveal next. But the fact that I was staring at my father was creeping me out. "Degamon. I need information. Questions need to be answered... and you're the one to answer them." No need to tell it I was planning on banishing it, if it hadn't already guessed or read those thoughts. "Why did you kill all the Unmarked? Why are you hunting us?"

A smile came over the demon. "Did you know that your blood is unique? Tasty with subtle flavors I don't recognize."

"Then you don't deny it?" I took the demon's silence as a yes, wondering if it could see the mark left by the archangel on my wrist. "Why? Why are you doing it?"

Degamon tilted its head thoughtfully. "Presuming I have this information you require, what is it worth to you?"

I scowled. "I'm not giving you my soul, demon. You can just forget it. So, what else do you want?" I knew this was dangerous territory. Offering something to a demon was never smart since if things went south, the demon could always use it against you.

But nothing would go wrong this time. *I* had its true name. It was bonded to me, not the other way around.

Degamon pulled up its head and smiled. "Give me your name, and maybe we can negotiate?"

"How stupid do you think I am?"

Degamon tugged on his shirt. "About as stupid as all the rest of the mortals who summon me." My demon-father grinned. "I have to assume you know the basic rules. You do not call upon me lightly. The possible dangers are far too great. A favor for a favor. It's how it works."

Jax shifted next to me. He looked wary but not frightened, and I drew some courage from that.

I stood my ground, feeling the effects of the adrenaline diminishing. "I do know the rules, Degamon. One, which all Netherworld beings are *obliged* to follow when summoned, is to offer assistance to the witch who called them."

"You're not a witch."

"I know that," I answered, a little peeved. "But here we are—and you get little me. Are we going to do this or not? Answer my questions and I'll send you back."

The demon said nothing as it crossed its arms over its chest, mimicking my father's character. Its black eyes roved from Tyrius to Jax and finally rested on me. "Does the council know of your dealings with demons? Not only are you acquainted with this demon Pokémon—"

"Did you just call me a Pokémon?" growled Tyrius, his ears back. "No. You. Didn't—"

"—but you have summoned a few other lesser demons in the past," informed Degamon. "I know the council laws. Death, should they learn that you have willfully brought demons into the mortal world."

"What do you want in exchange for the answer?" I demanded. Blood gushed to my head and I felt it might explode. "Answer me!"

"You are an aggressive bitch, angel-born." Eyebrows raised, the demon glared at me, its black eyes gleaming with sudden ire. "Once I am free of this magical circle, I *will* kill you. Just as I killed the others." The demon glanced over my apartment with open curiosity. "I know you are not well versed in the dark arts," it mused aloud as it raised its arms and motioned to the Seal of Solomon I'd drawn. "But I'll give you one for free."

"That's crap. It's trying to trick us," breathed Jax. "No demon would give anything for free."

I knew Jax was right, but I still waited to hear what the demon had to say before I banished it.

I felt Tyrius shift as he said, "I'll show you… *Pokémon…* you no good sack of demon crap…"

The demon's face was empty of emotion, and for a moment I thought it wasn't going to answer. "I've killed the Unmarked because I must," began Degamon. "Because I am commanded to do it. Because I am compelled to do so. I must kill *all* the Unmarked… including you."

Fear cascaded over me, and I shook. "You mean… someone else has *summoned* you?" My fear shifted to anger as I put the pieces together. Someone wanted us dead and had risked invoking a Greater demon to do so.

"Who summoned you? Was it a witch? A warlock?"

The demon smiled. "No more freebies, darling. If you want more, you need to give me something in return. Your name—"

"No."

"A piece of your soul, then," said Degamon with a grin. It shrugged. "I have to ask. I am a demon after all."

"No," I panted, half with panic, half with rage. "I told you—you can forget it—"

"Well, I *can't* give you what you want if you don't give me what *I* want" said Degamon. "You got the first one free. The rest, well, they'll cost you." It sighed at the look of horror on my face. "It's how it works," it said pointedly. It put its hands on its hips. "Really, what do they teach angel-born these days?"

"I'll do it." Jax's face was void of emotion. "I'll give you my name if you tell us who summoned you and the name of the demon who killed my sister."

"Ahhhh," breathed Degamon, eyes gleaming. It pressed the tips of its fingers together with both hands. "Now we're getting somewhere. Interesting."

I whirled around. "No way." Panic spiked through my veins. "I'm not letting you do this." If anyone could resist the ramifications of giving their name to a demon, it was me. I was already damaged. I could take it.

"It's fine," said Jax, though the creasing of his brow told me otherwise. "I want to know if it killed my sister. I've spent most of my life looking for her killer. This is my chance. I'm willing to give up my name to find out." The pain in his eyes wrenched at my heart.

"Besides, I'm not the one who summoned it, so it can't break free from the circle, right? I'm the only one who can. I have to do this." Jax gave me a look, and I could tell he believed the demon's claim on his name would disappear as soon as I banished it. But it still made me nervous.

"What will it be? Hmmm?" prompted Degamon.

"I hope he knows what he's doing," whispered Tyrius, his brow creased in concern, but Jax didn't take his eyes off the Greater demon.

Me too, I thought, my heart pounding.

Jax ran his eyes over the demon, and I saw only pure hatred there. "Just so we're clear, I'll give you my name if you tell me the name of the demon who killed my sister *and* the person who summoned you to kill the Unmarked. Agreed?"

"It's a deal." Degamon grinned and a sick feeling twisted my stomach.

"The names, Degamon," I ordered.

"Let us not be hasty, angel-born," said the demon. "His name first and then I give you the names."

"This feels wrong," warned Tyrius. "I don't like this. I don't like this one bit."

"Me either," I breathed. *But we needed those names.* I squared my shoulders. "Fine. But you are bound by this magic circle. It's a binding contract. You can't withdraw."

Degamon gave a wolfish grin. "That is correct. Do we have a bargain?" the demon prompted, excitement making its eyes seem bigger. "Say it, and you'll have your names."

"Agreed," said Jax, his lips tight in anger. I looked at his eyes. They were so green, my heart pounded, and I felt lightheaded at what he was about to do, even if it was only temporarily.

"Yes, agreed." I swallowed hard, glad that my voice didn't reveal the fear that was jumping through me. I caught a glimpse of Jax, his eyes pinched in worry. A nauseating mix of dread and fear shook my knees, and I held my breath so I wouldn't get sick.

But I had to fulfill my end of the bargain. Otherwise, we'd never get answers. Jax deserved to know the truth and we needed to know who had summoned Degamon.

Jax straightened his shoulders. "It's Jaxon Spencer."

The demon closed its eyes. A soft sound of satisfaction emanated from Degamon—a long, low rumble of contentment and pleasure.

Without warning, Jax jerked forward and I heard his sharp intake of breath. He gasped, his eyes flying wide open. His hand went to his chest. And then he went still, as though some force held him with an invisible string.

I blinked against my tears as Jax's face trickled in sweat, and his bottom lip trembled. He opened his mouth as if he wanted to scream but nothing came out. Gagging, Jax struggled to breathe. In a moment of panic, I thought the demon had lied and was killing him. But then Jax fell back, breathing harshly enough that I could hear it. Ashy and pale, he stood stock-still, but alive.

I straightened, and cold sweat dribbled down my temples and back.

Across from me, Degamon, was beaming and I didn't like it.

"Jax, you okay?" My throat was tight, and I felt a stabbing pain in my chest as though part of my soul had been taken right along with Jax's name.

Jax's eyes widened even farther. His lips parted, and he stood there, seemingly unable to even blink.

"Jax?"

Jax turned his head and nodded, his gaze distant, and I couldn't tell if he was in pain or not. Frowning, he studied the demon for a long moment. "So, is it you?" Jax's anger showed through his frustration and eagerness. "Did you kill my sister?"

"No," said Degamon in a voice as though it had surprised itself. "I did not kill your sister. The demon you're looking for goes by the name of Strax. It's a lesser demon, a rakshasa."

I bit the inside of my cheek. I hated being right.

Jax clenched his jaw. "And the name of the person who summoned you to kill the Unmarked?"

The demon remained silent, its black eyes on Jax.

I glared at the murderous demon and wished it would get a new shape already. "A bargain's a bargain," I said. "Give us the name—"

"I can't," it chortled. "I don't have it."

"I knew it," spat Tyrius. "It tricked us!"

I started. "It can't trick us. It's bound to the circle, to me." I gritted my teeth. "Degamon. I command you to tell me!"

"Command? Did you say... *command?* You, insignificant little speck of existence." My father's face started to warp, twisting his features to something more animal like in nature. "You don't *command* me."

"Banish it!" cried Tyrius. "Forget the names! Banish it before it's too late."

With a trembling hand, from both anger and fear, I yanked out my piece of paper. Holding out in front of me, I read the banishing spell.

"Per júdicem vivórum et mortuórum! Sed enim mundi Creator! Qui habet potestatem mittere in infernum! Degamon! Ut abire ex regno protinus!" I shouted. "By the Judge of the living and the dead! By that who has the power to cast into the Netherworld! Degamon! Leave this kingdom immediately!"

Degamon threw its head back and laughed, a horrifying guttural laugh that could only be demon. There was nothing human in it, and it chilled me to the bone.

"Bloody hell." Tyrius backed up from the circle, his fur sticking on its end making him look twice as large. "It didn't work. The spell didn't work!"

"That's impossible." I didn't like the panic in my voice. "You're bound to me! I know your true name!"

The demon's face lost its amusement and, its expression deadly serious, ran its attention over my face. "True. But you've made a grave mistake, little mortal, a mistake that'll cost you your lives."

I gripped my soul blade and took a step forward. I could kill it now. It was still bound to the magic circle.

Its black eyes fixed on my soul blade and then smiled. Fear tightened my stomach. "You cannot kill what cannot die. Your tiny angel weapon has no effect on me. Nor do your dark witch spells."

"You're still bound to the circle," I hissed. "And I can still vanquish you back to the Netherworld!"

Degamon shrugged. "But... am I bound?" questioned the demon, and my pulse pounded. "While your Seal of Solomon is correct, and would work on lesser demons, there are keys that can unlock and alter a summoning circle. Just like that one on your wrist."

My heart leapt in my throat.

Degamon sneered, making my blood pressure rise. "I was never bound to you, angel-born."

In a blur of limbs, Degamon broke from the circle.

CHAPTER
20

The three of us jumped back as Degamon landed outside the circle. Still in my father's form, it shivered as red and black vapors coiled around it. With its hands it pulled at its face and body, and its skin stretched like gum and melted wax, hitting the floor in clumps of hissing vapors. Nasty.

I knew some Greater demons were pagan Gods and Goddesses, but this thing was way too ugly to be either, or they had dropped their standards.

Degamon stretched to its full height, I guessed about eight and a half feet tall, as its head nearly grazed my nine-foot ceiling. Humanoid, it stood upright, a giant demon with seeping skin as red as blood and a mismatch of black fur along its back, arms and legs. It looked as though its flesh was still in the stages of decomposition. Taloned fingers brushed the floor, and its thin-fleshed arms dripped with red and yellow sores. Its head was the shape of an egg, abnormally large, with a mouth that was too big and filled with too many sharp, yellow teeth. The only thing that remained of my demon-father, were the eyes.

Its black eyes focused on me. "Angel brat," it snarled. "I shall take pleasure in killing you, in drinking your blood and tearing your flesh from your bones as I did the others."

"Screw you," I seethed and braced myself, feeling another wave of fever pour over me.

"Nothing personal," snickered Degamon, its lips stretched across its face to its ears in a gruesome attempt at a smile. "A job's a job's. Isn't that right, Hunter?"

It moved in a blur of red, faster than any demon I'd seen before, tearing up the floor boards as it came at me in a rush. For a moment, I was frozen, staring at the nightmare demon that I had unleashed upon the mortal world. Me. My fault.

Degamon charged and I spun, slipping away at the last instant. My pulse quickened, and the adrenaline spiked, but it did nothing now to hide my fatigue and fever. Even now, as I moved, I could tell it was with an added effort, more strenuous every time. I was weakening. Weakening for the first time in my life. And it scared the crap out of me.

Movement caught my eye, and there was Jax, whirling with cold grace in an onslaught of flashing blades. With detached efficiency, Jax caught the demon on the point of his blade. As he came down and around the demon, his blade sliced open the demon's hide in a powerful stroke.

Degamon hissed and backhanded Jax with the brute force of twenty men. Jax flew backwards and hit the kitchen cabinets in an explosion of cabinet doors and pots and pans.

"I've had enough of playing, whore," snarled Degamon, just as I heard Jax curse and get up. "I want what's mine, what's been promised. Are you going to give it to me, or do I have to take it from you—"

"Who promised?" I prompted. I knew it was a long shot, but maybe it would get cocky and answer.

Degamon whirled and dove at me. Maybe not.

The demon hit me before I knew it had moved. My face exploded into a fiery agony, and I crashed backwards into the small sofa. Without pause, I sprang back into the fight and skillfully avoided the flashing of its claws and fangs.

"I was sent to kill you," said Degamon. Black blood oozed from the cut Jax had given it and dripped down its side. "But in truth, killing angel-born brings me joy, so much so I'm willing to do it for free."

Degamon sprang in a storm of claws and fangs. It felt as if I were fighting a shadow. No lesser demon could move the way it did. I lurched back, but not fast enough. A swipe of Degamon's powerful claws caught me in the stomach and I tumbled to the floor. It was on me in a matter of seconds. I brought my knees up, protecting my stomach. We rolled on the floor, each trying to gain the advantage. With its emaciated, blistered arms constricting around my chest, the demon tried to muscle me onto my stomach. I could feel fetid breath on my face as I saw a mouth full of teeth lowering towards my neck—

Degamon howled and sprang back, releasing me, and I took a heavy breath.

"Come on! You bastard!" Jax stood behind the demon and the kitchen table, his face blotched in red spots. The tip of his blade dripped in black blood.

"Come to papa, daemonium!" yelled Tyrius, eyes flashing with demon magic. He slashed the air with his claws, a quick gesture, graceful with murderous mastery.

"Come on!" Jax yelled again, swinging his blade.

"With pleasure."

My chest tightened as Degamon leapt over the table toward Jax and Tyrius. The room suddenly resounded with a peal of thunder at the burst of battle. I saw flashes of red, streaks of fur, and sweeping arcs of steel. Shards of wood filled the air.

A wave of nausea swept over me, and I fell to the floor on all fours like an animal. Sweat trickled into my vision and my eyes burned. I blinked, trying to focus as the world around me tipped. I saw Degamon, wild and attacking with the grace of a skilled killer. Its arms lashed around, talons out like huge blades. Jax swung his weapon to keep the sharp talons at bay. Degamon's teeth snapped as it lunged at him. Jax thrust his blade, piercing the demon's neck with a glancing strike, enough that the demon reeled back in pain and fury.

"It's funny," Jax said, examining the demon. "I've fought my share of demons, but you are by far one of the ugliest SOBs. And what's with the smell? Man, you *stink*."

"No one bathes in the Netherworld," yowled Tyrius, his back arched as though he was waiting for the opportunity to pounce. "It's one of the reasons why I left."

Degamon opened its mouth and hissed. "You'll be bathing in your own blood once I'm finished with you."

"How original." Jax made a show of his blade as he twirled it skillfully in his hand like a baton. "It's not like I haven't heard that one before. For a demon as old as dirt, you need to get new material." Jax turned his head and our eyes met, his face scrunching in concern at the sight of my increasing fatigue.

Degamon grinned, and its lips cracked, coating its teeth in black blood. "I might not have killed your sister," it said, "but I know she screamed for her mommy as her innards were being pulled out of her and eaten while she still drew breath."

"Jax! Don't!" I yelled, having seen his face go pale and the deep fury in his eyes. He was lost in his own pain and anger. And that was a recipe for mistakes. He was going to get himself killed.

With a scream of rage, Jax raised his blade and dove at the demon in a savage onslaught of blades and kicks. Degamon moved like the wind, causing Jax to miss his target. He whipped his blade up and outward with frightening speed.

I heard a grunt from Degamon as it bounced back. Surprise crossed its ugly features. It moved its hand away from its abdomen, its talons dripping in black blood.

"You've got skill, tiny human," said Degamon. "You move like your angel forebears, but you're not quite as proficient as them."

"I'll take the compliment." Grinning, Jax crouched. "You haven't seen anything yet."

"If you were smart," snickered Degamon, circling Jax, "you'd give up the girl. I'm not here for you. Just her. Is your life worth hers? No, it's not. You barely know her. Leave now. No one will know. I just want the girl." The demon cocked its head to the side. "What do you say? Do we have a deal?"

Jax gave a confident jerk of his head, his mouth cutting into a cruel line. "You can take your deal and shove it up your big red ass."

Degamon stiffened. "Typical mortal response. So banal and unimaginative. It's almost irritatingly laughable in its simplicity."

"Bite me, you freakin' red bastard," said Jax, grinning like a fool, "was that *typical* enough for ya?"

I blinked, and my chest swelled with gratitude and surprise. I doubted another angel-born would have stood up for me like that. They would have left to save their own skin.

"It's your funeral," the demon breathed. "One more soul is like one more glass of wine. You can never stop at just one."

Jax shrugged. "I prefer beer."

A sneer twisted Degamon's face as it swung at him with its arms. Its jaws snapped as it came after Jax. He rolled to the side to avoid the slashing claws, but again and again, with a blur of claws and teeth, the demon struck. My heart caught in my throat as Jax twisted and leapt while its taloned hand lashed down at him, barely missing his face. Fear gripped me so much it hurt.

Degamon was going to rip Jax to shreds. I had to help him.

Powered by my anger, I staggered to my feet. Still clutching my soul blade, I took a steadying breath and crossed the room, my thighs pulsing with the effort to stay standing. My steps were labored, and I wasn't sure I could make it without tipping over.

But I had to. I had to help Jax.

Jax spun around, avoiding the deadly claws, but he was holding his left arm close to his chest. He'd been hurt. I could see the hatred flaming in his eyes as the need to kill this demon took him over the edge. He swung his blade faster and faster as Degamon charged to meet it.

Blood erupted everywhere, showering Jax's arms, his head, his clothes. Both red and black. The blood reeked, somehow, of death and decay. And then Jax fell, hitting the floor hard.

"Jax!" my voice sounded loud in the sudden silence. Degamon whirled at the sound of my approach. Its black eyes met mine and the smile it gave me turned my blood cold.

A flash of beige fur came out of the corner of my vision. Tyrius darted forward. He bounded onto Degamon's back, lashing out at the bigger demon with his claws. With his ears back, he struck the demon's hide, and a black welt appeared, welling black blood. Degamon hissed as it tried to get a grip on Tyrius, but the cat skillfully avoided the deadly talons.

I met Tyrius's eyes, and I knew exactly what the cat was thinking. He was distracting the demon for me, so I could finish it off.

Head pounding with the migraine of the century, I gathered what strength I had and went for Degamon, my blade angled towards its neck. The scent of rotten eggs filled the air around me, and I slipped on the blood on the floor—

Tyrius's strangled cry froze me into place. He cried out as Degamon's talons struck him, knocking him aside the way a tiger might strike aside a bunny. Tyrius flew across the room and hit the back wall with a sickening crunch. He slipped to the floor and was still.

Tears welled into my eyes. "You bastard!" my bottom lip trembled. "I'm going to kill you—"

Degamon's hand wrapped around my throat, lifting me off my feet. It pulled me towards its face. Its hot rancid breath was enough to knock out a grown man.

"Mortals are like maggots. You survive on diseased flesh and rotting meat. Strange how something so small and insignificant can be so... *feisty*." Its eyes rolled over my body, "A tender angel-born, flesh so soft and so, so tasty."

Degamon tightened its grip and the last of my air rushed out of my lungs. Without air, my arms hung loosely at my sides. My vision speckled with black spots.

"You'll never know who summoned me to kill you," said Degamon, the thrill in its voice at the promise of my soul made the hair on my arms stand on end.

I moved my lips, trying to tell the demon to go screw itself, but no words would come.

Degamon's grin widened at the sight of my despair. "I'm going to enjoy drinking your blood. I'm going to take my time with you, little mortal. The females always taste sweeter."

Looking up at the ceiling, I tried to draw a breath. But I couldn't. Cold panic swept through me as I tried to get air. It wouldn't come. My stomach muscles clenched in spasms, but I couldn't get a breath. I was going to die. Is this what death felt like? Alone, cold, and in pain…

Tears, either from the pain or the fear, fell freely over my cheeks. I couldn't die like this, basking in the foul breath of some Greater demon. It was embarrassing. It hurt like hell, but all I could think of was if the demon was on me, it couldn't hurt Tyrius or Jax.

I gasped for breath, still unable to find any. A shadow moved in my peripheral vision. It looked like a cat, but it also might have been a hallucination. Lack of air would do that to a person.

But as my black spots cleared for just a moment, I saw Tyrius, the Siamese cat standing, his eyes burning with demon magic and turning from their usual blue to a bright yellow. Darkness rippled around Tyrius like shreds of clothing in the wind, but that too could have been just my hallucination.

Degamon followed my gaze, and for a moment, I swear I saw surprise in those bottomless black eyes. Oddly, Degamon dropped me and I hit the floor like a stone. I crashed face-first on the wood floor, knocking my hip. I gasped as delicious air filled my lungs.

I took a shuddering breath, blinking through the tears. Through my blurred vision I saw a tiny form on the floor facing the giant demon.

Grunting with effort, I pushed myself up with one arm and with the other hand seized the hilt of my blade.

"Tyrius," I gasped, crawling on the floor. "No." He was going to sacrifice himself. I couldn't let that happen. I saw Jax on the ground, his nose bloody as he tried to sit up.

But the tiny cat ignored me.

And then something truly spectacular happened. Tyrius began to glow.

The baal demon seemed to glow with an internal light and expand until he became frayed at the edges. Still the light grew and grew. I averted my eyes at the sudden shining blur too bright to look at. Within a few seconds, there was no tiny cat shape left, but a large, gleaming black cat the size of a tiger.

I wasn't staring at a tiny Siamese cat. I was goggling at a three-hundred-pound black panther.

Tyrius the black panther roared, an actual deep, bone-chilling roar that shook my apartment. His yellow eyes blazed with deep hatred as he crouched low and hauled himself at the demon.

Degamon scrambled back, still in shock. The force with which Tyrius hit Degamon threw it against the floor. Degamon screamed in fury and panic as it tried to get the large cat off of it, but its weak arms were no match for the three hundred pounds of predatory muscle.

I watched, transfixed at the savagery with which Tyrius attacked. Claws as sharp as the finest sword sliced easily into Degamon's flesh. Black blood flew everywhere, as though someone had turned on a sprinkler of black water, showering the floor and covering me and Jax in it.

Tyrius mauled Degamon. With his large jaw, he went for Degamon's throat and clamped down. With a howl, the demon toppled to the ground, writhing and spilling blood across the wood floor. Degamon's eyes bulged out of his head as the black panther crushed its neck. Degamon thrashed and managed to kick off the black panther.

The two stared at each other without moving, and I wondered who would attack first.

There was a loud hissing sound, just as black and red mist coiled over the Greater demon until it disappeared under the cloud. Then in a flash of black and red vapors, Degamon was gone.

A deep rumble, seemingly a mix of a laugh and a growl, erupted from Tyrius the panther. His yellow eyes fixed on me, and for a moment, I wasn't sure whether to be frightened or happy. That was a *seriously* big cat. I'd never seen a black panther except on some National Geographic TV special on big cats. He was truly magnificent, surreal almost as though he'd stepped out of some mystical fairytale or *The Jungle Book*. His coat was like oil and rippled with tight muscles, his body perfectly proportionate with slightly larger hind legs built for speed and to climb and pounce. He was the perfect killing machine. His yellow eyes were like tiny brilliant suns, and I found I could scarcely look away from them.

Tyrius, the black panther, had saved our lives.

Jax was staring at the cat in awe, which surprised me. There was no fear or hostility on his handsome face, just a curious fascination.

Suddenly, the black panther shimmered with an internal glow until he became smaller and smaller. With a final flash of light, the black panther had disappeared, and the baal demon took his preferred Siamese cat shape again.

"How are you feeling?" Jax was next to me, eyeing me with worry, his face inches from mine. "You took quite a beating from that red demon."

"I've been better." I swallowed, but my throat felt like I'd swallowed a handful of razor blades. Degamon had released me, but my fever was still there. It was worse, if at all possible, and my energy was spent.

"I'm sorry you had to give that demon your name, Jax." My breath sounded harsh and my throat tightened as my emotions swung from one extreme to the next. "I'm so sorry. How do you feel?" I was worried about him.

Jax put a hand on his chest. "It hurt a little at first—like a fist around my heart. It was burning, and I couldn't breathe. But I'm fine now. I don't feel any different."

I frowned at him. Somehow, I knew he was lying.

Jax's eyes traveled to my neck and his brows rose in alarm. He lifted his hand as if to touch my neck but then pulled it back, thinking better of it. "Your neck is bruised," he said instead.

"That will heal." I knew normal scrapes and bruises would be gone in half an hour. I glanced at my right wrist and I hissed through my teeth. You could clearly see the outline of fingers. The skin was swollen and red. Transparent liquid seeped through the blistered flesh, like a second-degree burn.

"Holy shit, Tyrius," Jax swore as the baal demon made his way over to us. "That was awesome. That was so beautiful I almost cried."

Tyrius stopped and took a bow. "Why thank you, Jax. You weren't bad yourself."

"Did you know he could do that?" Jax asked me, a smile on his face. "I didn't know baal demons could morph into giant black panthers."

I shook my head, watching the baal demon closely. "No, I didn't know," I said as a smile of my own formed on my lips. "His transformation was as much as a surprise to me as it was to you."

"The black panther is my alter ego," said Tyrius, his voice sounding a little tired. "A baal's version of the Hulk."

Jax laughed and I pulled myself to a sitting position as Tyrius climbed over my thighs, his blue eyes sparkling. "You stupid cat," I cried, tears falling down my cheeks. "Why didn't you tell me you could morph into a badass black panther?"

Tyrius lay on my lap, purring. He smiled the only way a cat could smile and said, "You never asked." And with that, the tiny cat fell asleep almost immediately.

CHAPTER
21

"**Y**ou're sure your friends can help me?" I asked Tyrius for the second time as Jax took the next left and we drove up Rumsey Drive. I held on to the door's handle for support, as every time the car jerked I feared my head was going to explode. I was tired and part of me just wanted to curl up in the back seat and sleep. But Tyrius's constant worried eyes and sharp tiny claws that kept gripping my thighs kept my eyes open.

My body shook as my fever rose with every passing minute. I was soaked in my own sweat, but I was too feverish to care. It was getting harder and harder just to stay awake and alert. I felt ill, and my muscles ached like I'd been trampled by a horde of two-hundred-pound werewolves. Worse, my vision had started to go gray. *What the heck is happening to me?*

"If anyone can figure out what that angel did to you," said the cat, the tight anger in his voice pulling me out of my fever for a moment, "they can."

"I hope you're right." I didn't like all this attention on me, but I hated being sick. It scared me. "I despise feeling this way. I barely have enough energy to keep my eyes open."

Jax turned to look at me before focusing his attention back to the road in front of him. He'd barely said a word since we left my apartment, but his worry was written all over his face.

"I still can't believe an angel could do that," said Jax. "It's silly, but I was raised to believe that angels couldn't hurt a person. That if they did… they'd combust into flames or something equally lame."

"That's a myth, man," said Tyrius. "Don't you remember Lucifer? Asmodeus? They were once angels too but corrupted to the core. Angels do turn to the dark side. And I'm not talking about the dark side of the Force. Angels are not Jedi, and this isn't a *Star Wars* film. This is real. Some angels are worse than your most evil demon. Believe it."

I took a deep breath, trying to subdue another wave of sickness. "We have to alert the Angel Legion somehow. Tell them that one of their own…" I looked down at my sleeve, not wanting to touch or see the mark, "did this to me."

"Even if we could alert them," said Tyrius, "how are you going to explain how it happened? You summoned an *archangel*, Rowyn... an archangel by trapping him. To the Legion, that's sacrilege. Archangels are like their golden boys and girls—and you violated one. I wouldn't be surprised if what you did calls for the penalty of death. You *can't* tell them." His blue eyes fixed on me. "You can't tell anyone. You hear me? We tell no one... except my friends, of course."

"Tyrius is right," said Jax, his breath tight as he gripped the steering wheel. "We keep this between us. I don't see anything good coming from going to the Legion or the council. When things get complicated, it gets ugly. They won't understand your motives. And your estranged relationship with the council won't help us either."

"I know." My mood soured but I knew they were right. I'd done this to myself. If I hadn't summoned the archangel, none of this would have happened. I screwed up. Royally.

But that archangel had known what I was...

"The archangel Vedriel knew what leaving that mark would do to you. He did it on purpose." Tyrius's voice was bitter. "He knew you would summon the demon. It's the only reason he so willingly gave you the name. Think about it. He knew the demon would break the circle. He wanted it to."

"And hoped Degamon would kill me," I whispered, and another wave of the shivers shook me. Unease overwhelmed my fever. I had seen real hatred in the archangel's eyes before he'd grabbed me. His face had twisted into a satisfied smirk before he'd disappeared back to Horizon. I should have known the bastard had played me. He played me like the fool I was.

"I'm sure that's what the archangel intended," said Tyrius. "He wanted you to die, Rowyn. And whatever that mark is, it's making you sick. You better pray to your soul that my friends can remove it. I don't want to think about what might happen if they can't."

"Me neither." I gave Tyrius a false smile, but he only narrowed his eyes further. I met his eyes, feeling a pulse of shared fear as understanding flashed over him. For all accounts, I had been wasted by an archangel.

While we drove, I thought about what would happen to me if we couldn't figure out a way to remove it. The only plausible answer was death. My body was dying. I could feel it. Death inflicted by a celestial creature that was supposed to protect me— talk about irony. The only way I could describe my infliction was an incurable malignant growth. A cancer that was attacking my immune system, and I couldn't fight it. Me, the person who hadn't been sick a day in my life, felt like my insides were melting.

"Man," said Tyrius, "that archangel can hold a grudge. It's not like we hurt him. So, we called him up and he was stuck in a teeny-weeny circle for like... what? Ten minutes? Boo-hoo. You'd think we'd bled his angel relatives or something."

"We didn't hurt him," I said and took another labored breath. "But we did trap him in a seven-point star and threatened him." I shivered. "Well, at least *I* did. He's an archangel. He's proud and didn't like the fact that I held some power over him. That burst his big angel ego."

"Yeah, well, whoop-de-freaking-do," mewed Tyrius.

I felt a faint need to giggle and a smile curved over me. "Whoop-de. Whoop-de. Doo. Doo." I gave in to my desire to giggle. I was going mad.

"Come again?" Tyrius said, his tail whipping nervously behind him. He climbed over my chest, his face so close that I had to squint just to look at him.

Tyrius's whiskers brushed my face as he moved closer to inspect my eyes. A talking cat. A freaking talking, snappy little cat. "That tickles." I laughed again.

"What is wrong with her?" Jax whispered loudly. The worry in his voice made me feel all warm and fuzzy inside. My head rolled to the side as I let my eyes travel over to his face. His full, kissable lips, so close... so inviting.

"You're pretty," I said, smiling. "Pretty. Pretty. Pretty."

"It's the infection," said Tyrius, impatiently. "She's losing her mind. She's in between lucidity and irrationality until she either throws up or passes out. Hurry up, man, before we lose her completely or have to commit her!"

I pushed Tyrius away from my face, feeling some strength return to me. "I'm not crazy. I'm just tired." And a little embarrassed at what I had just said to Jax.

"Sure thing, Rowyn," said Tyrius. "Don't worry, we'll have you fixed up in no time. You'll be as good as new."

I frowned. I wasn't sure how to respond to that. I wasn't a car that needed fixing. I turned and looked out the window before I further embarrassed myself with my uncontrollable giggles and mouth.

The clock on Jax's dashboard said it was midnight by the time we got to Manhattan and into Mystic Quarter—the district where the paranormal lived and mingled.

We drove through Orchard Park in the East Village, the three-block park with a wall of fruit trees that hid Mystic Quarter from the rest of Manhattan. Every major city around the world had their own version of a Mystic Quarter. It was the only place in New York where mid-demons, half-breed demons and the rest of the paranormals could live in peace. That is, until one of them screwed up and the Sensitives came knocking.

Half-breed demons were the creatures that had once been human and had been subjected to one of the demon viruses, which then turned them into the different demon races—vampires, werewolves, faeries, leprechauns, witches and warlocks.

Once upon a time, demons escaped through the Veil and came to our dimension. They fed on human blood, possessed human bodies and mixed their blood with human blood. Soon, humans became infected with the demon viruses until they mixed their blood with others to make more of their kind. They were hybrids and were subsequently despised by other, *purer* demon species, like lesser demons and Greater demons.

To the outside mortal world, Mystic Quarter was the slums or a very poor and unwelcome place to live, which is one of the main reasons why they never even bothered to make the trip through the park. To them, the neighborhood was spooky and rumored to be filled with assassins and ex-cons, no doubt rumors started by the half-breeds to keep the mortals at bay. No one wanted to cross over.

There were occasionally cases of curious or drunk teenagers that crossed on a dare or just because they were stupid. Human fatalities were rare, and when that happened the Sensitives were called to investigate. Usually they were due to a vampire or a werewolf that couldn't control their innate need to kill.

"Here's good enough," informed Tyrius, staring out the window. "We walk from here."

Jax pulled his car to the curb and killed the engine. "Do you want me to carry you?"

"No," I said appalled that he'd even offered. "I'm not dead, just a little sick."

"Well, you don't look so hot," informed Tyrius and I glared at him until I stopped seeing two Siamese cats.

Burning with a combination of angst and fever, I fumbled for the handle and pushed the door open. Tyrius leapt out the door. My boots hit the concrete sidewalk, and using the door, I pulled myself out. I felt the blood rush from my head to my toes. The ground spun. Wide-eyed, I stared at the golden light from a distant street lamp post, willing myself not to pass out.

Jax drifted within my sight and I saw him rush over. I stepped away from him before he could offer me his arm, glad that I didn't fall flat on my face. *Just breathe...*

I felt something brush up against my leg. I looked down to find Tyrius watching me. "I'm fine," I lied, knowing all too well that the cat knew I was lying. "Which—way—Tyrius?" I rasped. I couldn't get enough air in my lungs. The effort of speaking was winding me.

"You proud and stubborn mortal." Tyrius watched me for a moment. "Follow me."

Steadying myself I shambled forward like a drunk behind Tyrius with Jax striding closely enough to catch me if I fell. I suspected that was his reasoning as to why he was so close and why I felt his shoulder brush up against mine, totally invading my space.

Tyrius led us down a dark narrow street, lit only with the same distant street lamp from two blocks away. When I neared another street lamp, I looked up and noticed that the bulb was broken. Accidentally or on purpose? Mystic Quarter was covered in darkness, the way the paranormals liked it.

The fresh air and just moving again seemed to have stifled my giggles for the time being, but it did nothing to relieve the feeling of weakness and constant fever.

The strong scent of sulfur and demon magic pulled me in every direction. It was everywhere—in the air we breathed, on the ground we walked on, in the trees and their flapping leaves, and coating us like a heavy blanket.

I willed my legs to move, but they were stiff with cold, like ice blocks that didn't want to bend at the knee. I was glad that moving hid my shaking. This malaise was the worst feeling in the world, and I was angry that it was happening to me.

Echoes of rich voices reached us, and the distant sound of a mocking laugh carried on the wind. Faeries. I'd recognize their scent anywhere—candy canes and butterscotch with an underlying hint of rotten eggs.

Faeries, just as beautiful and mystical as vampires, and just as wickedly deadly. They could spell you to believe you were the Queen of England and them a handsome prince, just to slowly drink away your soul, your life-force, making you their slave for as long as they wanted.

Worse—they ate cats and dogs. Whenever a cat or dog went missing, a faerie was usually the culprit. Humans were oblivious that their beloved pets went straight into the bellies of the faeries.

I hated faeries. More than I hated vampires.

Faeries always felt fouler to me and had more darkness in them, as though they possessed more of the demon virus than the other half-breeds.

Sure enough we ambled past a park, lit only by the light of the moon, with lush grasses and fruit trees that lined a large pond. Fifty plus faeries danced to some unheard music, or maybe it was just the wind. Who knew. They were weird like that. There was a bundle with a tail spiked above a fire pit, and my stomach churned.

They all stopped as they heard us pass, their cold faces screwed up in disdain. They barely looked at Tyrius, though no doubt they could smell the baal demon on him. After seeing what Tyrius could do, I wished he'd black-panther their asses. All of them.

I caught the sensual smile of a male faerie, his eyes rolling over me in a seductive way. I made a rude gesture with my finger and Jax laughed. The male faerie flashed his mouth full of pointed teeth. Yikes.

Seeing their hateful faces seemed to spark a little more strength in me, and for a moment I didn't feel like I was about to keel over and die. Not yet.

Mystic Quarter was colorful and bizarre, like walking into a circus Fun House. You never knew what to expect. A pack of werewolves was fighting in a circle, and beautiful faerie girls danced in front of curtained stalls that promised a good time. Gnomes stood in front of booths that sold glittering jewelry, and I caught a glimpse of a few sprites the size of large moths, stealing earrings and bracelets whenever the gnomes weren't looking.

A vampire couple walked past us, their hands clasped and cups filled with red liquid that I knew wasn't wine. A young witch with bright orange hair pulled a cart behind her as she traded charms, sang fortunes and whispered hexes.

More vampires in various forms of dress meandered by—some sporting modern fashions like me and Jax and some decked out in vintage mortal fashions with layers of skirts and lace. Not one of them bothered to look at us as we crossed paths. They didn't seem concerned or care that two angel-born waltzed among them.

I felt eyes on me. A leprechaun with more piercings than tattoos was leaning against the wall of a building, watching us. The moonlight reflected off his bald head. I stared back at him until he looked away. I didn't have to look to know there were probably four or five more leprechauns watching us.

The street sloped down, revealing more jumbled buildings all squished together as though from lack of space. Haphazard shops lined the street with bottles and boxes of poisons, potions, and charms sitting in the windows. Most witches set up shop here in the Quarter. Anyone looking for a dark spell or even a demon spell could find it here.

I stared at the window for a moment wondering if a dark spell could help me. What if I could find some potion or ointment to counter the archangel mark?

Before I realized what I'd done, my legs stopped moving and I planted myself before a witch's shop with a sign that said SEARCHING FOR LOVE OR FORTUNE? LOOKING FOR THAT REMEDY TO CURE THAT ITCH THAT JUST WON'T GO AWAY? YOU'RE IN LUCK. STEP INTO THE SHOP OF WONDERS!

"Are you okay?" Jax was next to me, looking at me as though I might faint.

A smile tugged on his lips.

"My offer of carrying you still stands, if you're interested."

God. Why did he have to be so damn good-looking?

I breathed in deeply. Part of me wanted to lean on him for just a moment and feel his strong arms around me to drink in their warmth. How long had it been since I'd let a man touch me?

"I'm fine," I muttered, careful to keep my face blank. "It's just... maybe..."

"Don't even think about it," said Tyrius as he doubled back, his eyes narrowed into slits. "Forget it, Rowyn. Just forget it."

I shrugged. "I didn't even say anything."

"You didn't have to." Tyrius eyed me like a parent about to scold a child. "I know you better than you think. I know exactly what's in that head of yours, and let me tell you that a dark spell can only worsen your infliction."

"But maybe it can help me?" I breathed through my nose. "What if you're wrong and all I need is in that shop?" I hated how desperate my voice sounded.

This wasn't me. I was the strong one, I was a Hunter. But I'd never felt so weak like this before either.

Jax looked from me to Tyrius to the shop, and understanding etched across his features. "Maybe she's right. Maybe this is all we need to heal her. A dark spell could counter the mark—"

"It can't." Tyrius's voice was final. "We don't even know *what* that damn thing is. How do you know adding a dark spell won't just make it worse? You don't. Half of what they sell here doesn't even work. Don't ask." Tyrius shifted his weight, his beige fur seemingly gleaming in the moonlight. "What the archangel did wasn't dark magic. It was *celestial* magic—whatever that is. I don't know about you, but I don't know much about it. Are you willing to take that chance? Are you willing to risk your life on a guess?"

I closed my eyes as another wave of dizziness shook me. "You're right. I'm just... so tired, Tyrius. I don't know how much more I can take." I cursed silently as I felt my eyes burn with moisture. I would not let them see me cry.

"I know, Rowyn."

I snapped my eyes open at the concern in Tyrius's voice.

"Help is close," said the cat. "Let's see what my friends have to say first. I trust them. They'll know what to do. Who knows. They might tell us a dark spell *can* help. But until I know for sure, I can't let you risk it."

"How much further, Tyrius?" asked Jax, though he was looking at me.

"Not far," said the tiny cat. "Just at the end of this block."

In silence, we followed the cat down the street. A few witches glanced our way, their faces cold and hard. I sensed their demon magic, the familiar scent of earth and vinegar wafting towards me. I was barely aware of my own body. Head down, I concentrated on putting one foot beyond the other. It was all I could do. The fever was pulling at me from everywhere inside my body at once. Sounds became muffled and my vision blurred again. I felt like I was walking in a perpetual dream state, not really in control of my body.

"That witch over there is looking at you," came Jax's voice next to my ear.

I looked up, surprised that he'd hooked his arm in mine, and I'd never even felt it.

"Hmmm?" I followed his gaze, and my body stiffened. If he wasn't holding me up, I might have fallen. My knees buckled, but Jax didn't seem to notice.

A witch with long wisps of white and gray hair and wearing a shapeless, weathered forest-green gown stood in the shadows across the street. Her small eyes were lost in the heavy wrinkles, but I could make out that one, milky white eye staring at me. I'd have recognized that face anywhere.

It was the dark witch I'd stolen the grimoire from. Ah, hell.

It could have been the fever, but I'd swear she was looking at me with a winning smile that seemed to say I'd gotten what I deserved. She lifted a thin, white hand and pointed at me, her lips mumbling as though in a curse. Shit.

"Do you know her? She seems to know you." Jax's face was so close to mine his chin rubbed against my face, his day-old stubble tickling my skin. His scent was musky and pleasant, and his deep voice sent tiny prickles over my skin. Or was that the fever?

I shook my head, careful not to bump my face into his, or accidentally brush my lips against his. He was that close—with such kissable lips. It would be a shame not to lean in and give them a try.

What was I thinking? I pulled my gaze from his lips before they got me into trouble. I was delirious, and I didn't have the energy to open my mouth. Breathing became difficult.

I didn't want anyone to know that the witch had found me. Was this simply the case of a strange coincidence? No. I didn't think so.

The old witch wanted her book, but I wasn't ready to give it back yet.

I would never have made it to the end of the block without Jax's help, without falling flat on my face. Tyrius bounded down the steps of a semi-basement apartment from a brown stone building. A sign above the stairs read THE LONE FAMILIARS.

Tyrius disappeared through the flap of a small cat door, left off the main door. I tried to smile but nothing moved. My facial muscles were numb like after a visit to the dentist.

Jax yanked the front door open and hauled me inside with him. There was the soft click of a latch as Jax closed the door behind him. I blinked at the sudden light coming from everywhere at once. As my vision adjusted, I realized the light was coming from dozens of computer screens.

The ceiling was low, and I set my gaze on the open space. It was lined with tables topped with computers, computer parts, yellow and red wires, black and white wires, and all manner of electronic devices that were alien to me. Books were cramped into the far wall and into teetering columns that grazed the ceiling. Bottles with orange and green and blue liquids sat on shelves along the walls. The room smelled of metal and mildew, with a faint rotten egg smell. It was one open room, no kitchen or bathroom, and it had the feel of a local geek shop that doubled as a lab.

Sitting on an antique Persian rug and looking up at us were two cats.

CHAPTER
22

"**B**emus. Mani. This is my friend Rowyn I've been telling you about," said Tyrius as he came around and stood by my legs. "And this here is her friend Jax."

The two cats eyed us. One was a Russian blue with yellow eyes, the spitting image of the cat in *Pet Sematary*. The other was an orange Persian with the signature squished face.

Baal demons. Their demon energy ran through my skin like a tiny electric current, just like Tyrius. They were large, too large and thick to be females, and the shape of their skulls told me they were males. I tried to say hello, but my lips were glued together.

"She needs your help." Tyrius moved around my legs, agitated. For the first time I saw how really concerned he was for me, and my chest knotted together in a tight ball. "She's been infected with something and it's making her sick. I didn't know where else to bring her."

The Russian blue raised one of its paws. "Say no more, my friend," he said, his voice deeper than Tyrius's. I detected a very faint accent that I couldn't place. "Bring her over to the chair here and we'll take a look at her."

Jax hauled me to the only chair in the space, next to a table that was covered in TV remote controls, but I couldn't see one single television in the space. I slumped into the chair, my hands on my lap, shivering and feeling cold and hot all at once. Jax had his hand on the backrest of the chair, like an overbearing body guard.

A flash of blue-gray moved in my line of sight and the Russian blue cat leaped up to the table, followed by the Persian and Tyrius. The three cats faced me. My head swam as I tried to focus on at least one of them.

"Can you tell us what happened exactly?" said the Persian. His voice was high and nasally.

"Yes," said the Russian blue. "What is the cause and nature of this infection?"

Tyrius looked at me and I gave a nod of my head. "It's angel," he answered, and I detected bitterness in his tone.

"Angel?" mewed the two cats together.

Tyrius sighed. "Archangel, actually."

"Let's have a look." The Russian blue leaned forward, his yellow eyes wide and curious.

Tyrius turned his head and looked up at me. "Rowyn? Show them."

I blinked slowly and took a deep breath. Gathering some energy, I raised my right arm and let it fall with a thud on the table. I stifled a laugh at how dead my arm felt. With trembling fingers, I pulled back my sleeve and I retched. The skin around my wrist had opened, and yellow liquid seeped from my blistered skin. It smelled like death.

The two baals hissed and spat and leapt back as though my arm was contagious. Their fur bristled on their backs, making them appear twice their size. I wondered if they were about to Hulk-out into giant cats, and what their forms would be.

"That is definitely very, very bad," said the Persian.

"Yup, definitely," agreed the other cat.

"Holy shit, Rowyn." Jax gave no warning as he gripped my arm, cursing softly. His touch was surprisingly gentle. All I could do was stare at the lines of worry that creased around his eyes. He pressed his palm against my forehead, his rough callused skin a welcomed feeling against the numbness I felt. "She's burning up." I felt a tinge of regret when he pulled his hand away. "Why didn't you tell us it was this bad?"

I didn't know, I wanted to say but could only shrug as my gaze fell back to my wrist. God that looked awful. The flesh looked as though it was burned and decaying all at the same time, like the flesh-eating disease.

Tyrius slipped next to my wrist and sniffed. He drew back his head and then sneezed. "You know what this is, don't you?" he asked the two baals, his face drawn in accusation. "What is this? And can you help her?" My bottom lip trembled, and my teeth chattered as another wave of the chills hit me, harder this time, and didn't stop.

"That's an archangel curse, that is," said the Persian cat. He sat and curled his tail around himself. "It's a rare kind of celestial magic that only archangels can do."

"Mani's right," said the Russian blue. "I've only seen a mark like that once before and…" the cat clamped his mouth shut and looked up at Tyrius, his eyes wider than I'd seen them.

"And what, Bemus?" growled Tyrius, his eyes darting between the two baals. "Tell me! If you know something, tell me! Tell me now, or you can forget the Dungeons & Dragons tournament."

Mani's and Bemus's little mouths dropped open, revealing tiny pointed teeth. Bemus cocked his head next to Mani and leaned closer and whispered, "Did he just…"

Mani's head nodded in quick successions. "He did."

After Bemus shot Tyrius a worried look, he straightened, looking regal. "It's called the Seal of Adam," he said, calmly. His yellow eyes met mine for a moment, and then his gaze moved to my wrist. "It was entrusted to all archangels, once upon a millennium or two, revealing itself as the first curse. They used it on half-breed demons as a means to control them since they could roam the Earth freely as part human—unlike their demon cousins, which could never stay in the mortal world for very long."

"When a half-breed bears the Seal of Adam," added Mani, "they must continually feed it, by submitting to the will of the archangel, otherwise they will succumb to the side effects of its immense power and—"

"Kill the human in them," interjected Bemus, "turning them slowly but steadily into a demon. It removes the humanity and sometimes the half-breed doesn't respond well to the curse... it kills them."

"Sometimes it can show up as a circle with the archangel's name, or a hand print like that one," informed Mani. "But the smell is always the same." He jerked his chin towards my wrist. "It reeks of the bowels of Horizon."

I would have blushed in embarrassment if I still had the will. Turns out I just sat there like a smelly, decomposing idiot.

Tyrius shook his head and looked at me. "Wait a minute. Rowyn hasn't experienced anything like that. Right, Rowyn?" I shook my head and he continued. "Are you sure it's the Seal of Adam? Maybe it's something else?"

"No, it's the Seal of Adam all right," said Mani. "I'd recognize that mark and smell anywhere. It's definitely the celestial curse. But she's not a half-breed, which I'm guessing is the reason the curse is reacting differently. It's very vexing."

"Agreed," said Bemus in a puzzled tone, as if he couldn't believe what he was seeing. "It's not supposed to do that to someone like her," said the cat, and I squirmed under his intense gaze. "You told us she was angel-born, a Sensitive like him—" the cat jerked his head to Jax, "—but different."

Bemus closed his eyes for a moment, and when he opened them, his demon magic flashed in his eyes, making them glow like brilliant stars. "She has the same angel-born energy, but I sensed something distinctively separate the moment she entered. A different energy. Like a layer of something else— something other than the curse. But it's so well interconnected, it's hard to pinpoint what it is."

"I sensed it too," agreed Mani. "A shade of another energy."

"Either way," replied Bemus. "It's not supposed to react like that for a mortal with an angel heritage."

"What are you trying to say?" Tyrius's voice rose, and I could sense a little fear in his tone. "That you *can't* help her?"

"What? No," exclaimed Jax, and I felt him shift next to me. "You *have* to help her. Look at her—it's not like we can take her to a human hospital. They'd just fill her up with human antibiotics and end up making it worse." Jax rubbed his face with his hands. "What about a spell? Can a witch help her? We just passed a few shops. Maybe they can brew a counter curse? A curse for a curse?"

Bemus lowered his head. "A dark spell would only worsen her condition, perhaps even kill her."

A tiny bubble of hope burst within of me. I'd been holding on to the hope that a curse could counter another curse. A cancellation of sorts. A nauseating mix of dread and pain shook my knees, and I held my breath so I wouldn't get sick.

Jax noticed the shift in me and angled his face to mine. I saw the recognition in his eyes at my dismay. "Are you sure?" he asked the baals. "You're absolutely sure?" I hated the despair in his voice. It didn't make me feel any better.

"We're sure," said the two baals together. Then Bemus added, "We've been witches' familiars for thousands of years before we gave it up. We know the effects a dark curse would have on a celestial curse— like adding fuel to a fire."

"Disastrous," said the Persian cat. "Catastrophic. And really messy, actually."

I jerked as Jax pushed down hard on the chair. "Then what?" he said. "We can't do *nothing*."

"No, we most certainly can't." Tyrius met my eyes, and I noticed that they were unusually moist. I looked away before I started my own waterworks.

The baals looked at each other, and then Mani broke the silence. "We'll do what we can, but first, you must tell us how she got the Seal of Adam. How did the archangel curse her?"

Tyrius began to retell the story of how stupid I was to summon the archangel. I was grateful he left out the part where I'd stolen the dark witch's grimoire.

Silence. The kind I hated. The kind where only bad news was brewing on the surface.

"Can you help her?" Jax's voice was strained and I tried to look up at him, but my head lolled to the side and rested on his arm. Fighting back the nausea, my body trembled from the fever. The adrenaline had spent itself out, and I was going to pay for it soon. The fear pulled my heat away, turning my sweat cold.

"Can you?" Tyrius was practically yelling. I'd never seen him like this, so agitated. "Please tell us there's something you can do."

"There's no cure," said Mani, and I felt nothing but an endless, hopeless darkness full of fear, pain, and defeat. "Once the curse has been laid, it can never be undone." The cat took a breath. "The only way to remove the Seal of Adam is to kill the archangel that gave it to her."

My mouth dropped open in horror. That was never going to happen. No mortal could kill an archangel. They were way too powerful. It was all over for me. I wasn't going to make it.

I sat as it dawned on me that I would forever be sick, until finally this curse took my life.

I felt Jax's hand squeeze my shoulder, and there was nothing I could do to stop the warm tears that leaked out of my eyes like a sprinkler. No one said anything as I sat there, sobbing like a fool. I'd done this to myself. Stupid. Stupid. Rowyn.

"But we can offer some temporarily relief," I heard Bemus say.

I looked up and through my blurred vision, the baals seemed to be smiling at me.

"Mani," said Bemus, "do you want to do the honors?"

Mani bounded towards me and settled next to my exposed wrist. I watched, silently, as the cat lifted its paw to its mouth and bit down. Black blood pooled around the corners of its mouth, and then the cat pressed its paw with its blood on my wrist, on the Seal of Adam.

I barely felt the pressure of Mani's front paw pads, warm and soothing as he pressed down on my wound. Soft vibrations echoed near me, and I realized he was purring. I took a slow breath. Then another. I flinched as I felt tingling and throbbing around my wrist, like the feeling of fingers and toes re-warming after being in the freezing cold for too long. A small electrical current ran through my body, through my veins, numbing the celestial curse. I stiffened, almost falling off my chair as I felt my strength shifting, and then slowly returning.

I sat up straight. It hit me like an adrenaline rush, and my heart pounded as my fever broke.

I didn't care that it was demon blood and that it had mixed with my own. It was probably forbidden to use demon's blood in such a way, but screw it. I felt better. Hell, more than better, I felt good. If I concentrated hard enough, I could still feel the effects of the curse, like a lingering weakness, but Mani's blood had given me temporary relief. And I gladly accepted it.

Finally, Mani withdrew his paw, watching me carefully and waiting for me to say something. I could feel everyone's attention on me.

"I feel better," I said, the relief in my voice as obvious as the loud sigh from Tyrius. I gave him a quick smile before I pulled my hand back and looked at my wrist.

Two things struck me. One, Mani's blood was completely gone as if it had evaporated, and two, the Seal of Adam was back to its bruised-like appearance. It was still ugly, with angry purplish-red fingerprints, but it wasn't oozing anymore, and it didn't smell. Well, at least I couldn't smell it.

"Mani. Bemus," I said, and I took a deep breath. "I don't know how to thank you."

"Don't thank us too soon," mewed Bemus, and I heard him start purring. "It's only temporary. You should be okay for another day or so. But if you tire yourself out or if you exert yourself doing whatever it is that you're doing, the effects will fade sooner. The harder you push your body, the faster it will go."

"Does this mean Tyrius's blood would have the same effect?" inquired Jax, his grip on the chair loose and relaxed. I could see spots of color returning to his face.

Tyrius looked at the baals expectantly. "Will it?"

"Yes," answered Bemus. "But you can't keep doing it because the effects will eventually stop working. It seems the curse begins to build a resistance to our blood after a while. You have maybe another three—four times tops before it stops working entirely."

"How did you even know your blood would work on the curse?" Tyrius's voice was mixed with relief and astonishment.

"Eight hundred years ago, my witch Belinda was cursed with the Seal of Adam," said Mani, his big eyes watering. "We tried everything to get rid of it, with cuts and burns and spells. Nothing worked. In the end, we found temporary relief with my blood until—" the cat shivered and looked away, his eyes pinched in some hurtful memory.

"Four times was the most it worked for Belinda," Bemus answered. "With luck, you might find something else to help build your own resistance to the curse, something that we failed to find in time for Belinda."

"And if we don't?" Jax's voice was almost a whisper. I looked at him, feeling both embarrassed at how weak he'd seen me and what I'd said.

"Who cares." Teeth gritted, I used the chair and pushed myself to my feet, surprised that I didn't feel dizzy or nauseated. "We'll think about that when the time comes."

"Right," said Jax. He exhaled long and slow. I could sense some of the earlier tension leave him. He rubbed his fingers together. "So, what do we do now?"

"We hunt Degamon." I was surprised at the growl that came from deep inside my own throat.

"We track it," I said as a tiny smile tugged at the corners of my lips. "Then we kill it."

"Where do you suppose we look?" asked Jax. The barest smile appeared on him. "The Greater demon could be anywhere here in this dimension or the Netherworld."

I pinched my lips, an idea forming in my head. We needed to be more creative since summoning was out of the question.

"Well, we know it's hunting me, right? Maybe we could set a trap and wait for it to show up—"

The door burst open, and there standing in the threshold with a look of panic on his face was Danto.

CHAPTER

23

"It took her! She's gone!"

The leader of the Vampire Court in New York stumbled into the small space. I could see his milky-white skin through rips in his neatly tailored black clothes, and blood, lots of blood. His eyes were wet, and tears and blood streaked his face. Clumps of his black hair were stuck to his face. He looked like he'd been in a fight and lost. Big time.

I'd never heard of Danto losing a fight, not with his super-vamp swiftness and strength. Plus, the head vampire was old and experienced, and in the half-breed world that meant power. I'd never seen him look so disheveled. The stoic vampire was a bundle of nerves. The only thing that didn't look out of place were his bare feet.

Danto's black eyes were wild in a helpless panic as he took in the space around him. He looked lost and a little bit mad. His eyes finally settled on me, and his features shifted from desperation to relief, as though he'd been looking for me. That couldn't be good. I shifted on my feet and waited.

Mani and Bemus eyed the vampire with semi-bored expressions, as though they were used to vampires busting into their shop looking like they'd just been to war with a couple of tigers. Tyrius had slipped to the edge of the table and crouched low like he was ready to pounce on Danto should the vampire do something stupid, like try to bite me.

But I was more worried about Jax. Had another vampire just charged in the shop looking mad and maybe just a little thirsty for blood, I might not have bitten my tongue to stop the moan from escaping my throat.

As it was, it was Danto. His vampires had attacked us and poisoned Jax with their claws. He'd nearly died and would have if Pam's miracle juice hadn't cured him. The kill-all-blood-suckers-look that crossed Jax's face was enough to tell me he wasn't about to let that go. Crap.

A blade was already in Jax's hand. Slowly, he lifted his head, a murderous look in his green eyes. Ah, hell. A small shift in his posture sent a stab of adrenaline through me. I could understand Jax's motive for wanting to hurt or even kill the vampire, but hurting Danto would start a full-on war with the New York Vampire Court. They'd think the council had ordered the attack on the vampires.

My muscles tightened as I reached out with my left hand and gave his arm a squeeze, hoping he would understand my warning. He looked at me and gave me a slow nod of understanding. I released a nervous breath through my nose.

"It took her! It took her!" Danto launched himself at me. The look of a madman marred his features, the whites of his eyes showing. He would have grabbed me if not for the tip of my soul blade stopping him short.

"Who took who, Danto?" I said slowly, my blade dangling close to his neck. He stood with his arms in the air, looking at the soul blade as though he'd never seen one before. I didn't trust vampires, even sad-looking ones. Not long ago, we'd barely escaped his club with our lives. His face had been triumphant and cocky then, the complete opposite of this frantic and anxious vampire.

"Just slow down and tell me what happened," I said, wondering why the vampire was even here. Vampires didn't usually seek out help from non-vamps. They tended to stick to their own, just like the other half-breeds. There had been cases where Vampire Courts, Faerie Courts and other half-breed courts sought the help from the council, but it was rare.

I wasn't part of the council. Seeing Danto here, looking as distraught as a father who had lost a child, was freaking me out a little.

I met Tyrius's belligerent glare and I knew he was thinking the exact same thing. This was bad.

"There were too many! Too many!" Danto cried in a panic. "I couldn't stop them!"

Jax was suddenly next to me, his own blade pointing at the vampire. But Danto made no indication that he'd even seen him. His eyes had never left my soul blade. From the corner of my eye, Mani and Bemus were sprawled on the table watching the exchange with great interest.

"Danto?" I repeated, twisting my blade, and the vampire's eyes moved to mine. "What are you talking about? And what the hell happened to you?"

Danto lowered his hands and curled them into fists. "It took her," he whispered, his voice cracking. "Too many. Just too many." Even upset he was still hauntingly beautiful, in a goth-rock-star kind of way, with his pale skin and raven hair. Damn those vamps, even disheveled they were hot.

"Cindy?" I asked. By the fear that flashed across his face, I knew I was right. "Who took Cindy? Was it another vampire?" I'd heard that some vampires liked to steal each other's mates. It was a feeling of pure domination, and to vampires it manifested as a twisted, addictive high. Great, Cindy had been stolen as a prize. I'd hate to be in her shoes, but the foolish woman had refused our help. That wasn't my fault. But it still didn't explain why he was here.

Danto shook his head, the motion making him look years younger. The vamp's eyes filled with tears and I was shocked at the emotions I saw cascade over his face. He just shook his head, trembling and sobbing.

Crap. Now I was feeling bad for a blood-sucking vampire.

"I tried to stop it," Danto blurted. He was so close I could see the tears trickling over his lips and into his mouth. "I tried, but... but I couldn't stop it." Shame flashed across his face. "It was too strong. Too many." He wiped a tear away with his hand. "They died trying to save her. They died because of me. *I* should have saved her. She was *my* mate!"

I took in Danto's blood-covered clothes and guessed most of it wasn't his. "Saved her from what? I can't help you if you don't tell me the whole story, Danto. If it wasn't a vampire, who was it?" I was confused as to why he was staring at me like I was his savior and the answer to his problem. But it didn't dampen the unease I felt in my gut. I had a feeling I knew what he meant.

"Why did you come here?"

"It said it wouldn't hurt her," continued Danto, as though he hadn't heard me, his voice trembling, "if I brought *you* to it."

I sucked in a breath through my teeth.

"Now we're getting somewhere," mewed Tyrius. "I knew twinkle toes didn't come here for the midnight special."

I turned my attention back to the vampire. The light from across the computer screens showed the lines of pain on his face.

"What did," I asked, my chest tightening, because somehow I already knew the answer. "What took Cindy?"

The vampire met my eyes and I saw true hatred there as he growled, "It called itself, Degamon."

Swell. My jaw clenched, and I lowered my blade. I had to give it to the Greater demon. It knew how to play me. It knew Cindy was important enough to me that I would risk seeking her out to try and save her. I was a fool like that.

"That's the one you had warned me about?" said the vampire. His lips were a stark red against his pale face, and his sculpted features were tight in determination. "Isn't it? The thing that's been hunting you... hunting Cindy?"

"Yes." I sighed, recalling the look of amusement on the red demon's face. "It's the same one." I felt a flush of regret pulling at me. If I had killed it, Cindy would be with Danto right now, probably enjoying herself with her pretty vampire.

"Isn't Degamon a Greater demon?" inquired Mani, his brows furrowed in thought. "The one that controls the legion of igura demons? The Greater demon that fought the demon Kutar at the Battle of Black Mountain and stole his favorite wife?"

"The very same red bastard," said Tyrius.

"And it's after you?" came Bemus's voice. I turned my head to better see his round yellow eyes on me. "Why is there a Greater demon after you and this Cindy character?"

"Long story," said Tyrius, his tail flicking behind him. "I'll tell you guys later."

"It brought its friends with it," said the vampire. "We couldn't hold them off. I should have listened to you," said Danto, his voice filled with horror. "She'd still be here if I had. But now she's gone, maybe forever, and it's all my fault. My own damn fault." He was silent for a moment. "I thought I was enough to protect her. I was a fool. I'm an ignorant fool."

"I'm not so sure about that," I said, feeling a slight throb on my wrist, a reminder that I wasn't as strong as I had first thought. I too had been ignorant, thinking I was somehow invincible, special. Danto wasn't the only fool in this. I was the capital fool. The fool of the century.

"Degamon's a very powerful Greater demon," I said, my gaze moving back to the vampire. "It came at me—at us—and we almost didn't make it. But we managed to get rid of it… for now." My eyes found Tyrius, and I swelled with gratitude at the special cat. He caught my expression and grinned, his tiny, sharp teeth gleaming in the light of the screens.

"What exactly did the demon say to you?" Jax's face was drawn tightly, and I still had the impression that he wanted to give a beating to the already beaten-down-looking vampire.

"It said—" Danto hesitated, seemingly gathering himself a little, "it *said* that it wouldn't harm Cindy, but only *if* I brought it the angel-born female that kept a baal demon as a friend." His eyes met mine. "It said to bring you to it *before* sunrise. It would keep Cindy unharmed and alive until I brought you. If I refused, if I brought an army of vampires with me to try and save her myself— Cindy would die. It wants you, Rowyn."

"Of course, it does." My gaze went to the door. Somehow, I had the feeling the vampire wouldn't have come alone. It was no secret other vamps saw us come in. They most probably told their lord the moment we stepped into Mystic Quarter. Danto looked desperate, and desperate vamps—just like people—did stupid things.

He might have wanted to take me by force—hell, that's what I would have done to save the one I loved—but I couldn't see or sense any demon energies other than the three baals and the one vampire. Maybe Danto did come alone.

"Well," Tyrius spat. "Sunrise doesn't give us much time to prepare. You do realize it's a trap. Don't you?"

Danto rounded on Tyrius. "Of course I know it's a trap, you idiot! But what choice do I have? I can't let her die. She's my mate. She's my… everything," he added with a whisper. "She's my love, my match in every sense." His eyes welled up in tears, and he raked his long fingers through his hair. "She's immune to the vampire virus," he said, and my breath caught in my throat. I shared a look with Jax as Danto continued. "Do you know how long I've waited to find someone like her? That I didn't have to *make* into a vampire because she didn't want? We could be together, and I never had to worry about biting her and her hating me for the rest of her long life." His breath quivered. "I want her back. I need her back."

Vampires weren't my favorite people, but his pain was real. It was raw. The demon took his true love away from him, and he was desperate to get her back.

But the exchange also told me what I had suspected. Cindy was exactly like me. She was immune to the vampire virus. Whatever we were, it was enough to warrant our deaths. We were different, and it made us targets.

I couldn't help but feel for the vampire. Watching Danto, I had come to the conclusion that he loved her unconditionally, with every fiber of his being. I'd never loved like that, and part of me envied him.

Damn. Danto was alone. He was in pain. He was being open and honest about his feelings. I couldn't just walk away. Yes, he was a vampire and had done questionable things, but I couldn't label him an evil half-breed. When I looked at his face, all I saw was honest and true pain.

I looked at Tyrius, reading the strain rolling over his back. "Yes, it's a trap," I said, answering the cat's critical stare. "And I'm sure it knows that we know it's a trap." My gaze darted over to Jax. "Degamon wants me dead, just as much as it wants Cindy dead. Someone summoned it to kill us. It won't give up until we're both dead. It can't. That's how summoning works. The demon will never stop hunting us." I shook my head. "But I'm not ready to die, and I'm positive neither is Cindy." I gave Jax a smile. "Besides, I just got a crap load of money that needs spending, and I'm in desperate need of a new wardrobe."

"Here, here," said Tyrius, and he flashed me his teeth.

Danto moved, and my eyes jerked to him. He didn't look dangerous. He looked helpless and frustrated, as if he was screwing up some courage.

"You'll do it?" he asked, relief coating his voice. It was obvious he didn't want to fight us, but he would have, if it meant saving Cindy's life. He would have tried to take me by force, and by the angry look Tyrius was giving the vampire, he knew it too.

"You'll come with me?" said Danto. "Even if you know it's a trap?"

Crap. I could see in his eyes that he already knew I would say yes.

My adrenaline pumped. "I'm not going to let Cindy die in the hands of that demon," I said. "Degamon needs to die. This is my chance at vanquishing the demon before it kills anyone else. I screwed up the first time. But I won't screw up again." I looked at my wrist, glad that my sleeve covered my angel curse.

"I love playing the hero and all," said Tyrius, his eyes pinched in worry, "but the last time we confronted the Greater demon, we almost got our asses kicked. How do we get Cindy back without getting killed? Are we just going to walk right in there and *demand* Degamon to hand her over?"

"We could fight him," offered Jax, his shoulders tight in determination. "We'd be better prepared than the last time."

"No, he'll be expecting that," I said. "We won't have to do that either."

Jax watched me, eyebrows high. "Why not?"

I steadied myself, my heart pounding at what I was about to say. "Because I have something better."

"Like what?" said Tyrius. "Catnip?"

I took a breath, trying to decide how I should word this. "Because I know who summoned it."

Silence soaked in, followed by a stirring unease. I clenched my jaw, glancing at the shocked faces.

"You do?" Tyrius's voice was flat, and a wisp of annoyance flashed over him. "Why didn't you say so? Why didn't you tell us?"

"Because I wasn't sure until now," I answered, knowing it to be true. "But it all makes perfect sense. I just can't believe it took me so long to put the pieces together. I'm usually not this slow." Again, I looked at my wrist, wondering if the curse had somehow given me brain-fog.

"Who is it?" Danto's dark eyes narrowed, and his mild fear shifted to hot interest. "Who summoned the demon?"

I swallowed hard. "A dark witch."

"N-o-o-o-o!" exclaimed Tyrius as he shot in the air like a rocket with fur. "The one you stole the grimoire from?"

I nodded. "The very same."

Mani looked at Bemus, eyes wide. "This is exciting!"

"I wish we had some popcorn," whined Bemus.

Jax was looking from me to Tyrius. "You stole a book from a witch? So what? What does that have to do with Degamon?"

"Because that's the book I used to summon the demon." I sighed. "It's her book. And she's not just any witch, she's a *dark* witch, and a really old and powerful hag. If anyone is powerful enough to summon and control a Greater demon, it's her. The book is filled with dark magic spells, demonic spells, and the very worst hexes and curses, a real treasure in the dark arts."

"And you stole it from her?" Jax whistled. "But how do you know it's the same witch? How do you even know she's doing this?"

"Because I just saw her outside." I saw the realization dawn on him. He knew I meant the witch he had pointed out to me. "She made sure I saw her too. She practically told me with her one good eye that she'd sent the demon after me." I stifled a shiver as I remembered the winning smile on her pasty, wrinkled face. She thought my days were numbered. But I wasn't finished yet.

"The witch wants me dead," I said, avoiding their eyes. "The only way to get her revenge was to summon the worst demon to do it for her."

"Shit." Jax raked his fingers through his hair, leaving the left side sticking out. "She could have just cursed you with some dark witch hex. Why the demon?"

"Because she doesn't know my name and you need a name for a curse to work," I said, feeling even worse than before. "Well, at least for the kind of curse she wanted to use on me." I sighed heavily as a new dread twisted my gut. "But she somehow figured out that I was angel-born and different. Somehow, she made the connection that I was an Unmarked. But without a name, the demon had to—"

"Kill all the Unmarked females hoping to finally get you," answered Tyrius.

My chest ached at the realization that I was the cause of those deaths. The Greater demon had always wanted to hunt me. To kill me. All because I had stolen that goddamned book.

I felt my throat and stomach knotting into a tight ball until it hurt. I felt the blood drain from me. I was cold and light-headed, as though the Seal of Adam was back with a force.

What have I done?

I looked up and found Danto's lethal glare on me. He looked like he was debating whether or not to vamp out and rip my throat out. Totally understandable. If Cindy died, that was on me.

"But when you summoned the Greater demon," asked Jax. "Why didn't it recognize you as its main target? Shouldn't it have known you were the one it was seeking?"

"No, even if it was staring at me in the face, it couldn't have known," I answered. "The witch never gave it a name. To the demon, I was just another Unmarked. For all we know, the witch told it to destroy us all, just in case. And it won't stop until we're all dead. No matter if it takes ten, twenty years... the demon will never stop."

A nauseating mix of dread and angst shook my knees, and I held my ground so I wouldn't collapse like an idiot.

Jax's eyes went serious. "And you're sure Degamon will give us Cindy for the witch's name?"

"Yes," I said, feeling confident. "We'll trade Cindy's life for the witch's name. The Greater demon will want to seek revenge on its summoner. It's why you never give the summoned demon your name. It can hold power over you. With the summoner's name, it can break the hold, destroy the binding and protection spells and kill the summoner."

Jax shifted next to me, his worried posture easy to read. "You sure about this? Don't you want to rest just a little."

"We don't have time to rest," I breathed as I caught Danto watching me. His eyes were calculating as he took in the scene, seemingly for the first time. I turned away from the vampire's intense stare and looked to the nearest monitor. "It's two in the morning. Sunrise is at around five thirty, right? Which gives us a little over three hours. We have sunrise to fall back on, if things go sour."

I sheathed my blade to my waist. This time I was going to kill the Greater demon SOB. "Where's the bastard?"

Danto's relief was visible as he exhaled loudly. But then the sharpness returned to his dark eyes as he said, "Fox Island."

CHAPTER
24

It took us about an hour to drive to Fox Island. I sat in the passenger seat next to Jax while Tyrius and Danto sat in the back, both leaning on the doors to put as much space between them as they possibly could. I'd been surprised Danto accepted a ride with us instead of following us in one of his many Range Rovers, which I had seen him drive before.

More astounding, Jax hadn't objected to giving the vampire a ride. In fact, he hadn't said anything at all as Danto pulled open the back door and slipped in quietly. At least he hadn't tried to sit in the front. That would have been awkward.

Jax's hands were stiff on the wheel, and a muscle feathered along his jaw. He was quiet. Too quiet. And it made me nervous.

He looked straight at the road, his face pale and shadowed in the darkness of the car. A storm was brewing in his eyes, a conflict of emotions ranging from guilt and anger to uncertainty, and I knew he was thinking of his sister. From what I'd seen, there was a playful side to Jax, but it was overwhelmed and overshadowed by his grief. And he had succumbed to it, letting his emotions control him. A part of me wished I could do something for his pain. I wasn't sure why. It's not like I knew him well, or that we'd be friends once this was over because I knew we wouldn't. He'd go back to whatever happy life he had before, to the welcoming arms of the council, and I'd never see him again. Just as well, I didn't have time for relationships.

My mood soured as I stared out the window. The Hudson River sparkled in the light of the moon. I could make out shadowed surrounding hills across the river. The mortal world was asleep, but nighttime was when half-breeds and demons came alive, feeding on the very darkness itself.

We were going to Fox Island for the sole purpose of putting an end to the Greater demon Degamon.

But something didn't feel quite right.

Why did the demon need to go so far away? And dragging an angel-born with it? Why Fox Island and not Brooklyn or Queens? What was so important about that place that the Greater demon would risk being seen or caught by guardian angels or other Sensitives?

My gut told me it was a trap, but it also gave us the whereabouts of the demon. I wouldn't pass it up. I caught Danto's face in the rearview mirror. He flicked his long bangs from his eyes. There were no more tears, and the faint tightening of his jaw was the only sign of his distress. While Jax and I had our soul blades and Tyrius had his black panther alter ego, I couldn't see any visible weapons on the vampire. Through the tears of his clothes, there was only pale skin. I couldn't see any leather holsters or even a weapons belt. It was a mistake to think that he could take down a Greater demon with just his good looks and sharp claws. What was he going to do? Try and seduce the demon with his pouty lips?

The chances that Cindy was still alive were slim. Why would the demon keep her alive anyway? It wouldn't. It was commanded to kill her. If by a miracle she was still alive, it was only because the demon was using her as bait to get me to come to it. We all knew it, but what other options did we have?

My mood worsened when Jax killed the engine and I climbed out of his car with the others. The solid thuds of Jax's car doors shutting echoed off the river and the stone faces of the buildings we had parked beside. I welcomed the cool night air and the faint salt breeze coming from the East River.

Leaning against the black Audi, I looked around at the rotten roofs, boarded up windows, and overgrown twisted, black, thorny vines that could skewer a leg sprouting from the cracks in the concrete street and forming giant impenetrable walls of death. Remnants of buildings collapsed into concrete rubble. Once it had been a booming amusement park, filled with the laughter of human children. Now beams and walls of abandoned buildings and rides stuck out like the skeletons of a giant beast, with only the whispers of a chilling wind. It was surreal. The park's once pulsating kinetic energy was eerily frozen in time.

The place was trashed by trespassers, tagged by vandals and reclaimed by Mother Nature. The deteriorating and collapsing Ferris wheels, carousels and roller coasters transformed with each passing season into rusting and rotting still-life portraits of benign neglect.

Fox Island was a small island just off Hunts Point in the Bronx, bordering the edges of the East River—a haven and breeding ground for demons.

Even the half-breeds stayed clear of Fox Island because it was overrun with demons. True demons, not half-breeds with a human heritage, but the real nightmares that sprouted from the bowels of the Netherworld. Demons and half-breeds hated each other, and a demon would kill a half-breed out of spite.

The streets and pathways were blanketed in a cold shadow. I sensed the darkness, the icy pull of death and the suffocating stench of rot—so thick, I could almost see it like a black mist. Unnatural. The place gave me the creeps. There were hundreds of demons here, possibly thousands. Great.

Tyrius was next to me. By the narrowing of his eyes and the line of hair that stuck out on his back, I knew he could sense them too.

"Lots of demons in this place," mewed the cat, reading my thoughts.

"I know," I said. "I can sense them too."

"Foul ones," said Tyrius, as he lifted his head towards a gust of wind. "It seems as though the entrails of the Netherworld came to Fox Island to party."

Jax moved to the back of his car and popped the trunk. My curiosity got the better of me as I heard the familiar sound of metal hitting metal and leaned over and took a peek.

My brows rose. "Damn, Jax. There's practically an armory in there. Where did you get all this stuff?" I took in a dozen or so soul blades, long swords, angry-looking hunting knives that could carve through steel, guns, rifles, shotguns, and huge bags of salt. The trunk was so packed with weapons I was amazed he could actually close it.

Jax gave me a sly smile. "I never leave home without my babies." He pulled out a thick, long hunting knife that looked a lot like a machete. The edges were sharp and stained. He slipped it into his weapons belt and began rummaging in his trunk. "You can never be too careful in our line of work. I believe in being prepared."

"Just a little overkill is all." A nice golden sword caught my eye. I wondered if Jax would let me borrow it. The gold would look great with my gold earring studs, and the blade looked sharp enough to pierce through stone.

Tyrius jumped up to my shoulder and leaned over. "Impressive collection, my man. Is that a Remington revolver? Whoa—those things are priceless."

Jax beamed, looking smug, and I rolled my eyes. "You know your guns," he said. "I'm impressed."

"I like things that go pow-pow," answered Tyrius.

"Okay, there, *boys*," I said as I lowered Tyrius to the ground, forgetting about the pretty golden sword. "Enough talk about toys. Let's be serious. This place is creepier than a Guillermo del Toro film, and it's crawling with demons." I spotted Danto, who stood with his arms wrapped around himself, his dark eyes searching the grounds. His bare feet stood out starkly against the dark concrete as he shifted from foot to foot.

"Rowyn, you need any extra weapons?" Jax leaned on his trunk. "You want a gun?"

"No, thanks," I said, cringing. I thought of that pretty golden sword. "I don't like guns. Never have. I prefer my good old fashion soul blades." I put my hands on my weapons belt, feeling the two soul blades. "Thanks, but I've got all that I need."

Jax reached in his trunk again and pulled out what I recognized as a double barrel shotgun. My mouth dropped slightly open as he moved next to Danto and handed it to him. The look of mild surprise on the vampire's face echoed my own.

"You know how to use it?" asked Jax, but I somehow suspected he knew the vampire did. Otherwise he wouldn't have entrusted him with one. "No one should meet this thing without some sort of weapon."

"I don't have a weapon," complained Tyrius.

"Tyrius," said Jax, looking down at the cat. "You *are* a weapon."

"I love it when you talk dirty, Jaxon." Tyrius flashed him his needle-sharp teeth.

Danto grabbed the shotgun easily with one hand, and in the same movement, with a flick of his wrist, he popped the gun open. The barrel opening swung on its hinge. "You've modified it," he said as he examined the inside of the double barrel. "Sawed off the tip. I've never seen cartridges like these. What are they?"

"Yeah, I modified it," answered Jax. His guarded expression shifted to one of pride as he looked at Danto. "It shoots salt bullets."

"Salt bullets?" Danto raised his brows. "Clever contraption." And with that, he flicked the shotgun shut and swung it over his shoulder. "Thank you."

Sporting the shotgun draped over his shoulder, Danto looked remarkably comfortable. Strangely enough, that look suited him, in an odd, goth-rockstar-vamp-cowboy sort of way.

Jax pinched his lips and gave a simple nod of his head. He reached in, filled his jacket pockets and jean pockets with boxes of salt cartridges, and then pulled out a smaller version of the shotgun he gave Danto, slipping it in his leather baldric. He pushed his trunk shut and moved to the front of his car, slightly little less tension in his walk.

I stared at this exchange, completely flabbergasted. What the hell had just happened? Jax gave his car a cheerful chirp and locked it.

When I looked down, Tyrius was peering at Danto with a curious expression. He looked up at me and said, "Now that's a first. Never thought I'd see the day when a vampire carried an angel-born shotgun—modified to shoot salt bullets." He shook his head. "The world's changing. Mark my words, Rowyn. There is shift. I can feel it."

"Maybe," I said as I hiked up my weapons belt over my hips. "Tonight, we have bigger problems. Come on."

The four of us walked towards the center of the amusement park. The sound of my boots hitting the pavement was loud in my ears. Apart from our tread, it was quiet, but the stillness seemed to hold a threat—a no humans or half-breeds allowed kind of threat.

Breathing deeply of the chill air, my skin rippled in goose bumps at the sudden shift of darkness around us, like stepping out of the heat and into an air-conditioned room. The darkness suffocated all light, all life. No grass grew on the island, and the trees I spotted were leafless, decaying sticks, a memory of what they used to be. No insects. No pests. Nothing. We were the only living things on the island. I shivered, feeling as though something was breathing down my neck. The cool air was quickly replaced by a thick, rotten egg smell.

"Which way?" asked Jax, who had taken the lead. Tension pulled his neck and shoulder muscles tight.

"Devil's Mouth," said Danto as he pointed with his shotgun to a maroon and green colored building in the distance that looked as though it were wearing a hat. Danto took a breath to say something but then stopped, shifting his shoulders as he changed his mind.

There were a couple hundred yards of fallen rides and debris between us, and I could make out what looked like a large field with mounds of dead grass and shrubs separating us from the building. Gray stones and ash sloped down to a barren landscape. The site was rough, covered with ash and heaps of weathered buildings and stone. Dotted in the landscaped were black, twisted trees.

It was the ugliest island I'd ever been to, and I couldn't wait to leave.

"We should hurry," said Tyrius, his voice edged with a little fear. "The demons know we're here. I don't think they'll bother us once we reach Devil's Mouth. If Degamon proclaimed it as his lair, then technically, all lesser demons should leave us alone. Technically."

"Technically." I knew that was a long shot. The creepy silence around us sent shivers rolling over me. Every now and again, I heard scraping, like fingernails on hard rock, and distant moaning. The wind brought forth a frayed chorus of faint wails and whimpers of things in pain. I knew the moaning and the cries weren't human. I could hear the distinct creature-like cadence that could only be described as monster in origin—demon, not human.

"This place feels like hell on Earth," I said, stifling a shiver. Yanking out my soul blade, I immediately felt more at ease with the familiar weight in my hand as I gripped my loyal companion. "A place of despair, pain and terror where the souls of the damned go to be tortured for eternity. Does the Netherworld feel like this? Like all hope is lost?"

"Worse," said Tyrius. "Even for demons, the Netherworld is a prison made of bone, flesh, blood and fear. It's one of the reasons why demons come here. They don't want to suffer the tortures of the Netherworld anymore. The mortal world is paradise for them. The ultimate escape."

"Fantastic," I said, my voice rough. My heart pounded as a ribbon of angst pulled through me.

"Be careful," said Jax as he pulled out his shotgun. "And stay frosty, people." He looked incredibly sexy with his leather jacket and a tight black t-shirt showing off his muscled chest, which was hairless and tanned. His weapons glittered at his belt. "Shoot anything that looks and smells like a demon—scratch that—just shoot anything that comes at us."

Together, we made our way swiftly through the rubble towards Devil's Mouth. The place was foul, and the ground was covered in a strange gray powder that looked more to me like the remnants of demon than sand or dirt. I resisted the urge to retch and kept moving. I didn't want to think about the demon bits I was stepping on.

Tyrius clearly shared the same thought as he was avoiding the powdery stuff, jumping from boulder to chunk of plaster or fragment of rotten wood.

We moved in silence through the rubble. It was a mass of smoking wood, stone and ash, charred like bones in a crematorium. Gray powder and ashes blew thickly across the land. I choked as some blew into my mouth. I tasted ash and something else I didn't recognize. Jax and Danto brought up their free hands to shield their eyes and mouths.

Even though I couldn't see them, I felt the presence of demons and death. I was used to it. I'd felt it since I was a child. My earliest memory was of a ghoul demon hiding in my closet, feeding on my pet hamster. It hadn't been pleased with me after I'd bludgeoned it to ashes with my doll. It had been my first kill. And I was four.

Darkness washed over me again, biting into my flesh. It was like a tug at my physical body, pulling at my insides, my skin. It was the feeling of death, of bitter cold, of a shitload of demons. And it scared the crap out of me.

A cold sweat trickled down my back, and my breathing became more labored. Instinctively, I pulled my sleeve up and looked at my wrist. The bruising looked the same. There was no blistering, but I could sense it throb in equal intervals, like a watch telling me that soon my time was up.

"What is that?" Danto was next to me even though I hadn't even seen him move. Damn those vamp stealth abilities.

"What is what?" I snapped, knowing exactly what he meant. Jax glanced over his shoulder at the sound of irritation in my voice. He looked about to interfere, but then changed his mind as he turned back around, his eyes scanning the darkness before us.

Danto was so close to me that I could smell the scent of blood and metal on him. He needed to take a step back.

"On your wrist, there," said the vampire, his voice like a purr, and he was still way too close. "You're not doing a very good job at concealing it, which I can tell is what you're trying to do. You keep looking at it, which defeats the purpose of a concealment. If you don't want us knowing about it, you shouldn't be working so hard at trying to hide it. So, what is it?"

My face burning, I pulled my sleeve and covered my wrist. "Nothing. Just a bruise." I could tell by the slight frown on his face that he didn't believe me. I guessed Cindy never got bruises either, or they faded away pretty quickly.

"Clearly, it's not just a bruise," said the vampire. "It gives off a certain... smell. I'm curious as to how you got... infected." I was glad for the darkness since my face went five more shades of red. Danto's eyes were pinned on me. "Did Degamon do that?"

"You don't give up. Do you?" I snarled and let out an exasperated breath through my nose. Tyrius whirled around from the top of fallen tree trunk. His yellow eyes shone in the darkness as they met mine. I could tell he was waiting for my signal to interfere. I gave him a slight shake of my head and the cat bounded ahead.

"I said it was nothing," I told the vamp. "So, it's nothing. Leave it alone, vampire, before I change my mind and leave your ass here... alone."

Danto narrowed his eyes at me and moved away, the shotgun swaying on his shoulders like he was born to use it.

Jax slowed his walk and I could tell he was waiting for me to catch up so he could talk. "Everything all right?" he asked as we walked side by side.

"Peachy," I growled. I didn't need to be reminded how stupid I was. I didn't want to think about the Seal of Adam. I just wanted to deal with Degamon. I'd figure out a way to get rid of the archangel curse afterward. If I wasn't dead, that is.

We made it to the clearing, my boots swishing above the ash-like ground. The demon energies around us were thick, the air crackling with static electricity, and my pulse quickened. Charred remains of buildings and dead trees blew around us, mixing with the ash.

Sticking out like pale fingers in a giant sea of ash were bones. Human bones, of all ages and sizes, lay sprawled along the ash-laden field, being slowly covered by ash as if they were being swallowed by a sand storm.

Tyrius lowered his head next to some scattered bones. "Those are human remains," he said, looking up at me. "It looks like there may be hundreds here."

"What?" I threw my gaze across the field. "This whole damn place is a graveyard." What I'd first thought was mounds of dead shrubbery was a feasting ground for demons. With this many dead, I felt a tearing ache, like a hole in my chest at the loss of life.

The taste of ash coated my tongue. My stomach twisted as I realized that most of us had been breathing the ashes—ashes of the dead mixed in with everything else.

Tyrius moved one of the bones carefully with his paw. "Some of these bones are old, maybe thirty—forty years old. Around the time when the amusement park was shut down. And there's more bad news."

"What?"

"This is grave dirt," commented Tyrius, who obviously didn't need a lab to tell the difference between regular dirt and grave dirt.

"Grave dirt," I seethed, my eyes traveling over the enormous space, the size of a football field, filled with grave dirt and bones. "I'm going to kill these bastards," I raged. Hard and strong, my blood pounded against my temples. "Damn these creatures. Damn them all to hell!"

"If only it were that simple," said Tyrius, his attention fixed on another bone. "This is where they fed. They brought their victims here, away from the rides, where they could devour their bodies and ingest their souls in peace, far enough away that no one heard their screams."

My eyes filled with tears. I knew Tyrius was right.

"Why keep it like this?" Jax looked like he was about to be sick. "Why not hide what they've done?"

"Because," said the cat, "they're trophies. Like all serial killers, the bones help prolong, even nourish, the fantasy of their kill. But above all, it's a show of strength, to show off their victims like a treasure. The bones of a human are worth more than gold to a demon. They're everything."

"How can this have happened?" asked Jax, his face in shadow, but I heard the mix of terror and anger in his voice.

"It's *still* happening." We all looked at the cat, but he was still looking at the bones.

"Why hasn't your council done something about this?" asked Danto, his dark eyes on Jax. "Isn't it your mandate to protect the human population from something like this? The vampire Courts wouldn't have allowed such a slaughter of their own kind. Makes you wonder if they'd known all along... and if so... why didn't they do anything to stop it?"

"Good question," I agreed looking at Jax, but he looked as perplexed as the rest of us. I immediately felt the rush of guilt at the accusation in my tone. It wasn't fair to accuse Jax of anything. He wasn't an elder in the council, an angel, or the Head of one of the Houses.

I was so lost in my anger towards the council, the Legion, and the demons, that I'd momentarily forgotten about my surroundings.

My demon senses went out of whack.

And by the time I'd felt them, it was already too late.

CHAPTER
25

A sea of demons stood between us and Devil's Mouth. It was as though darkness itself swirled and coalesced into shapes—wraiths and insubstantial figures, seething and simmering with death. Their faces churned with shifting shadows and hot tongues of flame, alive with hate, glowered from eternal night.

A scream caught in my throat as I looked out at the carpet of demons, the flickering limbs and rolling moans like wails from the dead and dying. The stench of death and rot filled my nose. It stuck to my clothes, to my hair and skin, like a thin mist. I tasted it in my mouth, on my tongue—rotten meat, carrion.

I'd never seen so many demons all at once, and it terrified me. My body tightened with fear. The sense of danger flamed through my very soul. We were surrounded.

This was hell on Earth—a piece of the Netherworld, the world of monsters and death and blood and nightmare—and we had front row seats.

"Looks like the road to hell is that way," I said, my gaze scanning the red glow in the eyes of some of the demons. Shifting forms intensified into burning embers.

Jax looked at me with a strange gleam in his eye and pumped his shotgun. "Good thing I'm in the mood for pain and chaos."

I took a slow breath. Heads jerked, and limbs thrashed in a jagged line dance. With a disharmony of rasping moans, the demons focused their craved and maddened eyes on us.

Tyrius climbed over a rotten tree trunk. "Shotgun on the big green giant with the beer gut and tail. What can I say? I like things with tails."

I felt Danto stir next to me. A fiery revenge burned in his gray eyes, and in the next moment they were black, making him haunting and dangerous. The vampire was silent, but the creases on his face said that he wanted to kill every last demon. Totally understandable.

"Okay, so we need to waste a couple hundred soul-eating demons to get to Devil's Mouth *and then* fight a super-human, soul-eating Greater demon to get Cindy back," said Jax, and then he shrugged. "No biggie."

Tyrius's tail flicked nervously behind him. "Anyone got any bright ideas just how we're going to get through this mountain of demon hide to get to the other side?"

"There's only one way," I said, my heart pounding as I anticipated how much it was going to hurt. It was going to hurt like hell. "That's forward... and through it. We need to make a run for it."

"A run for it?" echoed Tyrius.

"We don't have another choice," I said. "If we stop, we're dead. There're too many of them and too few of us. Our best option is to run and fight our way to the other side. We don't stop. until we're safely inside that building. We stop. We die. Got it?"

"I hate to stick a needle in this wholesome bubble of joy," said the cat, "but the chances of that happening and us not being torn to smithereens by those mad-hungry demons are slim." He looked at me, eyes wide. "I'm just saying, we might not make it."

Heart pounding against my chest, I moved my gaze to the black sea of rippling demons. "We'll make it." And then I added with more conviction. "We *will* make it."

"Of course we'll make it," said Jax as his eyes met mine. "But just in case we don't—"

Before I knew what was happening, he grabbed a fistful of my shirt and gave me a yank towards him. Off guard, I plowed into his hard chest—and he kissed me.

He took my mouth like a man starving for it, rough and hard. It gave me no choice but to hang on. But then his kiss turned gentle, and my mouth opened to let his tongue meet mine. Blasts and booms of heat assaulted me, and I rode that high, hot wave. It was unexpected, and it made me feel wanted. The passion in his kiss only added a sexy edge. Everything about the kiss—the heat of his lips, the strong grip of his hands—made me feel irresistible. And I liked it.

And then in the next second, it was over as he pushed me back gently and released my shirt.

Color showed on his cheeks. His eyes widened as he recognized the desire in my own. Flustered, I did what any respectable woman should do after being violated in such a fashion. I punched him.

"What the hell was that for?" I yelled, resisting the urge to wipe my mouth. "You just mouth-raped me!"

Jax cupped his jaw where I'd punched him, grinning. "Man, you hit hard," he said, still rubbing his jaw. "But it was worth it."

My argument died in my mouth. I was speechless. He knew I'd enjoyed it too. Damn him.

I narrowed my eyes as Tyrius laughed. I didn't have to turn my head to see the smirk on Danto's face.

Tyrius stood up on his hind legs. "With stout hearts, and with fervor for the death of these devils, let us go forward to victory!"

As though answering Tyrius's call, all at once, the demon mass descended upon us in a terrifying rush.

"Ah, hell," I said as the hundreds of clattering claws set me on edge. I gripped my blade until it hurt. "There goes my new outfit."

Jax turned around and flashed me a smile that I would remember for the rest of my life. My annoyance melted away. Grinning back at him, my fear was replaced by my deep hatred for these demons, at the destruction of life that surrounded us.

Breathing deeply, I pulled out another blade with my left hand, set my teeth in a defiant snarl, and charged into the mass of demons.

CHAPTER
26

I didn't know if the others followed. All I saw were shadows, claws, and fangs, and I wanted to destroy them all.

The first demon that crossed my line of sight was a shadow demon, a lesser demon that appeared as a dark shifting fog that could take on a solid form. The vaporous wraith solidified into solid bone and muscle, claws and fangs, into a frightening twisted beast covered with a leathery hide spotted with festering sores.

Shots sounded around me, and from the corner of my eye I saw Jax fire his shotgun into the demon stronghold, a mad smile on his face as he shouted, "Come and get it. There's plenty for everyone!"

I don't know why, but I liked him even better than before.

The shadow demon descended upon me in a frightening blow. With my blades gripped in both hands, I screamed with unleashed fury, driving the tips of my blades through the demon's chest as it rushed at me. Soft flesh and hard bone hissed at the contact with my blades. Demon blood splattered my face and neck. The shadow demon slid from the blades and hit the ground like a bucket of slop, its hide not entirely able to contain its contents. It bubbled once and then burst into a cloud of ashes.

I heard the hiss of a cat, and I whirled to see Tyrius scratching the eyes out of a big green demon that looked like a zombie sumo wrestler with a tail.

I burst down towards Devil's Mouth, slightly aware of Danto to my left running with a predatory grace and ease, barefoot and with a big-ass shotgun as he shot down two demons at a time.

The walls of demons closed in on us, the stench of rot suffocating.

I ran harder.

I knew there was a chance, when and if we reached the building, that Degamon might not even be there. The demon might have planned on having us killed to save the demon-sweat of doing it itself.

I ran harder still.

I could see Devil's Mouth more clearly, weatherworn and stained, spotted with years of neglect and the foul imprints of demons. What I'd first thought was a hat, were in fact ears, horns and a face. The devil's face. Devil's Mouth was a giant, painted face of the devil. And of course the entrance was through its mouth.

It was the only building still standing, apart from the skeletal remnants of the roller-coaster, carousel, and other rides that were almost unrecognizable in the rubble.

Degamon clearly had a sense of humor.

I raced toward the vile devil's head, the wails of the demons around me like the roar of a river, swollen from the spring rains. Only this river was swollen with soul-eating demons.

A shadow demon leapt out of some decaying brush. It lunged for Jax in a flash of leathery, long limbs marred with countless sores. He hadn't seen it. He was shooting at a shadow demon that had thrown itself at him.

"Jax!" I shouted, my warning lost in the loud boom of his shotgun. My heart caught in my throat. The shadow demon pounced—

And then Danto was there. He didn't falter as he ducked and twirled with inhuman speed, slashing down with his left hand and viciously slicing the demon's head clear off. The demon's body exploded into a cloud of ash the same moment its head toppled off its neck.

Jax gave Danto a surprised look, clearly acknowledging that someone he hated had just saved his ass. The two men shared a knowing nod, the kind that only men understood.

"Don't stop!" I shouted as I willed my legs to go faster. "Keep going!"

We ran. My shotgun-shooting companions flanked either side of me—a vampire, who was just as skilled with a shotgun as he was with his own razor-sharp claws, and an angel-born, who shot everything that came at us with just a hint of a crazy smile that spoke volumes of the kiss he stole.

I would deal with him later.

I couldn't see Tyrius, but I knew he wasn't far behind. Probably gouging the eye out of some demon. Good on him.

I spun as I sensed a presence behind me.

A creature of raw, red flesh and twisted body covered in blood shambled my way—a morax demon. It looked like a cross between a skinned gorilla and a giant beetle with glassy red eyes, a gaping maw, and claws itching to rip apart my new jacket.

I couldn't let that happen. So, I cut it down in three strikes. As soon as I found my footing, I was off again, shooting through the ash, bone, and debris like a cheetah.

"Why haven't you Hulked-out yet?" I yelled, spotting Tyrius sprinting a few feet ahead of me, in his preferred Siamese cat size.

"Because," panted the cat, "I can't just turn it off and on whenever I want. It uses up all my energy. I'll have to sleep after I use it to recover. I want to save it for my favorite Greater demon."

"How long does it take you to recover?"

271

"Couple of hours," said Tyrius as he ducked and skillfully avoided being squished by a two-headed demon that got blasted in the next second by one of Jax's salt bullets.

Tyrius sprang ahead of me. "Depending on how I use the power and whether I drain every last drop, two hours is best—incoming!" shouted Tyrius as he jerked his head at something behind me.

I sidestepped and whirled. Bringing out my blades like extensions of my arms, I swung them at the demon. The blades cut the worm-like demon's chest in quick successions. Just as it fell, another took its place.

All I saw was a blur as the tips of the claws scratched into my arm. The demon's mouth moved, a horrid pulpy mess of gray flesh that writhed like a slug. The demon made several gurgling, wet sounds as I sliced through its maw. Blood splattered my face as I stepped over the fallen demon and sprinted towards the entrance to Devil's Mouth.

We were almost there. Shotgun barrels glowing an evil red to either side of me, we took the last couple of yards.

I laughed as I ran even though I felt my legs begin to tire and the familiar weakness from the Seal of Adam on the edges of my body.

I brushed the feeling aside. We were going to make it!

Together, we burst into Devil's Mouth, tearing the night with our pants and howls of war, and I turned around, ready to cut down the demons that followed. But they didn't.

I whirled around, realizing it was darker inside than outside. Without the light from the moon, this place was pitch black. The darkness was dominant, and it felt alive.

"Uh, guys?" I whispered.

There was a sudden rush of light and I started.

Countless candles suddenly burned about the room, casting long and crooked shadows along the walls. Demonic symbols were painted on the ground and on the walls with large red stains. The only piece of furniture was a purple, month-eaten upholstered chair that looked like it belonged in the nineteen seventies. It was pushed up at the far end of the room and raised like a throne.

The room had a ceremonial feeling to it, like a ritualistic chamber where virgin human females were sacrificed to the gods.

In the middle of the room sat a table carved of blackened wood. The slab rested on the backs of wailing demons, their faces engraved with a look of eternal suffering.

And tied on top of the table was Cindy.

CHAPTER
27

Cindy turned her head at the sound of our approach. Her eyelids fluttered open, and her eyes widened, trying to focus. Her once shiny luscious hair was matted and clumped together with blood. Streaks of blood ran down the side of her face where she'd been cut, and her clothes were stained with dirt and blood. Her hands were red at the wrists, the blood that coated them still wet and running.

My skin tingled at the strong demon energies in the room. I scanned the area, but the only demons I could see, or had seen, were the ones left outside.

Cindy's eyes found Danto and her lips moved, but I couldn't make out what she was saying.

The air pushed next to me. I swung out my arm, but I missed. Danto was already across the room by the time I had raised my arm. Damn that vampire.

"Danto! Wait!"

I ran after the vampire but then skidded to a stop.

A wall of black vapor rose between Cindy and Danto. The vapors coiled and solidified, revealing a giant red demon with decaying flesh and tufts of black fur along its back, arms and legs.

In a rage, Degamon backhanded Danto across the face with a massive taloned hand. The vampire soared like a ragdoll across the room and slammed into the wall with a sickening crunch. His shotgun fell from his grasp.

The black mist shifted, and a dozen creatures of scale and claws and fangs stepped through the haze. Igura demons. Their black eyes burned with hunger. Gleaming death blades hung in their grip.

"Great, it brought its groupies," mewed Tyrius.

Encircling us, the scales of their bodies shimmering in the candlelight, the igura demons muttered in their demonic language as they tightened their circle around us.

"Angel-born," said Degamon as it flashed me its mouth full of sharp yellow teeth. "How good of you to come."

"There's nothing good about it, Degamon." I scanned the room for any other exits. There weren't any that I could see. "I like what you've done with the place—very supernatural chic."

A whimper escaped from Cindy. I flicked my gaze to her, and my insides twisted at the fear I saw in them. She didn't know this was all my fault. Stupid. Stupid Rowyn.

Degamon moved towards the table. It moved its long fingers along Cindy's legs, an idle smile playing on its lips. "Such pretty flesh for the plucking," it chuckled. A sick sound formed in its throat. "The female flesh is so much sweeter, tastier than the human males. Imagine my delight. Now I have two. I must thank you, half-breed," said the demon as its eyes found Danto, "for bringing me the angel-born."

"I didn't do it for you," came Danto's voice from behind me. I turned to see the vampire, blood trickling from a cut on his forehead. His body trembled with barely controlled rage.

"She is pretty. Isn't she?" Degamon purred as it leaned over Cindy, its black eyes fixing on me. "Pretty soft flesh, with a pretty soft soul," it said. With a sharp talon, Degamon sliced open Cindy's chest. I went cold as Cindy cried out. The woman's blood seeped through her white shirt.

"Bastard," I whispered, and Degamon smiled, a smile of terrible things to come.

Danto moved past me, but this time I was ready and reached out. I grabbed the vampire by the arm and yanked him back hard. He crashed into me and I held him.

"Wait," I hissed as Danto squirmed in my hold. When he finally submitted, and I was convinced he wouldn't do anything stupid, I released him.

"You must have assumed that I would never agree to let this pretty flesh go," said Degamon, eyeing Cindy like she was a juicy steak. "Yet, still you came, and still you brought the other female with you." Degamon watched us intently. "You came alone. Do you intend to fight me? You cannot defeat me, tiny mortals. You will lose. And with your deaths, I will bring forth more of my armies. There are countless lesser demons in the Netherworld, hungry for entrance to this world."

"We're not here to fight." I stepped forward. The igura shifted but did not come closer. "We're here to trade."

Degamon only smiled, a lazy smile, ripe with promise. "Trade? I already have your lives in my hands. Without your lives, there's nothing left to trade," gloated the demon. At that, Tyrius growled, which warranted a bigger smile from the demon.

"You'll want to hear what I have to trade," I persisted. "And then we'll walk out of here—the five of us. Including Cindy."

Degamon threw back its head and laughed, long and deep. Putting a hand against the table, the demon bent almost double. A thump of anger reverberated up through my feet to the top of my head. God, I hated that red demon.

"Is it supposed to do that?" whispered Jax, a hint of steel tightening his face.

I gave him a shrug. "Hell if I know."

"Oh, you are such a delight, angel-born!" said Degamon, clapping its taloned hands. "Dinner will have to wait. I'm always in the mood for entertainment." Its thick lips split in a nasty grin. "Tell me, what do you have to trade?" it mocked.

My heart raced. "The name of the one who summoned you."

"Really?" chortled the demon, though I could see the shift of interest on its face. "And you have *that* particular name, do you?"

"Yes, I do." I took a calming breath. This was going to work. I knew it was. I was almost dancing with excitement. "I give you the name," I said, "and we walk away free. With Cindy. Agreed?" When it said nothing, I continued. "I know how the summoner's name takes hold of the summoned. With this name—you're free. You won't be bound to them anymore. You won't be their slave."

"I know the rules, angel-born," informed Degamon, black smoke curling up from its back. "I practically wrote the book on summoning."

"So, are we agreed?" I pressed, the tension around me rising with every breath. I dared to look at the surrounding iguras. Darkness and rage sparked in their black eyes. Damn.

Degamon gave me a chilling look that scared the crap out of me. Its gaze dropped to Cindy and then back to me. "Agreed," answered the demon, its eyes glinting with eagerness.

I hid my sigh of relief, but my knees shook at the sound of Danto releasing a long breath. "The dark witch, Evanora Crow." I said her name loud and clear. There was no mistaking it. She was the summoner.

I waited. The blood was roaring so loudly in my ears that I could barely hear the growls from the iguras.

"I gave you the name," I said, my gut clenching. I hissed as the mark on my wrist throbbed suddenly. "Now it's your turn to keep your end of the deal. Let Cindy go."

The black mist that Degamon had brought with it coiled around him like a moving cape. "You think I'd let some half-breed order me around? And a dark witch at that?"

I took a breath, a ragged gasp in my throat. "Maybe." Oh crap.

Degamon licked its lips with its black tongue. "You are wrong, angel-born. It is not the dark witch, Evanora Crow, who summoned me. You came here thinking you had won, but you have lost. It was never the witch."

My jaw dropped. Heart pounding, I felt as if I was wrapped in quicksand. I couldn't move as my stomach lurched, the ground tipping at my feet. My breath came faster and faster as I felt a wash of panic. I'd been wrong. The dark witch had never summoned Degamon, and now I had killed everyone...

If the dark witch hadn't summoned the demon, then who? Who had it in for me? For the Unmarked?

"Uh... guys?" said Tyrius, and I felt him nudge up to my leg. But I was too shocked to look at him. "I think this is the time to come up with Plan B."

Degamon's expression was mocking, its black eyes spiteful. "A dark witch can't give me what I want."

Fear hit me like a gunshot. "And what's that?" I gripped my blade as I wavered on my feet.

"Flesh and blood and... oh, the sweetness of angel-born souls."

Moving too fast to readily follow, Degamon grabbed Cindy by the neck. The snap of bone was clear in the cold, dry air. My stomach lurched as Danto screamed and fell to his knees.

CHAPTER
28

This was far, far worse than I'd expected.

The iguras hurtled at us in a savage blur of fangs, death blades, and scales. I leaped sideways, grabbed a fistful of Danto's shirt, and hauled him to his feet.

"Snap out of it, or you'll die!" I smacked him across the face. "She's gone. You're not!" Cursing, I pushed him out of the way as an igura came tumbling towards us.

I blocked its blade with my own and sent a kick to its groin. Did it even have a groin? The igura stumbled back. Maybe it did.

"Behind you!" I heard Jax shout.

I ducked and spun, sending my blade across the chest of an igura. Warm blood covered my hand and arm as the demon's entrails flew out of its chest. It fell in a spill at my feet before exploding into dust.

And I smiled. Maybe we would make it out alive. Just maybe.

I launched myself at another igura, slashing with my soul blade as I went. I took another step forward, cutting furiously as I moved with the blade whistling as I swung it.

A deep growl sounded next to me, and I whirled to find a three-hundred-pound black panther tearing out the neck of an igura demon.

Brightness obscured my vision. I turned at the sudden illumination across from me and saw a ball of light in Degamon's hand. I retched as the demon ingested Cindy's soul. It caught me watching and grinned in delight.

I caught a glimmer of movement to the side, and in a wild dash, Danto hurled himself at Degamon. The Greater demon chuckled as it stepped toward the panting vampire and raised its clawed hand, aiming at Danto's chest. The vampire's strikes went wide as the Greater demon moved impossibly fast. It grabbed him and shoved him against the ground, his face smashing into the stone.

I watched in wide-eyed terror as Danto thrashed on the ground in one final attempt to pry himself free. The Greater demon held firm, as though it had been waiting for centuries to get its hands on the vampire. Degamon squatted over Danto, and with a powerful blow, hit him across the face. Blood flowed freely.

Danto rolled away from Degamon, his blood and saliva pooling onto the ground.

The idiot was going to get himself killed.

A shotgun cracked, and the weapon beat out a terrible, barking roar, salt bullet rounds flinging out and ricocheting from the walls in a crazy embroidery of terrible violence. Bullets tore demon flesh, splintered bone, and knocked the igura down and over—but still they came, until they were literally torn apart, broken into pieces.

My legs cramped, and I felt the beginnings of the Seal of Adam crawling back into my system. I knew I didn't have long before the effects would assault me, rendering me ill and too weak to fight back.

Movement caught my eye. I let out a scream as I deflected an igura's powerful strike. A muscle twanged near my spine, twisting and burning with every move I made. I was weakening. My body was screaming to stop, but if I stopped, I would die.

There were more of them—seemingly coming out of the black mist like a swarm of giant, butt-ugly flies. The demons, monsters from the Netherworld, came at me. Some carried death blades, but some just used their claws. They struck as they passed, their claws slicing into my flesh. They were going to rip me apart.

The hair on the back of my neck rose, and I whirled, just missing the tip of a death blade. I slammed into the igura, making the demon shriek in surprise. Blood pounding, I flung my blade toward it, and the igura jumped back, just missing my killing blow. The demons were closing in again.

Howling, cackling laughter echoed in around the walls. Degamon had Danto by the neck, the vampire's limp body dangling like a puppet in the demon's grasp.

Even if he was a blood-sucking vampire, I couldn't let him die.

I lost myself in the fury of the events, letting it overwhelm me. I charged. I hit the Greater demon in the back with my blade, pushing it through until I felt the blade hit bone.

Degamon cried out and released Danto. Up until now, my plan had worked, but now I had the Greater demon's full attention on me. Crap.

At the far end of the room, iguras rose angrily to their feet. Jax advanced relentlessly onward, firing his salt bullets. The loud blasts of shards tearing up flesh rang in the room. Jax followed them up with another pop from his shotgun. Three iguras tried to stop him, but Jax never stopped firing.

"I shall enjoy devouring your pretty flesh," said Degamon, taking a step closer. "Peeling it off you from the inside out."

"Chew on this," I snarled and flung one of my soul blades at its head. The demon was so swift that it scraped its cheek rather than wedging itself between its eyes. Damn. Black blood welled and flowed. It raised a taloned hand to examine it. "You're the last Unmarked. I will be free of my contract once you're dead." Degamon's expression changed. It was only for a second, but in that moment, I saw furious rage, arrogant pride, and violent bloodlust on its face.

"And after I kill you, I shall enjoy the fruit of what I was promised." It sounded convincing and it scared me.

I spat at the demon's feet. "You can go back to the Netherworld, you hideous prick." I stole a look over my shoulder to the entrance of Devil's Mouth and saw only darkness. The sun would be up soon. If we could just hang on until then, we could make it— maybe.

Degamon grinned. "The sun won't be up for another hour," said the demon, reading my thoughts. "Ample time for me to kill you ten times over… and your friends."

At that moment I realized I didn't hear the pop of gunshots anymore. I backed up, looking behind me, and saw Jax with his machete-like sword in his hand, his shotgun at his feet. He was panting, and he was favoring his left leg. Tyrius had retreated in a corner, facing three igura demons as they laughed and hacked at him with their death blades.

My heart all but stopped. We weren't going to make it.

"You don't have to do this," I said, fear making my throat tight. "I was wrong about the witch, but I can still find out the name of the one who summoned you. Let me help you. I can set you free. Never to be its slave again. Think about it. What's your freewill worth to you?"

Degamon said nothing as it advanced slowly, darkness rippling around it.

"You think your summoner will stop at this?" I said raising my last soul blade. "No. They're going to summon you for more favors because you're basically their bitch. Is that what you want?" I took the demon's silence as a yes. "You know I'm right." If the demon was smart, it would agree to this. Then maybe we'd all go home… alive.

"You want to be a slave for the rest of your demonic existence?" I prompted. "Because that's what's going to happen to you, demon. A slave."

"I'm a prince of the Netherworld," said Degamon in a voice that resounded in my bones. "I am no slave."

"Newsflash, dumbass. You are. You were the minute you were summoned and forced to do the summoner's bidding. If that's not slavery, I don't know what is."

A low growl rumbled in the Greater demon's throat. The glow in its black eyes intensified. "You talk too much, angel whore. I'm going to enjoy ripping out your tongue."

I stifled a shiver. I knew it meant it. "You're stupider than you look if you think after all this," I said pointing my blade, "that they'd let you off the hook. If it sounds like too good a deal, you aren't looking at the fine print. You always look at the fine print before you sign a contract. You think you won't be vanquished by the summoner? Why keep you around when you know its darkest secrets."

I knew I hit a nerve when Degamon lost its smile. "You know nothing, angel-born. And today you will die, never knowing who killed your parents in that house fire. And you'll never know why I was sent to hunt you."

I felt like my heart was going to explode. "So, tell me! Tell me why!" I shouted. My anger flared at the look of amusement on the demon's face.

Degamon licked its lips. "I'd rather not. I only wanted the Unmarked. And if a few of your friends die along with you, well, that's hardly my fault, now is it? You chose to bring them along for the feasting."

I made a rude gesture with my finger. "Feast on this."

The Greater demon sneered and then lunged for me again. Breathing hard with effort, I let my instincts flow and managed to avoid Degamon's killing blow. I dropped to the ground and rolled, tears in my eyes at the searing pain and fatigue in my body. How many minutes had gone by? Two? Three? Not nearly enough.

Sweat poured down my forehead and stung my eyes. I wasn't fast enough to stop Degamon as the giant demon tackled me.

My breath escaped me as I rolled onto the dirt floor, the demon's teeth and claws flipping and shredding and biting.

A foot slammed into my stomach and I cried out. The air shot out of me as the demon kicked me again and again. I hit the ground and rolled as I spat out a mouthful of blood and dirt.

Before I could move, Degamon brought its fist down onto my face. Black spots exploded behind my eyes. I heard the demon laugh as I crawled on all fours like a beast, trying to get away.

Something grabbed my leg and yanked me back. Struggling against the demon's grip, I felt a sharp pain at the back of my neck. Crying out, I kicked, and by the souls, I hit something solid.

With my legs free, I rolled to my feet, staggering as a wave of nausea hit me. I could make out Degamon moving towards me, but I couldn't see Tyrius or Jax, as my vision was plagued by a darkness on the edges.

I was going to die. My soul would be devoured by this Greater demon. I would never find out why my parents were killed. I would never know why I was Unmarked.

Terror like I'd never felt before took over. I covered my head as Degamon's claws swept upon me, and I kicked and punched blindly. Every movement was met with tremendous effort. My muscles burned with exertion. How much longer did I have? Minutes? Seconds?

Degamon pulled back and sneered. "Give yourself over to me, and I promise a quick death."

"You mean like what you did to Cindy?" I panted. My gaze fell on the young woman's face. Her lifeless eyes gave me the creeps and I looked away. "No thanks. I'd rather go down fighting. I might not be able to defeat you," *not with the Seal of Adam*, I thought, "but I can as sure as hell give you a few thrashings to remember me by."

Degamon gave me an incredulous look. "You angel-born always want to play the hero. But what about your friends' deaths? You want them to suffer too?"

At that moment, I heard a faint whimper. When I turned my head, I saw Tyrius still in the corner, two igura demons taking turns cutting him. Black blood trickled from his black coat. He was wet with it. I could see the bundle on the ground that was Danto, face bloodied and swollen. He hadn't moved an inch from where Degamon had thrown him onto the floor.

And when my eyes focused on Jax, a lump of fear knotted in my guts. Piles of ash heaped near his feet. He'd managed to kill a few igura demons, but he was limping. He swung his weapon tiredly at another two iguras that advanced on him. His strikes were too slow and too few.

"Give yourself away freely, and I will spare their lives. They don't need to die. Just you."

My breath escaped my lungs in a slow groan, lips trembling so hard I had to clamp down to keep the sound inside. My clothes were sticky and wet with my own sweat and blood. I was so tired.

"It would be more honorable to give in and die," encouraged Degamon. "Rather than letting innocents die. Unless… you forfeit your life and I will spare them."

A chill went down my spine. "Liar!"

Defiance and rage mixed in my blood. This wasn't fair. I swung my free arm, and it met with a red face with burning coals for eyes. The darkness rippled, and Degamon's gaping features appeared. But there were two of them. Damn it. I blinked my blurred vision until I could see more clearly.

How long did I have before another wave of the archangel-curse-induced visions took over? Degamon reached for my throat, and I flung myself backward. I felt a tug at the front of my shirt, the demon's claws just missed my chest.

My head throbbed, the Seal of Adam seizing control of my mind again, and I shook it to get rid of the multiple Degamons in front of me. The shadowy figure that was the actual Degamon laughed as it stepped towards me.

"Does death scare you, angel-born?" it mocked. "Knowing that I will devour your soul and you will never be reborn again?" The demon's laugh of delight shocked me. "I should find that liberating. Don't you agree? A real, true death."

"Screw you," I aimed my soul blade at one of the Greater demons. "Why kill us?" I gasped, as my wrist throbbed. But I just couldn't let it go. Could I keep it talking for another twenty minutes? "You said you knew," I pressed. "I'm dead anyway, right, so what does it matter if you tell me? Why do we need to die?"

"Because you were a mistake," said a familiar voice in a tone of intense satisfaction.

There was the sound of shuffling footsteps and I looked up to find the archangel Vedriel strutting towards me.

CHAPTER
29

The archangel Vedriel stepped from the shadows like he owned the goddamn planet. He was dressed in the familiar dark leather gear, wearing the same egotistical, punch-worthy grin. I guessed archangels didn't go shopping much. A long sword swayed behind him as he crossed the room, tangling in his long white locks that spilled down past his waist. His fair, glowing skin was a stark contrast against his black gear. His perfect features were held in arrogant dominance. He might be a powerful archangel, but to me, he'd always just be a conceited elf.

The Seal of Adam throbbed as if aware that its maker was in the room.

The remaining four iguras hissed and spat at the archangel as they cowered away from him as well as from Tyrius and Jax. When I met Jax's eyes, I saw the fear and confusion that echoed my own. Jax's face had gone pale—so, so pale.

It was obvious Vedriel had summoned Degamon, when with only one look from the archangel, the Greater demon stepped clearly away from me. He controlled the demon. Damn. What the hell was this? How could an angel, an archangel, warrant our deaths?

Anger twisted my gut, and blood pounded in my temples, the force almost making me vomit. I found my voice.

"You?" I accused the archangel. "But—how—why?" I swallowed hard. "How could you do this? How could you summon a Greater demon to kill your own descendants!" My soul blade was a welcome weight in my hand. It shone, coated with the blood of the iguras. And I wanted to cut the smile off the archangel's face.

"Why?"

Vedriel made his way over to the chair and sat, straight, shoulders back, looking down on us like a king gazing down at his court. "Because I must."

The iguras wailed and thrashed. Degamon was watching the archangel with a mixture of ire and fear, like it wanted to kill him but had no choice but to resist.

I jerked a quick glance to the side to see Danto pushing himself up, his teeth showing in a snarl, and his black eyes glittering in deep hatred. The archangel Vedriel had all but confirmed that he had ordered Cindy's death. My death.

I slid my gaze back to the archangel and raised my right wrist. "Thanks for the gift."

Vedriel crossed his legs at the knee. "Well, at least, now you can't say that the Legion never gave you anything."

"You're an archangel," came Jax's voice. It was strained and higher than usual. "This doesn't make any sense."

Vedriel pressed his hands together at the tips. "It makes perfect sense."

"How's that?" I staggered as another wave of dizziness hit me, figuring it was marginally more dignified than passing out and falling to the floor. "Enlighten us, archangel."

"With pleasure," Vedriel mused, playing with the shredded pieces of fabric from the arms of the chair. "Don't you know what you are? I would have thought you would have figured it out by now."

"What the hell are you talking about," I said, shivering violently as I looked over my shoulder at Jax and Tyrius, who were watching the exchange with a collective horror. Danto was pale, stiff, and looked like he was about to be sick.

"I don't speak archangel," I said looking back. "Spit it out. What?" The adrenaline was gone, and fatigue and nausea pulled at me. The igura demons were moving quickly around us, making me dizzy. My body was a solid ache, and part of me just wanted it to be over.

"Did you never wonder why you felt the presence of demons?" said Vedriel with a hateful smile. "Not just angels can sense the presence of demons. Demons are drawn to each other. They can sense other demons."

My mouth dropped open. "Liar. I'm not a demon. Stop playing your mind games." My blood chilled at the thought, and I could barely feel my legs.

Could it be true? Was I a demon? It would explain a lot...

Vedriel laughed. "Am I? No. I don't think so. I can see it in your eyes. You know exactly what I mean."

A throaty growl sounded and I felt Tyrius's large black panther body lean up against me, supporting me, as though he knew I was about to collapse.

I shook my head, the nausea increasing a hundredfold. "No. No. No. You're a liar. Liar!" I shouted.

Vedriel leaned forward. "Don't you know what you are? You are shadow and light. A shadow rises and light meets it. Creation and destruction. Angel and demon." The archangel's smile widened at the fear he saw on my face. "You are Horizon's super soldier. An experiment. A mistake. A mistake that I'm going to rectify." His pale eyes narrowed with anger that made my gut tighten and my archangel curse throb. "You became too powerful, see? Too unpredictable with your growing abilities," continued the archangel. "With equal amounts of angel and demon essence flowing in your veins, you are unmatched. The Legion couldn't have that. Think of the risks. Think of the threat you pose. You have all the strengths of a demon but none of their weaknesses—all packaged in the body of an angel-born. A very dangerous combination. You needed to be removed."

"But I'm not an experiment... I-I was born," I stammered, refusing to look at Jax and Danto, whose eyes were on me. "I wasn't made in a lab. My mother gave birth to me. My father witnessed it. He told me. I saw pictures!"

"Yes," said the archangel. "Just like all the other mothers, they gave birth to their own children. But they were unaware of the changes we made to the fetus. They slept while we injected the fetus with the demon and angel essence."

"You sneaked in at night and did things to a few pregnant women?" I shouted, spitting hair out of my mouth. "Do you know how sick and twisted that is? You sick bastard!"

Vedriel's pale lips pulled back in a sneer. "It was an experiment. But now the experiment is over."

My teeth chattered. My body trembled from the shock, the fever, and the spent adrenaline. Pulse pounding, I became lightheaded. Steeling myself, I set my will around my core, searching my body for answers and finding them. It was true. I'd always known it.

I was a thing. A monster. The Legion had created me.

If I wasn't angel or demon, what was I? What did that make me? A freak.

"The Legion allowed this?" Jax's voice sounded just as angry as mine. "Can't be," he said, shaking his head. "How could they do this to those innocent babies?"

"Not all the Legion, of course," Vedriel cocked his head to the side. "Only those who needed to know. Those who… participated."

I felt like a wraith, a thing. Maybe I was a demon. I gripped my faithful soul blade. "Why go through the trouble of summoning a demon? Why not kill us yourself?"

Vedriel shrugged. "Politics." His pale eyes moved to the back of the room where Degamon and his iguras waited. "Didn't want word to reach the wrong archangels. Sometimes to get things done, you need to be more creative." The archangel's expression was laced with a threatening warning. "You and the others," commented Vedriel, "are a waste of space and breath, a stain on the world. Unworthy of your birthright. You are not true angel-born. You're a mutation. A curse on the world."

I gritted my teeth, silent tears finding their way down my face. I couldn't help it. It hurt.

"You killed my parents." I shook from the fever and a deep rage that bubbled through my veins like a hot sauce. My pulse pounded as I let the pieces fall into place. "Why?"

"Because, just like you, they became meddling fools." Vedriel picked at his nails. "Too close to the truth, and we couldn't have that, now could we? Your parents saw the changes in you and they grew worried. They knew something was wrong. With you... and the others. They were asking too many questions. Talking to too many others. They needed to die."

I could still smell the charred remains of my house, the scent of ash and smoke and of burnt flesh. My parents had died because of me. Because of what the Legion had done to me.

"So you had them killed. You bastard!" Spit and tears flew out of my mouth.

And then I was moving. My legs pushed off the ground fast, surprising even me. The last of my strength pulsed through my muscles, giving me what I wanted, what I needed.

"Don't do it!" came Jax's voice, but I didn't care. I was going to kill that SOB or I was going to die trying.

I saw Vedriel stand up and brush a strand of white hair from his perfect face. I blinked as a sword appeared in his grasp. I didn't care how strong he was, or how stupid I was being. I just wanted revenge. Revenge for my parents. Revenge for all the others. Revenge at what had been done to me.

Without pause, I sprang, bringing my blade around. The archangel swept his sword up defensively as he plunged onward. Vedriel came at me, whirling with cold grace, an onslaught of a flashing sword and hair. With all my strength, I took my blade high and blocked his attack. Another strike came at me, and I ducked under it, coming up blade first.

Vedriel backhanded me with his other hand. Blood filled my mouth as I staggered back.

"I'm going to make you pay for what you did that night," Vedriel snarled. "You should have never summoned me like some subservient demon! You insubordinate fool!"

"Go to hell!" I lost myself over to the rage, to the grief, and became one with my soul blade. I knew I was going to die, but I would die revenging my parents.

Vedriel's cold fury-twisted face was all I saw as he came at me again. Everything moved with the slow elegance of a dance—the dance with death. I twisted, evading the killing thrust of the archangel's sword, but he moved like nothing I'd ever seen before, like the wind from a storm. And I was tired. So tired.

The archangel came around, closing the distance to deliver his own strike, but he didn't use his sword. Instead, he thrust out his left palm—and touched my shoulder.

There was a flash of white light. I couldn't get out of the way as something far more brutal than lightning hit me. I felt my feet leave the ground, and then I was soaring backwards in the air and crashed to the floor. I dropped my soul blade as pain like nothing I had known erupted through me. I tried to scream, but the air to fill my lungs wouldn't come.

"Only a fool thinks they can defeat an archangel."

Through my broken vision, I saw him prowl toward me. "You made a real mess of things," said the archangel. "I didn't want to have to get involved in such, *mortal* matters, but you left me no choice. I have to kill you myself."

In a flash of light, my very bones shattered as my body rose and then slammed onto the hard floor, again and again. I was crushed beneath another wave of torturous agony.

"Stop!" someone shouted. No, not someone— Jax.

I was dying. Hell, I had no idea it would hurt so bad. If I'd known, I wouldn't have thrown myself at the archangel without a plan. But it was too late.

Vedriel's face materialized through my tears. "You think you're worthy of the name, angel-born? Sensitive? You think you deserve anything at all, mortal? You're garbage. A mistake. Foul. A creature that should never have been."

Vedriel sneered as another volley of white lighting struck me. My back arched as I screamed in agony. I heard a pop and felt some of my ribs crack.

"You are the last super soldier," Vedriel breathed. "And after I clean up this mess and kill all your friends, the mortal world will be right again. The council will never know what happened to their angel-born. Soon they will forget," Vedriel raged. "What are you, compared to our kind, that you think you're worthy of us? Mortals shouldn't have powers.

What are mortals but bags of meat, blood, and bones? You're animals. You're nothing but meat for the worms."

I wanted to spit in his face, curse him, but I was being ripped apart from the inside out. I thrashed as I tasted blood in my mouth.

"Monkeys," mocked the archangel. "The lot of you. All scheming, filthy monkeys."

I screamed as searing pain burned my bones, my insides turning to jelly.

I wanted to die. *Let me die.*

"Your mortal soul means nothing. I will enjoy it being ripped apart by the very creatures you were sworn to kill."

Jax yelled something. Yelled it closer. Through my blurred vision, I saw Jax crouching for something. Then he was on his feet, a soul blade in his hands. He hurled himself at Vedriel, swift as a shadow, the blade aimed at the archangel's chest.

Not bothering to look, Vedriel lifted a hand, and a wave of white celestial magic shot from his outstretched fingers. It slammed into Jax's body. He was lifted and hurled backward, magic tearing through him like a bullet ripping a hole through paper. He hit the wall hard and slumped to the uneven stone ground, lying on his back.

I shivered again, this time so violently that my body shifted back, a flash of light and pain.

A blur of movement, and Danto was there, teeth out and claws, as he flung himself at the archangel. Vedriel sent the vampire a glare that would have sent ordinary men running. With a flick of his wrist, a beam of white light crashed into the vampire's chest.

Danto flew across the room. The clatter of broken plaster and wood echoed through the room as the vampire landed face-first on the dirt floor.

Vedriel spun and met a blur of claws and teeth as the big panther attacked the archangel viciously from behind. And for a moment, I thought Tyrius the panther had managed to wrap his jaws around the bastard's neck. But there was another flash of light, and Tyrius flew in the air and smashed hard onto the ground.

My pain intensified as I saw Vedriel wave his sword at the wounded panther. No. Not Tyrius.

Vedriel sneered at the baal demon. "You traitorous piece of filth," he seethed. "You're just as bad as these mortal beasts. Siding with a non-demon and half-breeds!"

He raised his sword. Something inside me snapped.

Get up. Rowyn. Get up!

With the last drop of adrenaline, I staggered to my feet. Something black winked at me from the ground. A death blade, fallen from one of the vanquished demons. Deadly and poisonous to angel-born and angels alike. Angels couldn't touch a death blade without poisoning themselves, without a death wish.

Shadow and light.

I wasn't just angel-born. I was also demon-born.

Making up my mind, I reached down and clasped the death blade by the hilt.

Immediately I was struck at the sheer coolness of the blade. It hummed with power. The black vapors coiled up my hand, up my wrist to my arm like snakes. For a moment I stood there in complete astonishment as I held on to the death blade's hilt, expecting it to melt my hand or at least burn. But the black metal felt cool against my palm.

I stiffened, but reached within, feeling for some thread of power. I didn't feel sick. I didn't feel pain. The blade felt familiar and strangely comfortable in my grasp.

And then I was moving again.

Vedriel pointed the tip of his sword at Tyrius's neck. "You'll wish you'd never met that silly angel-born." He raised his sword. "Demon filth—"

And I stabbed him in the back.

Vedriel cried out as I leaped back. The black hilt of the death blade sticking out of his back gleamed in the candlelight. Screaming, he dropped his sword and thrashed his arms behind his back, frantically trying to get at the blade. But he couldn't reach it.

The archangel swore, low and vicious. "What have you done!" For the first time, I saw real fear in Vedriel's eyes, and I was glad of it. Hell, I almost smiled.

And then, Jax, Tyrius and Danto threw themselves on the archangel.

They attacked with swift, wicked force. And one by one, they claimed the archangel. The sounds of claws and blades tearing flesh echoed in the room. I caught a glimpse of Danto's face, savage with rage and pain. And I saw Jax's face. There was nothing merciful on his handsome face, no glimmer of feeling for the archangel on his knees.

White light poured through large gaping holes in the archangel's neck, hands, and face.

"Don't do this," he pleaded, his features twisted, making him a lot less celestial and more mortal. "I'll let you live. No one will ever find you. I swear it. Please!"

My eyes found another death blade on the ground. I felt nothing as I closed the distance between me and the archangel. Tyrius shifted over, giving me space.

Vedriel's eyes widened at the death blade in my hand. "No! You can't! I'm an archangel! You will pay for this! All of you! You will be hunted and killed for what you've done!"

"I don't care." I plunged the death blade into his heart, pushing all the way in until the blade could go no further.

With the last of my energy spent, I fell back and landed on my ass.

Vedriel looked down, his mouth open in a silent scream. It was the final effort. The archangel's body shivered, and black veins spread over his arms, his neck and then his face and into his eyes until they were as black as the eyes of a demon.

Tyrius, Jax, and Danto all pulled back as the archangel started to convulse.

Then more white light spilled from his mouth, eyes, and ears until he was completely covered in light.

With a final scream, the archangel Vedriel burst into a million brilliant particles of dust.

CHAPTER
30

The rising sun warmed my face and I closed my eyes, letting it burn away the demon smut on my face and clothes. I smelled like a week-old garbage bin left in the sun for far too long. We all did.

The four of us sat on a stone pillar outside Devil's Mouth. The land was still barren, looking like the remnants of a nuclear explosion, but somehow the sun just made everything seem a little less gloomy and a little brighter—a promise of a new things to come.

The sun shone down from a brilliant sky onto the barren strip of the park, reflecting alongside the East River and making the waters sparkle like diamonds. My gaze traveled over the outstretch of land and debris, not surprised to see that all the demons were gone, having melted away into the Netherworld like mist burning away in the morning sun.

I didn't know how long we sat there in silence. Danto sat to my left with his arms crossed over his chest, his toes wiggling in the sunlight. The vampire hadn't said much, and I suspected he was trying to keep it together after what had happened to Cindy. His grief was still very fresh, and although his gray eyes were dry, his pain was etched deeply on his face.

Cindy. I felt a twang of guilt clenching my insides that we couldn't save her.

Tyrius was slouched on my lap, watching Danto's toes with the intensity of a cat watching a bird.

"What do you think happened to Degamon?" asked Jax, sitting next to me on my right, his long legs sprawled out before him. The sun cast a golden glow over his hair and skin, making him look very much like his angel ancestors.

I shrugged, looking away from those lips. "My guess is that without Vedriel—without its binding contract, the Greater demon had no business staying. It left after we..."

"Killed the archangel," said Jax, his eyebrows high on his forehead.

Killed the archangel, I repeated. Funny, I didn't feel any regret or remorse about killing Vedriel. I was glad of it.

My eyes moved to my right wrist, the skin smooth with my olive complexion. There was no sign of the archangel curse, no more bruises or blisters. The Seal of Adam had disappeared the moment the archangel had died. And I felt fantastic.

"Degamon doesn't care about me anymore," I said. "With its summoner dead," I swallowed, "the contract is nulled. It will never hunt me again." I met his eyes. "But it has your name, Jax." It was tainted with demon smut, and I was worried about him.

Jax sighed and pulled his gaze away from me. "I know. Let's hope it doesn't call me up on some *nighttime* favors just yet," he laughed. "I'm still a little sore. Don't know how well I'd perform."

I scowled. He wasn't taking this seriously. I didn't think Jax understood the severity of a demon possessing one's name. But that conversation would have to wait for another time.

It was hard not to think of the kiss we'd shared—the one he stole—with him so close to me. I leaned a little closer to his musky scent. I suddenly became very aware of his thigh pressing up against mine, and I didn't move an inch. I wasn't sure what the kiss meant, now that we'd made it out alive.

But it had been nice, very nice.

Jax kept his bad-boy smile in place, seemingly oblivious to my worry. "Are you going to stay this time, or are you going to leave again?" he said, changing the subject and staring at me through his long eyelashes.

My face warmed and it wasn't due to the sun. "I'm staying," I answered, knowing it was the truth, and I felt Tyrius's eyes on me. "My grandmother needs me. She's all alone and she's the only family I have left." I sighed. "I have a feeling the Legion's not finished with me either. I'm the only Unmarked left."

"That we know of," mewed Tyrius. "There could be more, and there could be more of a *different* kind. Who knows what the Legion's been brewing all these years."

I knew he was right. There were probably more of Horizon's soldiers but different from me. Something that we hadn't seen before. Something worse.

"We killed an angel," I muttered, stroking Tyrius's head, suddenly a little more nervous. The words felt strange coming out of my mouth, like I still couldn't believe it.

"An *archangel*," corrected the cat, purring loudly.

"We killed an archangel."

Tyrius crossed his front paws. "Yes, but he was a very *bad* one."

I shook my head. "Doesn't matter. The Legion won't see it that way. To them, we just murdered one of their sacred archangels. There'll be hell to pay."

"With Vedriel's death," said Tyrius, "his allies will come looking for us. They'll try to kill us… because of what we've done. All of us. Vedriel was just the beginning."

"Let them come," I said, my pulse pounding. Tyrius leapt from my lap as I stood up. "I'll be ready for them." I was angry, furious at what the Legion had done to me and to the others.

"Me too." Jax swung his shotgun on his shoulder, his eyes alight with determination. "I'm with you on this."

"You can count me in as well," said the vampire, surprising me. He stood up. The traces of pain were gone, and all I saw was the vamp's elegant grace marred by retaliation. His eyes fixed to me with a shocking intensity, and I swore I saw a flicker of admiration in there.

Tyrius purred. "Same here. We do this together. The four of us. Like it or not, we're a team now."

A smile crept to my face. The thing was, I didn't vanquish the archangel alone. I had done it with the help of three unlikely allies—a broken vampire, a baal demon and an angel-born warrior … and me. Horizon's hybrid super soldier.

"I don't know about you guys, but I'm in the mood for drink. There's a pint of beer somewhere with my name on it. Hell, make that three. I don't even care if it's in Mystic Quarter. Who's with me?"

We all laughed as we began the long walk back to Jax's car. Together. And I wouldn't have wanted it any other way.

I had always known there was something inside me… it had always been there… and now it was awakened.

I was lost for a long time, not knowing what or who I was—but now, I know what I am.

I am shadow and light.

Slipping a soul blade into my weapons belt around my right hip, I reached out for the death blade I used to stab Vedriel and slid it around my left.

Horizon's armies will come after me. And I say, let them come.

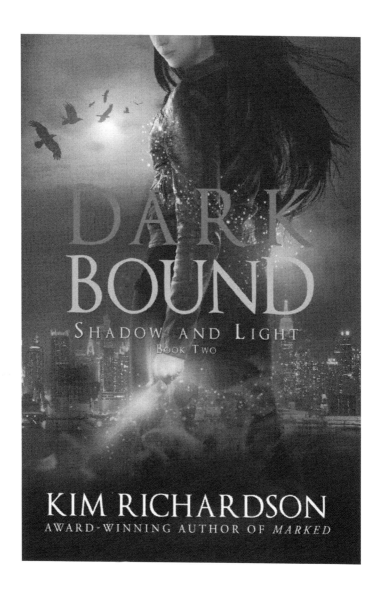

SHADOW AND LIGHT
BOOK TWO

KIM RICHARDSON
AWARD-WINNING AUTHOR OF *MARKED*

CHAPTER

1

NOTICE OF FORECLOSURE.

Damn. I held the letter in trembling fingers. It didn't matter how many times I'd read the stupid notice. It always said the same thing; the bank was threatening to take my grandmother's house.

My gut clenched, and a sick feeling weaved its way into my being. I sat in my usual spot at my grandmother's antique wooden table. Suddenly cold, I stared out the kitchen window to the falling rain, forcing myself to breathe. The cool autumn wind drafted through the open window and I clenched the paper so I wouldn't hyperventilate.

This can't be happening.

"Rowyn, put the notice down before you give yourself a heart attack," commented Father Thomas sitting across from me, his beautiful voice, rich in tones and resonant. "The words won't change no matter how many times you read them."

I let the notice fall on the table and glanced at the priest. He'd been on one of his regular visits to my grandmother's when I popped in this morning to check on her.

Father Thomas was one of Thornville's local priests, but also a modern-day Templar Knight. They called themselves Knights of Heaven, and they were a team specially appointed by the church to investigate all the "unusual crimes" that happened in the city and the surrounding areas, specifically New York City. They waged a secret war against the church's enemies—demons, half-breeds, ghosts, and other supernatural baddies that posed a threat to the church.

He wore his usual dark ensemble of black slacks and a black shirt, the white square of his clerical collar stark against the deep tones. He was a few inches taller than me with a drool-worthy, athletic physique gained from hours at the gym and somewhere in his early thirties. His strong, handsome features complemented his dark, intelligent eyes, and his olive complexion framed by his raven hair spoke of his obvious Spanish ancestry.

Tall, dark and handsome. Yup. El padre had the full package. I wasn't even sure I was allowed to say or even *think* a priest was hot. Would God strike me down and send me to the Netherworld for thinking Father Thomas was a tad pretty?

Father Thomas is hot.

Father Thomas is hot.

Father Thomas is hot—yup, still here. *I guess it is allowed.*

"Father Thomas is right," said Tyrius, sitting on the table, and I pulled my eyes from the priest. "We've all memorized what it says. Now we need to figure out what we're going to *do* about it."

The chic Siamese cat looked regal with his carefully refined features, elegant black mask, and black-gloved paws. The concern in his voice mirrored my own. Tyrius loved my grandmother deeply, and this notice had us both on edge.

I glanced at my grandmother, standing with her back to the oven. The sign above her kitchen cabinets read LIFE'S TOO SHORT. LICK THE BOWL.

She wore a calf-length sweater dress with her white hair tied loosely in a long braid. Her face was paler than usual, and her eyes were a bit sunken, lacking their usual mischievous glint. The age lines in her face that I once found so comforting were deeper, making her appear tired and older. The sadness that clouded her eyes brought my heart into my throat.

"Can the bank really do that?" asked Tyrius, his deep blue eyes flashing. "Can they really take her house?"

"Yes." Father Thomas shifted in his chair. "The loan agreement was signed with the client's consent for the bank to take the necessary action should the client default on payments." I heard the frustration in his voice. "And that means they have every right to repossess the house if the payments stop."

"When does the bank take possession?" asked Tyrius, his voice carrying a new concern.

"If we don't cough up twenty grand," I said, my fingers drumming on the table, "in seven days from today."

A sullen silence descended, and I leaned over with my elbows on the table, letting my head fall in my hands. I'd been so wound up in my own affairs with the archangel's death, the deaths of the Unmarked, and my confusing feelings about Jax—I'd never even noticed the strain happening at my grandmother's. I was a fool. A selfish fool.

My thoughts were rambling now, panic making it hard to breathe. I needed to focus. I needed to figure this out.

I needed twenty freaking thousand dollars.

Since I hadn't actually *vanquished* the Greater demon Degamon, I wasn't entitled to the full ten thousand the council had originally offered. But having solved the murders, the council allowed me to keep the five thousand they'd given me up front. Jax had explained Degamon's involvement to the council, in a lie that we had agreed upon. He told them Degamon was hunting the Unmarked because their souls were more potent and held more life-force than regular mortals or angel-born.

I don't know if the council bought our fabricated story, but the killings stopped, and so did the council's attention on me. Good. That's how I wanted to be—left alone.

Most of that five thousand had gone toward three months' rent, overdue bills and a desperately needed new wardrobe. I'd put the remaining five hundred dollars in a savings account, hoping to save up for a car. I hated having to take the bus and subway to get around. I was a Hunter. Taking the bus was bad for my image.

Screw my image. I had five hundred dollars to put towards my grandmother's debt. Now I had to figure out a way to get nineteen and a half thousand in less than seven days. Damn. How the hell was I going to pull that off?

"I say we rob a bank," said Tyrius, and to my surprise Father Thomas laughed. "What?" said the cat. "You think I'm kidding? Do you know how easy it would be for me to hack into the bank and transfer some cash to Cecil's account?"

"No one's robbing a bank," I growled, though I was tempted, just for half a second. But with my grandmother's strong moral fiber, she would never agree to it.

Jaw clenched against a New York-sized headache, I glanced at my grandmother, my heart breaking at the pain I saw. "Why didn't you tell me?" Twenty grand meant she hadn't been paying her mortgage payments for more than a year, plus interest.

My grandmother wiped her eyes, and I strained to keep my own waterworks at bay. "You had so much on your plate already, with you moving back here and then that Greater demon Degamon on a killing spree and that insufferable council meddling in our affairs again. I didn't want you to worry."

"Too late. I'm worried." Although I'd been open and honest about the encounter with Degamon and why it was after me, the memory still sent my heart pounding.

I shifted to the edge of my chair, wondering how I could have missed this. "Grandma, I thought you and grandpa had some money put away?" I said. "A pension and some lucky savings?"

"Lucky savings?" My grandmother gave me a tight smile. "I needed a new roof. Water was leaking through cracks in the foundation, so that needed to be fixed. Don't get me started on the plumbing." She sighed heavily. "It's an old house. Old houses always need repairs, just like this old body. If it's not a hip replacement, it's a window replacement. I've stretched that small pension as far as it will go. It just wasn't enough."

A knot of worry tightened around my middle. I couldn't let my grandmother lose her house. I had to do something.

"I'm so sorry, Cecil," said Father Thomas as he leaned back in his chair. "I'll make inquiries about a possible loan from the church. There has to be something we can do to help."

"No." My grandmother's expression was hard and she straightened. I recognized that stubborn pride. Guess I got it from Granny. "Stop fussing about me." She set her coffee mug on the counter. "It's just a house. It's got a roof and walls. That is all. If that goddamned bank wants it so badly, they can take it. I just don't care anymore."

Father Thomas startled at the foul word coming from such an innocent-looking old lady, and I smiled at the hint of the badass angel-born she'd been in her younger years.

Of course she cared. I cared. "It's not *just* a house, grandma. You poured your life into this place. It's the house you bought with Grandpa. It's the house Mom grew up in. It's the place where I can transport myself into memories of her and Dad and Grandpa. Memories are all I have left of her... of all of them." I gritted my teeth until my jaw hurt. "The bank's not getting those memories," I added and blinked the moisture from my eyes.

"So, what's your master plan, then?" Tyrius cajoled as he shifted atop the table.

"I'll get a job," I announced, surprising myself. "A real, human job." God, that sounded lame to say it out loud. The thought of a human job was foreign, disturbing and even a little creepy. Could I even pull it off?

Tyrius's bark of laughter caught me off guard, and I frowned as he cleared his throat and said, "You? A real job? That's as hilarious as rainbows shooting out of my ass."

I stiffened in my seat. "What? You don't think I can?" Heat rushed to my face and part of me wanted to knock him off the table.

"Never said you couldn't." The cat's smile was brief but sincere. "It's just... well... what skills do you have? Apart from killing demons and that one, lame-ass archangel... what else can you do?"

My eyes flicked to my grandmother as she stared at the table without blinking, her expression far away and distant, and I nearly lost it.

"I *can* get a regular job," I protested, nearly shouting. "My people skills are a little rusty. But how hard can it be? I'm loyal. Dependable. Kind."

"That's great," commented Tyrius. "Now, all you have to do is learn how to catch a Frisbee and you can work as a Golden Retriever."

Father Thomas laughed and I scowled at the cat. "You've got a better idea?"

Tyrius grinned in a way that made me want to pull out his whiskers. "We could *borrow* money from the bank. They wouldn't even notice. Easy-peasy."

"No."

"It would be so-o-o-o easy, so ridiculously easy."

"Tyrius, we are still not robbing a bank," I said, watching Father Thomas smile at the cat because he thought he was joking. He wasn't. I knew if I said yes, Tyrius would probably transfer small amounts of cash from several different accounts so as not to draw any attention and then stash it into my grandmother's. But she wouldn't go for that. And neither would I.

The cat made a face. "Fine. Have it your way then. But the idea of you behind a desk is as unnatural to me as a swimming cat. It's just plain wrong. You wouldn't last a day."

I rubbed my temples. "I would." *I didn't even know where to start.* "I will get a regular job if it means I can save this house. I'll do it."

"Do you have a résumé?" Father Thomas's mouth quirked, and he touched his clean-shaven chin with the back of his hand.

If he wasn't so pretty, I would have slapped him. "No." My face warmed. Hunters didn't have résumés. We got our jobs by reputation. Not that it mattered now.

"Rowyn, be reasonable." My grandmother tilted her head, and a brief look of pain passed over her features. "Tyrius is right. You're angel-born, a Hunter. The human workplace is no place for my granddaughter. You won't fit in."

I don't fit in anywhere, I thought sourly. No big surprise there.

With a troubled look, my grandmother exhaled. "I'm sorry you're losing this place, Rowyn, but there's nothing else we can do."

Now I felt guilty. "Yes, there is." I pushed my chair back and stood. "I'm not giving up. I *won't.*" I glanced at my grandmother and I swear I saw hope flitting behind her eyes. "I'll figure something out," I said, my throat closing. "Just don't do anything rash until you hear from me. Okay?"

"Where are you going?" my grandmother called as I walked out of the kitchen and rushed down the hallway.

"To get the money," I whispered to myself. My head throbbed as I pulled open the front door and stepped out into the morning rain onto Maple Drive.

Yes, my life was a bag of disasters, but it needn't be for my grandma. She was all the family I had left, if you didn't count Tyrius. And I sure as hell wasn't going to sit back and do nothing.

I *would* get the money. Even if I had to hurt a few people to do it.

ABOUT THE AUTHOR

KIM RICHARDSON is the award-winning author of the bestselling SOUL GUARDIANS series. She lives in the eastern part of Canada with her husband, two dogs and a very old cat. She is the author of the SOUL GUARDIANS series, the MYSTICS series, and the DIVIDED REALMS series. Kim's books are available in print editions, and translations are available in over seven languages.

To learn more about the author, please visit:

www.kimrichardsonbooks.com

\

Printed in Great Britain
by Amazon